Unveil the Vow

Karen Hembrough

Unveil the Vow

Paperback ISBN 978-1-957497-77-8

Cover Photograph by Rebekah Cloninger

Published in the United States of America

Dedicated to my daughters,
Tara, Tasha, and Tiffany

1

COLUMBUS, NEW MEXICO, 1915

Pulling her by the hand, the Mexican children wanted Audra to come and play ball with them. "*Amiga, amiga, vamos a jugar,*" they chanted. The children of the Mexican ranch workers saw the young woman as their playmate rather than the adult daughter of the ranch's owner, Daniel Kirk. They played until all were exhausted. Audra walked to the veranda and stretched out in her hammock. She felt comfortable in the warm New Mexico sun. The winter day wafted a light breeze. Her orange cat, Petula, lay beneath her, and she brushed its fur with her fingers. As she rested in the hammock, she picked up a book and gingerly held it in front of her.

A deep voice interrupted her, "Audra, come quickly!" She threw the book onto the tile floor and ran to her grandfather, Dr. Richard Kirk, who lived at the ranch. "A messenger has just come with the news that there has been an accident at the Gordon ranch." The doctor hurried to the stable and hailed a ranch hand, "Ramon, *por favor*, hitch up the surrey!"

Audra had become her grandfather's medical assistant as an adolescent. Dr. Kirk, a widower, was a compassionate and gentle man, and highly skilled in his medical practice. Audra aided him in the consultations of his patients in his clinic in Columbus. She had a God-given gift for medical science. For a woman so young, she had amassed much knowledge in the healing arts. Dr. Kirk was an excellent mentor, and his granddaughter was quick to learn. Her delight was to read medical journals. Even as a little girl, she wanted to be a doctor.

With a black bag in hand, Dr. Kirk climbed into the carriage, also helping Audra. The ride was not far, only a couple of miles. As they bounced over the bumpy road, Audra reflected, "I will soon be twenty-one years old, and I have received many compliments on my beauty. Some touted, 'You could be a fashion model in a high society magazine. Your flawless, ivory skin is comparable to that of a china doll. Your pretty face, framed with long, red hair, is thick and wavy. Your delicate features are accented with rosy cheeks. You are tall and slender and walk with statuesque grace.'"

As she contemplated her life, Audra turned to the doctor. "Grandfather, please pray for me. I have rejected four proposals of wedlock. Young men have come from three counties to court me, but none of them has suited father. He did not favor any of them. He has been controlling and domineering in regards to my future. He has an obsession to find a son-in-law that he can claim as his own son. The man must be spiritual with qualities of virtue and ambition. I wonder if this ideal man really exists. So far, father has taken charge of my life in respect of procuring a beau, and it perturbs me!"

"Yes, I will pray. Daniel, my son, is deeply religious and

moral. Daily, he prays and reads the Bible. He will do the right thing. Your mother, Elizabeth, is a sweet and amicable woman. What is her opinion?"

"She has attempted to encourage me that God has a unique plan for my future. However, most of my female friends are already married, and some of them even have a child. I have prayed for wisdom in regards to a husband. Yet the nagging fear of becoming an old maid is plaguing me. I will attend the medical school in El Paso in a few months. Maybe I will find a suitable husband among the medical students."

Audra thought about her older sister, Raquel, "At age twenty-five, she is still beautiful with auburn hair, pale skin, and fine features. Despite father's great displeasure, she insisted on marrying a man who was not a believer in God. Raquel was attracted to Wade Conner, a man of stocky build and brown hair. Before their marriage, he was solicitous to her and polite. Yet not long after the nuptials, Raquel discovered the true character of her husband. Wade is often intoxicated and callous to her and to their small children."

As the surrey came to a halt at the Gordon ranch, Audra stopped her daydreaming. A group of neighboring men had gathered at the ranch to build a barn. Young Jared Gordon was the victim of a fallen timber. The men had carried him to the house where he lay delirious with a laceration on his head.

Dr. Kirk examined the young man thoroughly. He checked for any broken bones and found none. The doctor then quickly debrided the gash and called to Audra, "My dear, you may now suture the wound. You are as skilled as any professional."

"Yes, I would be glad to do it." She stepped up without

any nervousness and sewed up the lesion.

The man's wife, Debra, tried to speak to him. "Jared, can you hear me?" However, he was confused and would not respond. Thereafter, he turned away from her and closed his eyes.

At his bedside, the doctor, Audra, and Debra prayed in unity for his healing. Then Dr. Kirk stood over the young man and spoke in a loud voice, "Jared, wake up!"

Opening his eyes, he was fully lucid and asked, "May I have a drink of water?" Debra, his wife, began to weep and rejoice over her husband's recovery.

~~~~~~~

Shiloh Ranch, owned by Daniel Kirk, was a cattle domain on mostly arid, desert land. However, there were enough fertile acres and a creek running through the land to support a large herd. The ranch was located near the village of Columbus. In 1915, the small town was a site for the railroad and border crossing with Mexico. The army garrison, Cavalry Camp, adjoined the settlement. The military post housed 350 soldiers. There had been border conflicts with Pancho Villa and his bandits, plundering and killing Americans.

It was a humid, cloudy day when Daniel Kirk, a robust man in his 40s, drove his truck into Columbus to do some errands. The dirt streets were filled with horses and carriages, army trucks, and some Model T cars. He stopped on Main Street and became acquainted with two soldiers, Lieutenant Matthew James and Corporal Kenton Lott. They had come into the town from the garrison.

Lieutenant James spoke with enthusiasm, "Mr. Kirk,
~~~~~~~

we would like to invite you to come on the morrow for the evening meal and to stay for the gospel meeting."

Corporal Lott bragged, "Our chaplain, Sergeant Derek Rands, is a mighty preacher. The mess hall will be packed with the enlisted men for this occasion. It keeps the soldiers out of the bars and from drunkenness."

"I gratefully accept your invitation with the utmost anticipation. I am a man of faith, myself."

"Very good, sir, we shall expect to see you there."

Derek and his friends, Matthew James and Kenton Lott, were a tight-knit group at Camp Cavalry. While other soldiers played cards or rolled dice at night, these enlisted men often read the Bible. The three soldiers had ownership of their horses and trained them for war in combat maneuvers. Derek's horse, Rio, would follow him like a dog. The men purchased grain for their mounts so that the beasts were strong and sleek. The big animals were powerful in speed and endurance.

Derek affirmed to his comrades, "We have prepared our horses for battle, but the Lord will bring the victory."

The three soldiers were impeccable in their appearance and manners: clean-shaven, hair trimmed, and genteel speech. The soldiers regularly practiced Kung Fu martial arts together. They would often lift large stones to increase their brawn and toughness. Because of their physical strength and sobriety, some of the soldiers called them the 'army gods'.

The troopers in good humor would say, "Take notice of the macho men, the combat kings."

When his companions encountered their teasing, Derek

would tell them to respond in this manner, "Smile and wave, boys."

The sergeant was accustomed to ironing his military uniform. He used a flat iron on the wood stove in the kitchen of the mess hall. A few of the soldiers would razz him in fun. "Here comes Mr. Perfect. His hair is perfectly combed, and his pants are perfectly pressed."

Derek would only grin and boldly declare, "Only the Lord is perfect. Trust in Him. He will never leave you nor forsake you."

It was a diversion for these army buddies, but they seemed to want to hear it again and again that God cared for them. Many of the recruits would come to the sergeant for counsel and prayer when they had problems or fears. Derek had a sterling reputation as their chaplain, and the enlisted men trusted him. His counseling schedule was continuously filled with appointments.

~~~~~~~

Daniel Kirk returned the next evening to the garrison. In the mess hall, he encountered his newfound friends, Lieutenant James and Corporal Lott. They invited the rancher to sit with them at a table, and Sergeant Rands joined them. A plate of food was brought to the rancher; the army rations of beef stew was tolerable. However, the conversation was stimulating as Daniel conversed with the enlisted men. The rancher noticed that the three soldiers were tall with broad shoulders, dark hair, and handsome features.

"Are you men related?"

Their reaction was to snicker and to chuckle as they looked
~~~~~~~

at one another. Lieutenant James turned to the rancher. "No, but we are comrades of like mind and like goals. We share the same philosophy of life."

Daniel surmised, "Birds of a feather flock together?"

"Yes, exactly. We are also keen on mastering the martial arts." Corporal Lott gave him a cocky grin.

"That is a rare sport and not the usual fighting technique for the army. Tell me about it."

The two soldiers pointed to Sergeant Rands. "I trained with a Chinese master of Kung Fu in San Francisco. It took three months to develop my skill."

"How interesting. How long have you been a chaplain for the army, Sergeant Rands?"

"This is my second year. My father is a pastor and also the Indian agent for the Apache reservation. I was raised with Bible teaching. I learned the art of counseling by watching my father deal with the Indians. When I joined the army, I applied for this position. When I was chosen, I knew it was a divine appointment."

At the appointed time, the soldiers came pouring into the mess hall for the Bible meeting. Lieutenant James, with a guitar and Corporal Lott on drums, led the men in singing hymns. Chaplain Derek Rands' message was on the ministry of angels: "Angels will protect you and go forth to serve for your sake."

He preached with zeal, and the anointing of God flowed through his message. The enlisted men listened with rapt attention. The rancher was inspired by the music and the message. Daniel perceived that the chaplain, Sergeant Derek

Rands, had tremendous influence in the lives of the soldiers.

After the meeting, Daniel expressed his appreciation to his friends for a most enjoyable evening. He then turned to the chaplain, "Sergeant Rands, it is my wish to invite you to our home at Shiloh ranch for Sunday dinner. You will meet my wife, Elizabeth, and my daughter, Audra."

"Thank you, sir. I have no other plans; I would be pleased to come."

Daniel had desired a husband worthy of his daughter, Audra. The father had an inkling that this soldier was the appointed man. He began to pray for the will of the Lord in this endeavor.

After the rancher arrived home from the garrison, he was anxious to talk with Audra and Elizabeth. His eyes twinkling, he spoke in an animated voice, "I just had the most enlightening experience attending the gospel meeting at the army post. Audra, I am excited to tell you that I have finally found your future husband and my son- in-law! His name is Sergeant Derek Rands, and he is the chaplain at Camp Cavalry. He is near to your age, twenty-five years old."

Audra shrieked, "Father, are you crazy! This is presumptuous and preposterous!"

Elizabeth chimed in, "What do you know about this soldier to make such a rash judgment?"

"I saw him interact with the soldiers during our meal in the mess hall. His sermon in the evening meeting was excellent. Sergeant Rands has the aplomb and boldness of a fearless leader."

Raising her eyebrows in dismay, Audra exclaimed, "Father, do I not have a choice of whom I will marry? They arrange marriages in India, not in America!"

Her father persuaded, "Daughter, when you meet Sergeant Derek Rands, you will come into agreement with me. And by the way, he is a handsome man."

"So, when will he come and sweep me off of my feet?"

"I have invited him for Sunday dinner. My darling, put on your prettiest silk dress."

"My dear wife, prepare a banquet for our honored guest. At last, my 'son' is coming."

On Sunday, Sergeant Derek Rands rode on horseback from the garrison to the Kirks' ranch for the dinner invitation. Audra sat on the veranda to watch for Derek. When the sergeant entered the stone walkway and his eyes beheld Audra, he was amazed by her beauty. She was wearing a deep rose silk dress. Her long, red hair was curled and fastened with garnet clasps.

She, too, was a bit awed by the dashing soldier in uniform who stood before her. She took a deep breath and found her voice, "Welcome to our home, Sergeant Rands. I am Audra, and we are happy to have you as our guest."

"Please, call me Derek. It is an honor to be here."

In the dining room, Daniel seated his daughter next to Derek. The soldier was courteous, but not overly attentive towards her. The conversation at the table revolved around politics and the war in Europe. The rancher inquired of the sergeant, "What do you hear of the border conflict?

"Pancho Villa's raiders from Chihuahua have again attacked and looted along the northern border of Mexico. Yet the Columbus citizens doubt that Villa will attack here because of our military presence."

Audra was curious. "Derek, tell us about your background."

"I lived for ten years on the Apache reservation, where my father is the Indian agent. In the past, the Apache were nomadic hunters. Now, they live off the land, raising sheep and goats."

After the dinner, Audra challenged Derek to a game of checkers. With little deliberation, she won. With a look of surprise, he asked, "How did you become so proficient at this game?"

She darted him a sly grin. "Grandfather taught me. Let us play again, but with a bet. If I win, you shall take me horseback riding in the desert. The cacti are in bloom."

Derek's face reflected a cunning look. "If I win, you will make chocolate eclairs for me."

The game was intense, and the sergeant was the winner.

Audra laughed. "It seems as though your sweet tooth won."

Upon leaving, Derek expressed, "I am grateful for your hospitality and the good company."

~~~~~~~

One morning as they were chatting over breakfast, Elizabeth mentioned to her husband, "It is a tradition for my friend, Susan Dodd, to visit at Thanksgiving. She will come to the ranch next week with her nephew, Ian. Susan is anxious for Ian to meet Audra, since the young people are the same age and have similar interests. He will also be attending the
~~~~~~~

medical school in El Paso."

Frowning, Daniel replied, "I am not in favor of Ian's visit, but I will grant it for your sake, my dear. I want Audra to focus her attention on Sergeant Rands and not on this man."

The two guests arrived by train from El Paso. It was a warm afternoon when Elizabeth, Dr. Kirk, and Audra met them at the station. Introductions were made, and the merry group journeyed to the ranch in the large surrey with Dr. Kirk driving. Elizabeth turned to Susan, "We must catch up on the present and reminisce on the past."

Silently, Audra studied Ian as they traveled to the ranch, "He appears to be in his twenties and physically fit with ash blonde hair and hazel eyes."

Ian began to flirt with Miss Kirk. "I must say, Audra, your beauty makes me want to do an Irish jig."

"You flatter me. Tell me about yourself."

He boasted, "I am a nurse, and I practically run the old folks' home. The residents call for me more than any of the other workers." Then he teased, "You will be under my spell by the end of my stay, too."

She giggled. "We shall see about that."

As the surrey entered a bend in the road, a hawk flew out and into the path of the horses. It spooked the big animals, and they began to gallop at top speed. The women were jostled and began to shriek. Struggling, Dr. Kirk yelled, "Hold on, I am having trouble controlling this team of horses."

Ian offered, "I may be stronger. Let me help." Taking the reins, he began to pull the horses in tow, and the wild ride ended. The young man was able to stop the animals, but one bay was still nervous and rearing up. Stepping down from the carriage, he grabbed its bridle. Then he began stroking the horse's neck and talking to it, "Be calm and rest easy, my friend." Taking out a bag of jelly beans from his pocket, the horses nibbled them from his hand. Glancing at the passengers, he announced, "The sweet candy has made the horses forget their fright; we will now travel on towards the ranch."

A friendship developed between the two young people during the three-day visit. However, Audra's parents cautioned her, "We have noticed that Ian seems quite conceited. He brags a lot about himself and his accomplishments. Though we will be polite to him, we do not enjoy his presence."

Later in their privacy, Daniel commented to his wife, "I am glad that we are in agreement in the hope that our daughter will marry Sergeant Derek Rands."

After church, the Kirks noticed that Ian was flirting with a group of young girls. As they watched the young man's behavior toward the opposite sex, they concluded, "Ian is a classic philanderer."

Audra beckoned him, "The family is waiting at the surrey."

But he was hard put to leave his admirers. "I will be along shortly, just a few more minutes."

Before Ian departed for El Paso, he kissed Audra's hand and complimented her, "You are every man's fantasy. I anticipate seeing you in the future at the medical school."

"I will look forward to it." And she smiled brightly at him.

Audra assessed the relationship, "It has been diverting to spend time with Ian. I am attracted to his upbeat personality and jovial attitude. He might be a prospect for a husband. Yet I must remember that he is a flirt and possibly a womanizer. A man's integrity is of utmost importance to me."

~~~~~~

The sun was shining as Raquel and her children left for the short trip to Shiloh Ranch for Audra's twenty-first birthday party. Ranch workers, Pablo and Maria Lopez, would also attend and stay for the weekend.

The Kirks were meticulous in preparing for the party. Thirty people had been invited, including soldiers from Camp Cavalry. A Mariachi band had been hired for dancing. Strings of colored lights hugged the walls of the patio. Wrought iron tables were covered with bright Mexican serape cloths and adorned with colorful crepe paper flowers.

The guests arrived in all of their finery. They entered the patio to view a long buffet table filled with Mexican enchiladas, tamales, mangoes, and papayas. Dessert included a large butter cream cake that was decorated with pink candy roses. Elizabeth Kirk had ordered ornate flamenco dresses from Spain for her daughters to wear for the occasion. Audra and Raquel, along with their parents, greeted and circulated among the guests. It was a very festive party.

When Audra spied Derek and his two soldier friends, she pulled Raquel aside. "Sister, that is the soldier I told you about. Father sees him as his chosen son-in-law and my future husband. Every time I meet the sergeant, I get nervous inside. He is cordial, but his demeanor is rather serious and aloof, not a man to reckon with. I have tried to flirt with him on occasion, but I have been rebuffed. I find him arrogant,
~~~~~~

so now I am just nonchalant toward him."

Raquel peered at the men. "The sergeant is handsome, and so is the older soldier with him."

"Why didn't Wade come to the party? You look ravishing in that dress."

Her sister appeared grieved. "Wade feels guilty that we owe father money for our debts."

Audra sighed. "I have greeted everyone here except the soldiers. If Derek wants to talk to me, then he will have to come and find me.

On the other side of the patio, the soldiers were conversing. Lieutenant Matthew James stared across the way. "Who is that auburn-haired beauty with your girl, Audra?"

Derek appeared amused. "Audra is not my girl, and the other woman is her sister, Raquel. She is married and not happily so, I have heard."

"Really? Thank you for the tip."

"Be careful, Matthew. Don't rush in where angels fear to tread."

The band was playing, and the guests were beginning to dance. Derek searched until he found Audra. He extended his hand. "May I have this dance, Miss Kirk?"

"Yes, you may, Sergeant Rands."

Audra wanted to say no, but she had to be polite. When the dance was over, she sought to escape, but Derek led her to his table. "Would you come and chat for a few minutes?"

She nodded. "Of course, I would be happy to."

Also seated at the table was Corporal Kenton Lott, and he, too, asked Audra to dance. She was more at ease with him than she was with Derek.

As the group conversed around the table, the band announced the Mexican Hat Dance. Audra expressed excitement, "My sister and I have always liked this dance!"

She gazed up at Derek. "Would you?"

"Absolutely."

Audra then surprised Matthew James. "Lieutenant James, would you be willing to be my sister's partner just this one time? Her name is Raquel."

"I would be pleased."

When she went to get her sister, Matthew confided to Derek, "I don't know one thing about this dance."

He snickered. "Neither do I, just follow the others. We came here to have a good time."

When Raquel came to join them, Matthew observed that she was prettier up close than at a distance.

Audra announced proudly, "This is my sister, Raquel." Then she introduced the soldiers.

Raquel responded, "It is an honor to meet you, and thank you for your service."

A partner was also found for Kenton. The couples danced the Mexican Hat dance and had a hilarious time. When the dance ended, Derek took Audra's hand and led her back to his table. It was obvious that he was not going to let her circulate.

Finally, she requested leave of him, "I will see you in a while. I must visit with the other guests." She flashed him a smile as she looked back at him.

Matthew asked Raquel to sit at their table, but she declined. "I am married, and I must put my small children to bed. I usually read them a story before bedtime."

"I am very adept at reading stories. Would you allow me?

Raquel gazed at him quizzically. "Well, yes, if you wish."

She led him to the nursery where a young hired girl was playing with the children. Sofie, four years old, and Andrew, two years old, looked up, astonished to see a soldier come into their room.

Their mother smiled brightly. "Children, this is Lieutenant James, and he will read your story tonight."

Happy at this prospect, the children giggled. Matthew marveled that they accepted him so readily. He read a fairy tale about a beautiful princess who was forbidden to leave her castle until a handsome knight came to rescue her. He used much expression in his voice to the children's delight. When he finished the story, they wanted him to read it again, which he did.

When Raquel tucked them into bed and kissed them good night, Sofie begged, "I want that soldier kiss me goodnight."

Then little Andrew echoed his sister, "I want him kiss me, too."

The lieutenant looked at Raquel, who nodded yes. When they left the nursery, he turned to her, "I enjoyed the time with the children. May we talk for a few minutes?"

She hesitantly answered, "Yes." And then she led him to the parlor.

Gazing at the lovely young woman seated across from him, he spoke, "Tell me about your life."

Raquel bit her tongue, and her eyes beaded with tears. Matthew immediately went to sit beside her, his hand on hers.

"My life has been very unhappy except for Sofie and Andrew. My husband, Wade, is not affectionate to the children or to me. He is lazy, and his whiskey and tobacco habits consume our money. Father pays a middle-aged couple, Pablo and Maria Lopez, to help us on our ranch. They live in a small dwelling near us. They are loyal and love the children and me. Yet it is a meager existence. My parents do not know all of this, and I do not wish for them to know. I am sorry. I should not have told you my problems. I do not want your pity. God gives me joy in the midst of the suffering."

Frowning in anger, he offered, "Raquel, if you ever feel that you must leave, send for me, and I will come and get you and the children."

Her smile was sweet. "Thank you, but I shall not. We must get back to the party. You go first, then I will come later. We must not be seen entering the party together. I cannot abide any rumors."

Matthew looked into Raquel's brown eyes and studied her appearance one more time. He wanted to remember her beauty and elegance.

While visiting with the guests, Audra noticed that a young, dark-haired woman was talking to Derek. The girl smiled up at him. "I am Penelope Adams. I asked someone your name. Do you dance, Sergeant Rands?"

"Yes, but I am much too old for you. Corporal Lott, would you please dance with Miss Adams?"

"I would be honored." And so, he led her to the dance floor.

After the dance, Kenton invited Penelope to sit at their

table to chat. He surmised, "This young lady is quite witty and very much of a flirt."

Derek wondered whether he should seek out Audra or if he was giving her too much attention. He rationalized that it was only a dance, and so, he went to find her. Thereafter, he asked her to stay and chat, which she did. After the party ended, Matthew sought out Raquel to tell her goodbye. She was flattered that he had made the effort.

As they prepared to leave for the evening, Derek warned Matthew, "My friend, do you remember the commandment that says not to covet another man's wife?"

"Yes, I do. I have been casting down the imagination of Raquel's pretty face and sweet demeanor. Yet I have prayed for the Lord's will to be done."

Raquel received the same warning from Audra, "Raquel, remember that you are married. Do not become infatuated with Lieutenant James. Yes, he is handsome and charismatic, but do not let that beguile you."

"It was wonderful to spend a few minutes with him tonight. He seemed to genuinely care about me."

"Sister, guard your heart."

"Do not be concerned about me. I will not be tempted. By the way, you seemed to enjoy Sergeant Rands' company this evening." Raquel had a smug look on her face.

"Oh, sister, I experienced the charming side of Derek tonight! He was interested in my medical work, and we talked about many subjects. He made me feel like I was the most important person on earth."

~~~~~~~
~~~~~~~

The Kirk family attended the church meeting on Sunday. They were pleasantly surprised that Reverend Barr had invited the chaplain to be in charge of the meeting. The pastor, an army veteran, was acquainted with Sergeant Rands.

Derek's subject was on prayer: "The Lord will hear your prayer, and He will answer."

The congregation was favorable to his message, and many of the parishioners shook Derek's hand upon exiting the church.

After the meeting, Daniel Kirk invited the three soldiers to dine at the ranch. Audra greeted them as they entered the spacious dining room. Matthew and Kenton were seated and began some stimulating dialogue with Daniel and Dr. Kirk on politics. Raquel and the children were also present. Derek followed Audra to the kitchen, where Elizabeth was preparing the meal. The lady was a gracious hostess.

He offered, "Mrs. Kirk, may I carve the roast for you and help in any other task?"

"Yes, I would be most obliged to you." She wiped her hands on her apron and smiled in appreciation.

While waiting for the dinner to be served, the soldiers entertained the children. They would lift up Sofie and Andrew and swing them around. There was much giggling and laughter. It was the Christmas season, and the children were particularly fascinated with a Nativity manger scene that was set up on a low table.

When dinner was announced, Raquel found that her father had seated her next to Matthew at the end of the long table. She caught her father's eye and gave him a stern look. Then, silently, she tried to still her nervousness.

The lieutenant was very attentive to her. "It is my pleasure to see you again."

"As is mine."

Matthew and Raquel talked about many things and found that they had much in common. Seated next to Audra was Derek, and their conversation was amicable.

After the dinner, Audra played her mandolin, and all joined in singing Christmas carols.

When Raquel announced that Sofie and Andrew were to take their nap, the children begged, "We want that soldier to read our story." They pointed to Matthew.

Sofie had a book in her hand. "Grammy gave this book to us."

Their mother was nearby and stated, "It is the Nutcracker, a story about a little girl at Christmas. The book was written in Germany in 1816. The pages are illustrated with colorful pictures of a little girl, a soldier, and a sugar plum fairy."

As Matthew read the story, Raquel began to remove the hairpins from the tight chignon of her hairstyle. The thought came to her that it might be unwise to let her hair down in front of the soldier. However, it was giving her a headache. Staring at her, Matthew resisted his attraction for her. His conscience warned him, "It would be better not see Raquel again, even in the company of her family."

Before leaving the dining room, Derek expressed his thanks, "Ladies, you have served us a delicious meal! I will help clear the table." He entered the kitchen and rolled up his sleeves to wash the pots and pans.

In the mid-afternoon, Matthew and Derek left for the garrison, but Kenton was reluctant to leave the presence of the pretty Miss Kirk. He suggested to Audra, "Would you care to take a stroll in this nice weather?"

"Yes, I would. Let me get my hat."

As the two walked, their conversation was congenial. They seemed to regret the end of the visit.

2

It was Monday morning after a diverting weekend. Raquel, her children, and the ranch workers left Shiloh to return to her home. She dreaded going back to the place where there was so much strife.

Inside the main house, Raquel encountered Wade in a sullen and sulking mood. He was not glad to see her or the children. Telling no one, he had sold all of their cattle and Raquel's horse at the livestock auction. He waved the money of $700 in front of his wife's face. It would be their cash money for the coming year. Wade proudly showed her his purchases. "Here are my new boots and Stetson hat." He did not reveal his box of cigars and bottle of whiskey.

Raquel commented, "The items are superb. By the way, did you pay the bill at the general store?"

Gazing at her scornfully, he gruffly replied, "No, and I don't intend to! You can sell your mantel clock, and the rose china dishes, and pay the bill."

"I certainly will not. I insist that you pay the bill!"

He then took the money and stomped out of the house in a huff.

The children ran to hide.

Raquel took some deep breaths to compose herself, but then she began to cry. She fretted, "Wade's liquor habit has taken a toll on our family. I have tried to be a good wife, but now I wish that I did not have to continue in this loveless marriage. Even when Reverend Barr came to counsel with us, Wade immediately ran him off."

Hugging her children, Sofie and Andrew, their mother comforted them. Thereafter, she entered the cellar to get a jar of jam for their breakfast. In moving the jars, she encountered a tin money box that was far back on the shelf. Her husband had secretly hidden it there.

When she came up from the cellar, she noticed that Wade and Pablo were in a heated argument. Wade had cursed him many times, telling him to leave, but he would not. Pablo worked long hours on the ranch. It was his initiative that sustained the family's livelihood.

Wade demanded, "Put my tools in the wagon. All of the livestock are sold. You no longer have a job here on the ranch."

Pablo was flabbergasted. "Why did you do it?"

"I am headed to California to be with my brother, and I need every penny."

"Has *Señora* Raquel agreed to this?

"She does not know, and I will give her no money, either. She can go live with her parents. I was never cut out to be a family man."

Pablo was shaking his head defiantly. "No, I won't do it!"

With his fist in Pablo's face, Wade threatened the man. "You will do it, and you will tell no one if you don't want trouble."

Looking at the ground with a frown on his face, Pablo brooded, "What should I do? Should I sneak away and tell Daniel Kirk? If Wade abandons his family and moves far away, then Raquel will be rid of the surly man. Maybe this would be best."

At 4:00 the next morning, Wade staggered into their bedroom. He had a disgruntled look on his face and yelled, "What did you do with the money, Raquel? One hundred dollars is missing from the tin box!"

"I put it aside to pay the general store."

"Go get it, now!

"No, I will not. We owe that money."

Wade, who was inebriated, tripped on a shoe and fell to the floor. He passed out due to his intoxication.

Running out the door to the Lopez home, Raquel instructed Pablo, "Prepare to leave for father's ranch."

"Yes, I will hurry and hitch up the team of horses to the wagon." He perceived her distress.

In the main house, Raquel gathered the children and dressed them for travel. She put their clothes and her Bible into a trunk and grabbed the rifle. In a whisper, the disillusioned wife vowed, "I am determined that I will not tolerate any more anxiety. I will not live here again with Wade unless he gets free from the liquor."

Maria took Raquel's hand to comfort her and spoke in Spanish. "God will help you, my dear."

She embraced the older woman. "I appreciate your kind words."

They were ready to leave when Raquel shouted, "Wait,

I must get something from the cellar!"

Entering the underground room, she retrieved all of the money from the tin box. It was dawn as Pablo, Maria, Raquel, and the children traveled to Shiloh. They left Wade to lie on the floor. Raquel did not look back. She prayed for wisdom about the decisions she would have to make in the near future.

As they approached Shiloh ranch, the workers wondered at this early morning arrival. By the time Raquel encountered her parents, she was in tears, telling them what had happened. Elizabeth took the children and put them back into bed. They were sleepy and did not know of the turmoil of the morning.

The family gathered around Raquel to support her. Elizabeth begged, "Please, daughter, you must get out of this marriage. Think of your children."

Deep in thought, Daniel suggested, "Raquel, we will go to the lawyer's office this morning. You must file for a divorce."

Audra implored her sister, "Do as father and mother say, Raquel. You are worthy of a righteous man such as Lieutenant James."

Dr. Kirk was present. "Has this situation been going on for a while?"

Her gaze strayed, not wanting to meet her grandfather's eyes. "Yes, for almost five years."

Pablo and Maria were included in this inner circle. Pablo raised his finger to speak. In Spanish, he related, "Wade plans to settle in California. His aim is to abandon Raquel and the little ones, leaving them destitute."

When Raquel heard about Wade's plan to desert the family, it clinched her decision. "Yes, I will file for a divorce."

Father and daughter traveled to Columbus to the lawyer's office. Raquel filled out the paperwork to obtain a divorce and also a document relinquishing parental rights.

~~~~~~~

At the Conner ranch, Wade had discovered that Raquel had taken all of their money. He schemed, "If I pretend and make a plea to Raquel to quit the liquor, I can get the money back. Later, I will sneak off and leave."

It was mid-morning; Wade had been in the house packing up supplies to take on his trip to California. To his surprise, the sheriff rode up on horseback and approached the young man, "Are you Wade Conner?"

"Yes, what do you want?"

"I have a summons for you. Your wife is filing for divorce. You will need to meet with her at the lawyer's office this afternoon."

His countenance fell; he looked like he had seen a ghost. Wade fretted, "Since my plan to leave with money has failed, I must make a convincing plea. Right now, I am 'between a rock and a hard place'."

Later, at the lawyer's office, a certificate of divorce, and also a document relinquishing parental rights were ready.

Raquel nervously asked, "Father, am I doing the right thing?"

"You are unequally yoked with an unbeliever. If an unbelieving husband wants to leave, let him leave."

When Wade saw his wife, he immediately begged, "Raquel, please forgive me." Blubbering and wiping his eyes with his handkerchief, he pleaded, "I am sorry. I will work
~~~~~~~

hard on the ranch and stop drinking whisky. I promise to go to church with you."

"I understand that you planned to leave the children and I in poverty."

"No, no, my intention was to go to California to buy an orange grove and then to send for you and the children. I had in mind to give you $200 to live on.

"Lies, all lies.

"My dear wife, I am truly sorry for the past. I no longer want to go to California. If you would give me a chance, I want to stay here and be a loving husband and father. And I will buy another horse for you."

Unflinching, Raquel retorted, "Wade, I will not be deceived nor manipulated by your promise to reform. In the past, you expressed sorrow for your liquor habit, but you did not stop. I was so worried on the nights that you did not come home. Here, sign the divorce papers."

Wade glanced at Daniel Kirk who stood beside his daughter. "All right, and Kirk, you give me $1,000. Then I will sign divorce papers."

"No, I will not."

"Then I ain't signin nothin. The ranch is half mine. I deserve some money from that."

Anger filled Daniel's eyes. "When I purchased that ranch, I put it in Raquel's name. You have no ownership in it."

Desperation overtook the young man. "I have to have some money to get to California!"

Studying him, Daniel replied, "I will think about it. The court will award Raquel a divorce anyway for abandonment."

Wade saw the futility of the situation. He had lost the battle, and he had to accept their terms. He signed the divorce papers.

When he saw the document to relinquish his parental rights for Sofie and Andrew, he sneered. "Sure, let another man raise the brats." Thus, he signed that document, too.

Daniel informed Wade of the terms of his departure, "I will bring the horses and wagon to town to you tomorrow morning, and we will meet here at the lawyer's office."

When father and daughter left the office, Raquel was shaking and clinging to her father's arm. "Father, I feel weak and sick to my stomach."

"Do not worry about the future, my dear. You will stay with us at Shiloh. I will take care of you and the children."

The next day, the father and daughter motored into Columbus and met Wade at the lawyer's office.

Daniel had carefully considered, "If I give Wade money, it will be a bribe to get rid of him for good."

So, he took out an envelope from his pocket. "Here is $500 for your trip to California." Then the rancher warned him, "Son, do not return to Columbus or go near Shiloh. My ranch hands are aware of the circumstances. You may be harmed if they see you. I cannot be responsible for their actions."

"I understand. Sir, you have been good to me. I especially liked the Winchester rifle that you gave me last year for Christmas. I guess that I'll not be able to take it with me."

Coming to the lawyer's office, Raquel brought Sofie and Andrew with her. Wade wanted to see them before he left. He was starting to second guess his decision about leaving his son and daughter behind. He got down on one knee and reached out his arms to them. "Come to papa." But the children turned away from him. They clung to their mother's skirt.

She reminded him, "You did not hold them as babies. When they tried to climb onto your lap, you pushed them away."

Wade hung his head in shame.

The lawyer offered, "I have some candy in my desk drawer."

Giving it to Wade, the father finally coaxed his children to come to him. With an arm around each of them, he hugged them and wept. "I did not realize how precious my little ones are to me."

Having the last word, Raquel declared, "Wade, I have forgiven you, but I never want to see your face again after today. I have an order of protection against you. If you come near me in the future, you will be arrested."

Outside of the office, Pablo was waiting to take Wade to where they had left the horses and wagon. It was located on a side street not far away. The young man left with him, but Daniel tarried a minute longer to thank the lawyer. Suddenly a terrible thought came to him. Pablo hated Wade and might seek revenge. So, the rancher quickly exited the office and started running down the street. When he turned the corner, Wade had his back against the wall, and Pablo was about to punch him with his fists.

Daniel yelled at him in Spanish, "*Pare*! Stop!" He did so hesitantly; the rancher reprimanded him in harsh tones. "*Compadre*, do not use violence to punish! Let the Lord avenge!"

Standing by in silence, Pablo showed no remorse.

Wade started to walk to his wagon. But before getting on board, he suddenly stopped. "I need to talk to Pablo." He motioned to his ranch hand.

Pablo postured, figuring that he would be rebuked.

With Daniel interpreting Spanish, Wade spoke to the man "Pablo, *perdóneme*. I am sorry for the way that I have treated you these past years. Thank you for helping us. You had strong character not to leave. If it had not been for you and Maria, we would have starved."

Pablo nodded that he accepted the apology.

Turning to Daniel, Wade expressed, "I appreciate all that you have done for us." Then he nervously asked, "Would you pray for me and my life ahead?"

"Yes, son, I will." The rancher put his arm around him and prayed. Then he spoke, "Son, there is food, a canteen, and a bedroll under the wagon's buckboard for you. Go in peace."

"I'm very grateful." But Wade was puzzled. "How can this man be kind to me when I have been such a failure in regards to his daughter."

Wade journeyed until twilight and then stopped to have some supper. He was pleasantly surprised to find cans of beans, bread, cheese, and a jar of honey under the buckboard of the wagon. He also removed the bed roll and felt something hard in it. To his astonishment, Wade pulled out his Winchester rifle.

Emotion overtook him, and he groaned, "I am the prodigal son, yet my father-in-law has blessed me."

~~~~~~~
~~~~~~~

An appointment was made with the court, and Raquel appeared before the circuit judge one week later. Pablo and Maria came as witnesses. When the judge was informed of Wade's abandonment, he immediately granted the divorce.

The young mother was free from the sordid marriage that she was entangled in. For Raquel, joyful thoughts flooded in, "I will start a new life without Wade and not look back. It will be very liberating to be free from the stress and fear that he caused me."

On the Sunday thereafter, the family prepared to go to church. During the week, Elizabeth had fashioned a fancy, turquoise, chintz dress for Raquel. It was very detailed with ornate trim. Audra walked into Raquel's bedroom and found her sister lying in the bed and the gorgeous dress laid on a chair.

Audra expressed concern, "Sister, are you not well?"

"I feel a little nauseated. I don't think that I can go to the church meeting today."

"Could you be pregnant?

"Maybe. I would only be a few weeks. What if the church ladies ask about my separation?"

"Tell them the truth. The reason for the divorce was Wade's abandonment. I will bring you some biscuits and tea. You must go by faith. Derek is preaching today."

Audra brought breakfast to the room. Then she dressed the children. After eating, Raquel was feeling better and got up from her bed. She was shaking as Audra helped her to dress, apply makeup, and put on jewelry.

Pleased with herself, Audra gave Raquel an admiring glance. "You are the epitome of beauty, sister. The horses and surrey are waiting. I will walk with you. Come children. Take Aunt Audra's hand."

When they arrived at the church, Audra looked around for Matthew and Kenton. She wondered, "Why are they not sitting with our family?"

A Christmas play was presented by the older children. It depicted Christ's birth with 'Joseph' and 'Mary' holding a real baby as Jesus. The congregation joined in singing the old, familiar carols.

In his sermon, Derek spoke on the power of love and unity among the brethren.

After church, a group of young men crowded around Audra. Derek thought, "I can understand why they are interested in her. She is exquisitely beautiful and charming."

Finally, she was able leave her admirers and find her sister. As Audra, Raquel, and the children exited the church, Raquel caught the eye of Matthew in the church yard. He nodded to her and then turned away.

Audra observed this. "Raquel, did Matthew James just snub you?"

"Yes, I believe he did."

"He brushed you off like he would brush a fly from his arm." But the children would not be snubbed. When Sofie saw Matthew, she raced across the church yard, yelling, "James, James!" She reached up her arms to him, and he picked her up. She put her arms around his neck and gave him kisses on the cheek.

Following his sister, Andrew was trying to climb up the soldier's leg. Kenton stooped down and picked him up and snickered. "Children certainly do remember who gives them attention."

When Raquel went to collect her children, Matthew greeted her formally. Kenton was more cordial.

Smiling at the soldiers, she stated, "Father has asked me to invite you for dinner along with Derek."

The corporal nodded in affirmation. "I gladly accept, Miss Raquel."

She peered up at Matthew. "Will you come to dine with us today? I have important news to tell you."

He declined the invitation, "Thank you, but I am unable to attend. I have other plans."

Raquel felt forlorn. Matthew had been formal and almost cold in his attitude toward her.

As they were leaving, Kenton turned to Matthew. "Why are you not coming to the dinner?"

"You shall not covet another man's wife. Isn't that reason enough? Her appearance is quite elegant today."

"Very enticing."

"Yes, that is why I need to stay away."

A hearty dinner awaited the family and guests at the ranch. It was a merry group, especially since Raquel with Sofie and Andrew were among them. Audra was seated at the table with a mysterious grin on her face. When Derek came to sit next to her, she hastily put a pine cone in his seat. He sat down on it and then jumped up, startled. He held it up, and everyone began to laugh. Mirth filled the atmosphere.

After the meal, Audra asked Derek if she might talk to him privately in the parlor. They entered the large room, and she motioned for him to sit on the Victorian couch with her. Silently, she challenged herself, "I will break his reserved composure."

He was curious. "What is it that you wanted to discuss?" Audra started giggling and flirted, "Sergeant Rands, you are so dashing and debonair, I just wanted your attention. Maybe you would like a little kiss?"

Moving close to her, Derek placed his hand on her back drawing her towards him. She blurted out, "I was only teasing. I didn't really mean it!"

Before she knew what was happening, Audra was locked into his embrace, and his lips were on hers. She yielded to the pressure of his mouth on hers and was a bit shaken when he finally released her.

"I did not expect this."

"Next time you need to think before you speak." He had a smug look on his face.

"Derek, I seriously need your help. My sister is no longer married."

His eyes collided with hers. "Really?"

"Yes, Wade abandoned Raquel and the children. The judge has granted her a divorce. Father will explain it all to you later. I think that Lieutenant Matthew James is interested in my sister, and I approve. What Father will not tell you is that Raquel may be pregnant. I don't want Matthew to come to court Raquel and then find out later that there may be a baby involved. If he courts her and then rejects her, she will be devastated. You must tell him now so he will not be deceived.

Derek snickered. "Matthew James is a man of integrity. If he wants to pursue Raquel, no baby will deter him."

Smiling sweetly, she replied, "Thank you for saying that. It makes me happy."

The scent of Audra's perfume lingered, and Derek contemplated, "I must not be thinking about her. I regret the kiss, even though it was satisfying that she yielded to me. My career is of utmost importance. I will not let himself get entangled into a romantic web."

Thereafter, the two re-entered the dining room. Raquel, seated across from Kenton, was laughing at a story that he was telling.

Audra glanced at them, smiling. "It is so wonderful to see my sister joyful again."

Turning to the corporal, Raquel asked, "Would you care to take the children to swing on the oak tree?"

"I can think of nothing better that I would like to do."

The young mother scrutinized Kenton. "He is quite charming and winsome."

After the soldiers left, Audra relived the kiss in her imagination. "I very much liked the kiss I provoked, and the feel of Derek's mouth on mine. I am beginning to come into agreement with father about the sergeant. My future plans are to go to medical school for a year. But after that, I want to be married."

~~~~~~~

At Cavalry Camp, Derek informed Kenton, "I want you to know that Raquel was recently divorced and also that she
~~~~~~~

might be pregnant."

"That is astounding news! I must find Matthew and advise him of this turn of events."

Searching for Matthew James, Kenton was informed that the lieutenant had gone into Columbus for the day. It was not until evening that he encountered his comrade to tell him the news of Raquel.

With a cocky attitude, Kenton spoke, "Matthew, you really missed out today by brashly refusing to go to the Kirks. I spent part of the afternoon with Raquel. I amused her at the dinner, and entertained the children. It was a splendid day."

Giving his friend a stern look, the lieutenant warned, "Did you not remember that she has a husband?"

"Oh, by the way, she no longer has a husband. She recently obtained a divorce, on the grounds of abandonment."

Wiping the sweat from his brow, Matthew was almost stupefied. "Circumstances have turned to my favor. I am free to pursue her."

The corporal snickered. "I guess so. If she does not choose you, I will be next in line."

Scratching his head, Matthew debated, "This very evening, I am anxious to go and see Raquel. However, it is already getting late. It would be dangerous for me and my horse to travel in the dark."

Kenton strutted away like a proud peacock. He reflected, "I may be a corporal, but I have upstaged an officer."

Later, Matthew met up with the sergeant. "I suppose you know the news from Shiloh. I am ecstatic."

Derek advised, "Wait a minute, brother. Raquel may be

pregnant, possibly only a few weeks."

Giving him a cocky grin, he replied, "You think that would stop me from pursuing her. I have prayed for this young woman, and the baby will be mine."

"I predicted that you would say this."

"Does Ken know about this?"

"Yes, and he is of the same opinion as you."

Lieutenant Matthew James planned to call on Raquel the following evening, but the garrison was commanded into a lock down because of a border threat. It was indefinite when he would be able to leave the post to visit her.

~~~~~~~

In the cool of the evening, Audra was in a solemn mood and conversed with Raquel about the present circumstances, "Sister, I told Derek that you might be pregnant. So, I am sure that he has told Matthew."

"Oh, no, you didn't!" she shrieked in horror.

"Sister, it is better that he knows now. You would not want him to think that you deceived him."

"Yes, you are probably right. Three children would be a great responsibility for any man."

Each day thereafter, Raquel dressed and groomed carefully in case that Matthew might come to call. Each evening, she fretted, "Again I go to bed with sorrow in my heart. I was so sure that he cared for me."

In the meantime, suitors began to come and inquire about her. The news was out about Raquel's divorce and that she was the owner of a ranch. The county newspaper had posted the divorce in the court house section. A steady stream of
~~~~~~~

men came from three counties to call on her.

Daniel Kirk screened each of the men before introducing the prospective suitor to Raquel. The older fellows were immediately eliminated. Her father quoted the proverb, "You can't teach old dogs, new tricks." All the men interviewed were in favor of being a father to Raquel's children. It was like a merry-go-round; the proposed courtiers came and went. Although many of the possible beaus were handsome and prosperous, Raquel did not seem to be interested in any of them.

She directed her concern to Audra, "Five days have gone by, and Matthew has not come. Marrying a divorced woman might be considered shameful. After all, I understand that some men could not handle that stigma. I have resigned myself to the fact that I will not see Matthew again."

Trying to assure her sister, Audra encouraged, "Have faith and do not give up, he will come."

On the sixth day, the rancher was in his office when a soldier knocked on his door. It was Lieutenant Matthew James, and Daniel called for him to come in. "Good evening, sir. Thank you for seeing me. I will cut to the chase. I have come here to talk to you about Raquel. I would like your approval to court her with the motive of marriage."

Daniel challenged him, "Raquel is alone with two small children. Are you a hero come to save a damsel in distress?"

Matthew gave him a cocky grin. "If she needs a hero, I'd be the man. I would climb a tree to rescue a kitten."

The father let out a jovial laugh. "So, you are one of the few noble men."

"Sir, for a long time I thought that the army was enough to fulfill my life. I am thirty years old, and now I want a wife and children. Raquel is a fine lady, and her children are a delight to me. Though I serve in the army, I am a man of means with other investments."

"You need to know that Raquel's ranch was bought contract for deed. I have three more years of payments."

Undaunted, he nodded, "I will accept that responsibility."

"Several suitors have already come this week to court Raquel. I am sure that more young men will come. My daughter can have any man she wants. If she chooses you, I assume that you will treat her well."

On the other side of the house, Luisa, the hired girl, started running down the hall to Raquel's room. "*Señorita* Raquel, *señorita, el soldado está aquí*! The soldier, he is here!"

Dropping her needlework, Raquel opened her door. "What soldier?"

"*Señor* James. *El habla con tu papá. Date prisa, preparate*!"

"Luisa, are you telling me to hurry and to prepare myself for my guest? Well, I don't want to hurry and meet Matthew. I am angry that he has waited so long to call on me."

Dragging her feet, Raquel chose an ornate dress. She powdered her nose, dabbed on perfume, put on jewelry, and took her time combing her hair.

"Let him wait. I waited for him," she fumed.

When Luisa mentioned the name, Lieutenant James, Sofie and Andrew started running about the room and clapping their hands. Raquel hushed them, "I know that you are excited, but you must calm down. Let's go and see your aunt.

I do not want to talk to Matthew alone." So, the children accompanied their mother to the parlor where Audra was playing her mandolin.

Looking up to see her sister donned in a fancy dress, Audra asked "What is the occasion?"

"Matthew James is talking to father in his office."

"That is wonderful! I told you he would come!"

A little later, a knock came on the parlor door, and there stood the lieutenant. The children ran to him, and he picked them up and hugged them. Audra smiled as he entered the room.

Remembering that Matthew had snubbed her only a few days earlier, Raquel was cool in her greeting, "Good evening, Sir."

After the three of them visited for a short time, Audra took the children to the nursery.

When Matthew and Raquel were alone, the soldier looked intently at the lovely young woman seated before him. Concentrating on what he wanted to say, he blurted out, "Raquel, you look beautiful tonight!"

"Thank you for the compliment."

"I am sorry that you have gone through a divorce. Actually, I am not sorry, but I did pray for you. How are you coping?"

"Things are going very well. The children have adjusted to life here on the ranch. They seldom ask for their papa. He was not a doting father. Thank you for inquiring. How are things at Camp Cavalry?"

"We are still on alert for Pancho Villa and his Villistas. I would have come to see you sooner, but I had no choice in the matter. All soldiers were detained at the camp for these past three days." Finally, he broached the subject of his coming. "Raquel, it would be my honor to come calling on you. I have admired you from a distance ever since Audra's party."

"Matthew, last week after church, I invited you to dinner to tell you crucial news. You seemed to care about me. You told me that if I ever needed you, you would come for the children and me. It was just words, empty words. Your caring attitude was all a pretense. Last Sunday I wanted to talk to you. I wanted your comfort and your strength, but you turned away from me."

In exasperation, he sighed. "My word is true. I would have come for you. You only had to ask. I am sorry that I did not listen to you. I was struggling with the issue of lusting after you. You are a most desirable woman. I did not want to sin against God in coveting another man's wife. Would you please forgive my callousness?"

"Yes, of course, I understand."

Beginning his plea, he placed his hands on hers, "Raquel, your father has given me permission for a courtship. Would you be interested?"

"I will think about it and let you know what I have decided. Now, please excuse me, I need to help Audra put the children to bed."

He offered," I could to read them a story."

"My sister probably has already read to them. Your presence will only make them want to stay up longer." Raquel walked Matthew to the door. "Good night, Lieutenant James."

"It was my delight to see you again." Riding his horse back to the fort, he thought about Raquel, "It might be harder than I thought to win her love. Yet I have made my prayer, and God will help me. In reality, there will be fierce competition for her hand of matrimony, especially since she owns a ranch. My only bit of satisfaction is that I am the one she wanted to comfort her."

A few days went by, and Raquel did not contact Matthew of her decision of a courtship. He surmised, "I might be out of the race to win the heart of this alluring young lady."

3

One evening at the family's supper, Daniel enthusiastically made an announcement to Elizabeth and Audra, "The Apache Indians and their culture have always held a special intrigue for me. Derek's discourse has piqued my interest in this indigenous people. I have a desire to teach the Indians ranching methods. My dear wife and daughter, how would you like to go on a real adventure? Our annual outing this year will be to go on a mission trip to the Apache reservation."

Elizabeth dropped her teacup, and the tea spilled onto the table, staining the lace cloth. "Are you serious about this, Daniel?"

"Yes, my dear."

Audra twisted in her chair. "This news grips me with uncertainty. I am not sure about leaving grandfather and his medical practice. He has a tendency to overwork and to become exhausted. How long would our stay be, father?"

"With travel time, we will spend about three weeks on the reservation."

Elizabeth nervously brushed back a wisp of hair. "How primitive will our living quarters be, an adobe house?"

He chuckled. "No. I have communicated with the Indian

agent, Garth Rands. Next to the agency, they have a home with guest rooms to accommodate us. There is also a church on the compound. My goal is to teach the Indians ranching methods. We could be a blessing to the Apache people."

Suddenly Audra gave a little squeal. "I am ready for the quest of serving the Apache!"

Her father assumed a serious demeanor. "Indian Agent Rands is much obliged for our offer of help and he and his son, Derek, will meet with us next week at the garrison, to discuss the trip. The sergeant will teach us greetings in the Apache language."

Her confidence flowing, Audra added, "I am already fluent in Spanish, learning the Apache tongue will be an easy task for me."

Elizabeth suggested, "I could teach the young women to sew clothes for their children."

Her husband smiled. "Yes, that would be helpful. We shall pray and lift this mission up to the Lord. Today is the 12th of December. My intention is to be ready to leave Shiloh in one month."

~~~~~~~

On the following week, the Kirk household was busy preparing to celebrate Christmas; the railroad had delivered a load of pine trees for the town. The parents also screened more suitors who came to call on Raquel. In the midst of this, she received a letter from Wade.

Dear Raquel,

I write this letter with much repentance. I am terribly sorry for the way I treated you. I dream of holding you in my arms again.
~~~~~~~

Nothing can surpass your beauty and grace. I sorely miss you and our children. Enclosed is money for your needs. My brother brought me to church, and I prayed with the pastor. I now have Christ in my life. I don't drink hard stuff. If you can forgive me, my promise is to love and cherish you always.

With unending devotion,

Wade

Showing the letter to Audra, Raquel asked, "What do you think of this plea, sister? Wade now attends church and has sworn off liquor. He wants to come back here and make us a family again. I am confused as to what decision I should make."

"You need to pray and seek God. If it were me, I would never, ever trust him again! I am happy for his new life, but I would not return to him. What if he regresses to his old degenerate ways and habits? Raquel, you told me that there were several nights that Wade did not come home. Where did he spend those nights?"

"He told me that he was drunk in the jail."

"I will contact Derek and ask him to come with me to the tavern. I want to talk to the owner and investigate. I will plan a trip to town for tomorrow. Anyway, I think that you seriously should accept a courtship with Matthew James. I believe that it was a rendezvous made in heaven the night you met him at the party. He came to call on you knowing that you might be pregnant. None of the other suitors had any knowledge of your dilemma. Matthew clearly loves you and the children. Can you not see that he is a noble man? He is a mighty warrior, not just in the army, but in the kingdom of God."

"I am not sure. Knowing Matthew for such a short time, fear has assailed me. I do not want to rush into marriage. I made that mistake before. I do know one thing. I wish to be married when this baby is born!"

~~~~~~~

The next day Audra had her horse saddled and rode to meet Derek at the tavern in Columbus. She told him about Wade's letter and her suspicions, "I do not want my sister to make a serious blunder."

"I am in agreement with you. She has gone through a trial, and she deserves a better future."

The two united in prayer, "Lord, in Jesus name, we ask that the truth would come forth about Wade."

The two entered the tavern, and Derek introduced Audra and himself and shook hands with the owner. With an air of authority, the sergeant inquired of the man, "Sir, I am here to ask you for any information about Wade Conner."

Audra added, "He was married to my sister."

The owner gave them favor and related a full disclosure of Wade's time at the tavern, "My niece, Doreen, is a barfly. She has a room upstairs in the tavern. My wife and I took her in because her family had disowned her. Doreen does tend bar, but she makes a living mooching off the men. Wade spent some nights with her. She bragged that he had promised to take her away with him. She was bitterly disappointed when he left the area without her."

Derek expressed their thanks, "We greatly appreciate your forthrightness, sir."
~~~~~~~

After the couple left the tavern, they walked their horses toward the drug store. Derek turned his eyes to Audra and asked, "May I buy a soda pop and a pastry for you at the store's fountain?"

Her smile was sweet. "That sounds refreshing, and thank you for accompanying me today."

"The pleasure was all mine." Flattery was in his words.

Giving her sister the information about Wade from the tavern owner, Raquel gasped, but shed no tears.

Only anger and sorrow were apparent in her face. "So, Wade was unfaithful to me. He defiled the marriage bed with his adultery. This is the last insult, and it clinches my decision. I will never go back to him."

Another week had gone by, and Raquel had not contacted Matthew of her decision for him to come courting. He told his companions, "I am anxious to speak to Raquel. I might be out of the race to win the heart of this young lady, but I plan to tell her of my intentions. I don't want some young 'buck' to come in and 'sweep her off her feet'."

With a box of chocolate covered cherries in hand, Matthew went to visit her at Shiloh. He brought up the subject of courtship, "Raquel, I know that many suitors have come to call on you. Would you mind telling me where I stand with you? Do I have a chance? If you have met a man that you are interested in, then I will end my pursuit. Is it futile for me to continue to hope? I love you, and I will love your children. I would wish to adopt Sofie and Andrew. I know about the baby, and it would truly be my own child. I am well able to support you with a good life."

"Matthew, you are a man who shares my faith, and I am impressed with you. You may call on me; yet we have only known each other briefly. Could we spend some time talking about our life and future to see if we are suited for each other?"

With a look of victory in his demeanor, he replied, "Yes, that would be splendid."

4

It was January third; the new year of 1916 had come in. The mission trip to the Apache reservation was quickly approaching for the Kirks, and there was excitement in the atmosphere

Daniel Kirk discussed some specifics with Ramon, his ranch hand, "Our truck, full of goods, could not navigate the rutted dirt roads of the reservation because of the rainy weather. Therefore, I have obtained a covered wagon for travel. Please load the trunks, the medical supplies, the tools and seeds, and the treadle sewing machine with the bolts of calico fabric."

The appointed departure day for the mission trip came. Daniel informed his wife and daughter, "We will leave for Cavalry Camp today with our personal belongings. Ramon will take the horses and wagon ahead to be left at the garrison. Our plan is to spend the night at the army post and then leave at dawn the next day. It will be a two-day journey to the reservation. Agent Rands will meet us at the army post."

The Kirk family was settled in their guest rooms at the garrison when a messenger brought a telegram to them in the afternoon. It read, "Dr. Kirk is gravely ill. Come home."

Daniel informed Derek of his father's illness, and then he and his family left immediately for Shiloh. When they arrived at the ranch, Dr. Kirk lay on his bed with a high fever.

When the family checked on Dr. Kirk's health the next day, he had malaise and was still spiking a fever. The doctor made a plea to his family, "Do not cancel the trip to the reservation because of my illness!"

Advising his wife and daughter, Daniel stated, "The mission trip must be postponed until a later time"

Expressing concern to her parents, Audra objected, "I will not cancel! May I go alone to the Apache reservation if it is permitted? It is a lifetime opportunity."

Astonishment was Daniel's reaction to her declaration, "No, I will not allow it!"

Aghast, Elizabeth gasped. "It is unthinkable!"

Yet Audra persisted, "Mother, father, please pray, it is a chance for me to help this people."

Shortly thereafter, her father, with a proud look, responded, "Audra, we prayed about your bold plan and submitted it to God. It has been a struggle for us to let our adored daughter go alone to the reservation. However, if Agent Rands will permit it, then you have our blessing."

Audra was elated. "I am very appreciative; I love you both! It is my dream to serve the Apache."

The Kirks journeyed again to Camp Cavalry to consult with Agent Rands, but it was reported that he had been detained at the reservation. He was expected to arrive the following day.

Addressing Audra, Daniel gave her a parting piece of

advice, "My dear, I insist that you remain at the garrison to wait for the agent's arrival. You may have further contact with Derek. I will leave a message for the sergeant concerning Dr. Kirk's continued illness. I will also ask the sergeant to arrange for a guest room for you and to look after you until you can meet with the Indian agent. You could suggest that he practice the Apache language with you in his free time. If Agent Rands tarries in coming to the garrison, do not fret. It will give you and Derek time together to continue your friendship. If you must return home, telegraph me, and I will send someone for you. I may wait a couple of days. An attachment between you and the sergeant may form."

Seeing through the pretense of her father's words, Audra challenged him, "Father, that is manipulation, and I am embarrassed by it. Derek Rands has made no overture of affection to me. He is only polite."

"I'm just trying to be a good father who wants the best for you." Daniel grinned, and his eyes twinkled.

Indian Agent Pastor Rands would come soon to Camp Cavalry, and Audra mulled over her plan, "The agent has the authority to let me come alone to the reservation. I have much ability to serve there as a nurse. So, I must ask Derek for favor with his father before he and the other soldiers go out on their morning maneuvers."

Tightening her wool shawl around her, Audra walked out into the chilly dawn. With her head up, she walked boldly to the barracks. She considered, "What I am about to do is risky, but it might be my best opportunity to make my plea." As she neared the barracks, she could hear the snoring of the men, and she questioned herself, "Is it rude to try and see Derek at this early hour? Could I send in a message? What if my plan backfires?"

As Audra approached the door, it suddenly opened, and a soldier on his way out collided with her. Surprised and half asleep, the startled man cried out, "What in tarnation is wrong, Miss Kirk?"

She whispered, "I have to see Sergeant Rands. "

The soldier was Corporal Kenton Lott, and he almost pulled her inside the barracks. The wind was cold.

Looking around, she could barely see the forms of the men on their beds.

In a low voice, the amicable soldier informed her, "The Sarge's bed is in the middle of the row. I will lead you to him, but I don't want any part in waking him up."

She murmured back, "I don't think this is a good idea. I will wait outside."

But the corporal took her hand to follow him anyway. In the dim light, she tripped over a pair of army boots in the aisle. She fell on top of a sleeping soldier and almost turned his cot over. The astonished man screamed, leaped up, and grabbed her. He held onto her with a tight grip. It woke up the entire army barracks. There was an immediate uproar with a soldier shouting, "What the heck is that woman doing in here?"

Audra cringed and tried to escape, but some soldiers blocked her way. The sun was coming up and light was now streaming in through the windows. The men could see that it was the young lady, Miss Kirk, demurely beautiful even at this hour. They scrambled to pull on breeches and shirts. Then laughter and snide remarks arose among the ranks within the barracks. The soldiers found her intrusion quite amusing.

A soldier yelled to her, "What the deuce do you want, Miss?"

"I want to see Sergeant Rands," she timidly responded.

Derek came forward, bare chested with shirt in hand.

"Do you mind?" He motioned for her to turn around while he pulled on his shirt. Audra turned pink, yet trying to remember his muscular chest and the biceps of his arms. Derek studied her intently. "Why are you here and at this hour?"

"I needed to speak to you before you went out on maneuvers, to ask for favor with your father. I did not want to enter the barracks, but a soldier persisted in bringing me in while he looked for you."

"What soldier?"

Corporal Kenton Lott raised his hand. "That is true, sir, I couldn't leave a precious little thing like her to shiver in the cold."

"So, you're her accomplice?"

"No, sir, but I will be her advocate."

Derek rolled his eyes.

Facing him, and in a repentant voice, Audra begged forgiveness, "I am truly sorry, sir, for the intrusion."

Major Howard, a scruffy man, fifty years of age, came forward to speak, "So, Missy, you wanted a little *tête-à-tête* with the Sarge, eh? Ain't that sweet. Well, Missy, before we let you go, we want to see you kiss the Sarge, here. Call it a little token for waking us up."

The men all chimed in with their hearty approval and catcalls. Audra blushed, but approached Derek and kissed him on the cheek.

The major did not like the kiss. "No, that ain't good enough. We wanna see a real romantic kiss, don't we boys?"

A soldier yelled out, "Show us how it's done, Sarge."

Derek hesitated, but he quickly saw that it was no use to argue.

Major Howard demanded, "Go ahead, man, kiss the girl!"

Coming near to Audra, Derek placed his hands on the back of her shoulders, gently pulled her close, and gave her a long and tender kiss. She obliged and gave no struggle. The moment was so intense for her that she gripped his forearms to keep her balance.

The soldiers were enraptured with this scene and began to clap, whoop, and holler. As the men dispersed, Derek looked intently at Audra. "What is so important to cause this ruckus?"

She winced at his choice of words. "Derek, sir, my parents will permit me to go alone to the reservation."

Raising his eyebrows, he could hardly fathom the news. "Truly, your parents will allow this?"

"Yes, and my plea is that you will give a favorable word to your father for me."

"We will discuss this when I return from maneuvers."

He thought for a moment. "You play the mandolin very well. There will be a hymn sing tonight in the mess hall. Would you sing a hymn with your instrument? It would be of some recompense for the fracas you caused today."

Her smile was winsome. "Yes, I would be delighted."

As Derek walked Audra back to her room, she kept thinking about the kiss, "It was very exhilarating, even under the circumstances. Maybe I might choose this soldier as a future husband."

In the garrison compound yard, Derek found Audra later in the afternoon. She was reading her Bible under an elmwood tree, and he joined her. "What is this about a plea?

"My plea is that I might come to the reservation alone."

His eyes viewed her delicate face, and it was alluring for him. "Audra, I admire your desire to help the Apache people. Let me paint you a picture of the obstacles. You are a young and pretty woman. Therefore, the Indian men will lust after you. The Indian women will be jealous of your elegance and ignore you. The children, of course, will love you and seek your attention. Even if you were married, going alone might be unpleasant."

Arguing, she insisted, "But I would be living with your parents in their home."

"My father and mother cannot be your nursemaids. My father will never permit you to come alone. I never would have imagined that your parents would allow this."

"So, you will not speak a word for me of your favor?"

He shook his head. "No, I am sorry, I cannot. You need to go home and go back to your nursing."

"I am not only a nurse. I am a doctor's assistant, sir."

"My apology, Miss Kirk."

~~~~~~~
~~~~~~~

It appeared that every soldier on the post was in attendance at the hymn sing. Word had gotten around that Miss Kirk would sing and play her mandolin.

As she entered the mess hall, Corporal Kenton Lott came up to greet her with a big grin and complimented her, "Miss Audra, you are more beautiful than a *de' Medici* painting."

"Thank you for the compliment, sir. My mother prayed that I would be as fair as Job's daughters."

Nodding, he replied, "I certainly believe it."

Audra stood alone in front of the soldiers who stared at her, expectant to hear her sing. She prayed, "Lord, in Jesus name, help me not to be nervous and that I have the Spirit of the Lord where there is freedom."

Three soldier musicians with drums and guitars accompanied her on her mandolin. She began with a favorite song, the Battle Hymn of the Republic. When the men started to sing the chorus, glory, glory, hallelujah, it sounded like a mighty choir. Her next song was a solo, Amazing Grace.

The enlisted men shouted, "Sing it again." So, she sang it again. The last hymn was What a Friend We Have in Jesus. As the soldiers raised their voices to sing this song of praise to God, the presence of the Lord filled the place. After the hymn session ended, the soldiers lined up with many accolades and thanks to Audra for her music.

Derek also praised her, "You gave an excellent performance tonight, Miss Kirk."

~~~~~~~

Leaving at dawn, Agent Garth Rands made the long
~~~~~~~

trip on muddy dirt roads from the reservation to the fort. He arrived in his truck at the garrison mid-morning. Derek and an officer came to greet the Indian agent.

Garth Rands was a tall, handsome man of forty-seven years of age. His charismatic personality and astute wisdom made him respected among the Apache. As Indian agent, his judgments were impartial; the Indians trusted him to always carry out justice on the reservation. He was a powerful figure in the Apache nation, and no one in the tribe dared to challenge his authority. Through much prayer and ingenuity, he had accomplished building a large church next to the agency. As the pastor of the church, he taught them the Bible. The fruit of his ministry was evident in that many on the reservation had begun to prosper. He often taught that Jesus came to earth give them an abundant life.

Speaking to his father, Derek related, "Audra's parents had to return home quickly to care for Mr. Kirk's father who had suddenly become ill. Therefore, she desires to go the tribe alone."

Dismayed, Garth Rands almost shouted, "It is absolutely out of the question! She is a young, white woman coming into the reservation without protection."

"I told her as much, but you must talk to her."

It was almost midday when Audra was called in to converse with Agent Rands. She nervously hurried to the office where the agent was to speak with her. His kindly manner quickly turned into an interrogation. "Miss Kirk, why do you want to come to the reservation without your parents? Is this an adventure for you?"

"No, sir, I want to serve the Apache with my medical skills."

His facial expression was stern. "Do you have faith to come?"

"Yes, I believe it is the Lord's will."

The agent looked at her intently. "Would your beauty not cause trouble and be a snare to this people?"

"No, sir, it would not!" Her attitude was adamant.

Fighting hard not to lose her confidence, she considered, "I must stay calm and keep my faith."

With her hope diminishing, Agent Rands reiterated the same potential problems that Derek had given her. Almost ready to dismiss her, he hesitated. "Miss Kirk, I do not think it would be wise for you to come alone, but I will pray and give you, my answer."

It was early afternoon, and the soldiers were resting a bit after their meal in the mess hall. Their horses were put out to pasture, and all was quiet at the fort. Some of the men were carrying water to their gardens. Others were cleaning their saddles and repairing their gear.

Still thinking about the riot she had created in the barracks yesterday morning, Audra reflected, "Why is there always drama wherever I go? I guess it's my willful personality that brings me attention. At least I redeemed myself in the hymn sing last night. The soldiers raved about my singing. Yet I am aware that only the anointing of God can bless the music."

Not yet hearing back from Agent Rands, Audra anxiously awaited his decision. Strolling across the army compound yard and headed to her room, she saw a gathering of soldiers.

Kenton beckoned her, "Derek is teaching Kung Fu techniques for combat to the recruits. A great number of them want to learn the skill. It is much desired for the enlisted men, and Derek is quite adept in this style of fighting. His Chinese master had taken a special interest in the him, seeing his strength and keen ability. When he enlisted in the army, he has continued to practice this fighting art. Lieutenant Matthew James and I have become his protégés."

With the group of onlookers, Audra watched the soldiers sparring and mock fighting. Viewing the exhibition of physical strength and strategy, she mused, "It is fascinating to see Derek in action and his prowess in the martial arts."

When the session ended, two young soldiers noticed that Audra had been at the demonstration. They had heard that this young nurse wanted to serve the Apache nation and to enter the reservation alone and unaccompanied.

Derek was nearby when a soldier, Private Lane, called to her, "Miss Kirk, may we talk with you? We have a remedy that will enable you to go safely go to the tribe." He grinned from ear to ear and his eyes twinkled.

Audra approached the soldier. "What would that be, sir?"

"You need a husband for your protection, a covering. The Indians will respect that."

Laughing at the jest, she inquired, "Are you volunteering, sir?"

He chuckled. "No, but the Sarge here will do the honor. His father, a pastor, can perform the vows."

Private Rentz also chimed in, "Yeah, the Sarge thinks you'd make him a splendid wife. Ain't that so, Sarge?"

Hesitating, but with a mischievous grin, Derek answered, "Well, yes, my lady. I am at your beck and call. Your wish is my command."

Audra joined in the jest, "Would I be loved, Sir Knight?"

Derek looked directly into her eyes. "Yes, you would be loved."

"Then how can I not accept, sir." Smiling, she seemed to enjoy the farce.

As she walked away, she heard the young men laughing and guffawing. With a nonchalant aspect, she concluded, "If they want to make fun of me, then I will play the game and turn it back on them. I had the last word. If the Lord wants me to go to the reservation, He will help me. Yet I must push the words from my mind that Derek has just spoken. Those words perturb me and like a clock, they keep ticking and ticking in my brain, 'You would be loved, you would be loved, you would be loved'. I wonder what would it be like to be loved by a man of such authority as Derek Rands. I imagine that it would be amazing."

Leaving the scene, Derek felt convicted in his spirit about joining in the jest, "It is dangerous for me to flirt in such a manner. It is like holding a fire cracker too long, before it goes off. I have not allowed myself to be entangled with a woman, and I certainly will not start now. I am already casting down the imagination of Audra's pretty face. I cannot be thinking about her, when in reality, I handle several strategic matters at the army post. This duty requires my utmost attention, and I must keep myself focused on the business at hand. The officers include me as one of their advisers. I do not disclose my age since I came up in the ranks so quickly. Though some of the older soldiers seem jealous of my ability, all have shown me respect. Humility is a virtue, and at times I have to resist my own cocky attitude. I prayed for the wisdom of Ahithophel who advised King David. The Lord gives me wisdom in every task I tackle, and the men follow me. I have had success in every arena of life, and I credit it to my faith in the Bible."

~~~~~~~

The day was hot and Audra was resting in her room when a letter was placed under her door. She read it quickly and then read it again. "Oh Lord, I praise you," she whispered. She threw the letter in the air and danced around the room. She hugged herself in delight and started singing, "My spirit is soaring and my soul is roaring." Then she dropped to her knees in prayer.

Quickly dressing into her purple silk dress, she adorned it with her cameo broach and earrings. Then she anointed herself with perfume and was almost shaking as she combed her long red tresses. With anticipation, she thought, "I must look ravishing. This will be one of the most important days of my life. It is too amazing, too marvelous, for it not to be the Lord."

Thereafter, she carefully folded the letter and placed it in her dress pocket. It was late afternoon, and the sun was yellow orange, going down in the west. Audra timidly knocked on the chaplain office door where Derek was working. He was visibly surprised to see her. Her brown eyes measured him and the soldier appeared handsome and dashing.

He stood up politely as she entered. "You wish to see me,
~~~~~~~

Miss Kirk? Please be seated."

Taking a deep breath, Audra commanded her heart to stop beating so fast. Nervously, she broached the subject of her coming. "I came to give you, my answer!"

"Your answer?" He looked puzzled and stared at her quizzically.

With animation, Audra began to speak and the words tumbled out, "It is with much joy that I accept your proposal of marriage. I hope that I am worthy of you."

Derek's eyebrows went up in acute astonishment, and incredulity flashed across his face. His relaxed demeanor changed to a soldier at attention, ready to address his commander. Taken aback, he slowly considered this encounter, "At this moment, Audra seems serious, even though she had entered into the jest a few hours earlier."

His ego goaded him to ask her a few questions, "I need to know why you would want to marry me. You want to go the reservation that much?"

Not stammering, she answered boldly, "I think it would be very exciting to be married to you."

His eyes widened as he studied her. "Is that what you want from me, excitement?"

"I would love and honor you all of my days."

Gazing at her matchless beauty, Derek fought the temptation he felt. However, he continued to question her, wanting to know where this would lead. "You are serious about this, Audra. You have counted the cost?"

"Very much so."

"Maybe this is an infatuation, and you will grow tired of

army life, away from your lavish ranch."

His face was so somber that fear began to encompass her. "It would be no sacrifice for me. I would gladly leave it to be your wife."

"And you would give up attending the hospital medical school?"

She winced at that prospect. It had been her dream. "I would marry you today. My husband and my children will be my priority."

Silently, Derek reflected, "How very flattering and satisfying it is that she will give up all to be with me. Yet I see that I am on a dangerous path." But he continued to quiz her, "Wouldn't I need to ask for your father's permission?"

"You are my father's favorite, and he would choose you, as I also do."

Derek felt a twinge of guilt and silently made a decision. "The intrigue of the game has gone far enough. I know that I must end it before I wound her. I hope that she will see the logic of the situation." So, he began his speech, "Audra, what kind of man would I be to marry you, impregnate you, and keep you from your dream of becoming a doctor? Should I let my lust overcome my honor?" He frowned and shook his head. "I am a military man with an ambition and a career ahead. My aspiration is to be the commander of an army post someday. God has promised me my destiny. I cannot have a wife and baby holding me back and dragging me down."

Blinking back hot tears, she reached into her pocket and pulled out the letter. "Then why did you write this, to continue the jest?"

He grabbed the letter. "What is this?" His brows knit together, and he seemed dumbfounded as he read it.

Dearest Audra,

Though I did not seek it, you have captured my heart. Your charm and beauty enthrall my very soul. I must have you as my beloved wife. May I have your hand in marriage? I will love and cherish you, my darling. With unrequited love,

Derek P. Rands

There was fire in his eyes and disgust in his voice, "I did not write this, nor is my middle initial P. The young soldiers played this trick, and they will be reprimanded. I am truly sorry for their malevolent deed."

Trembling and visibly shaken, Audra quickly realized that she was the brunt of a cruel joke. Sadness and embarrassment settled upon her demeanor, but she would not let herself cry. The tears froze in her eyes. As she approached the door to leave, Derek put the palm of his hand on the door to stop her. She turned to face him, no defiance in her eyes, only sorrow.

Seeing her distress, he contemplated, "Though I would like to comfort her and press her into my broad shoulders, I cannot. Things might escalate in a manner that I will regret. I must break this magnetism between us once and for all. So, he assumed an aspect of smugness. "Were you looking forward to being in my arms tonight?"

She gazed up at him unflinching. "Yes!"

Audra's reply was totally not what he had expected. Her answer goaded Derek to react. As she tried to brush past him, he pulled her into his arms. He kissed her on the lips with such fervor and passion that it sent her senses reeling. It was not a tender kiss, but a kiss of possession. She would have fallen had she not been held so tightly in his arms. She tried to twist away from him, yet he still held her in his iron embrace.

Breathing deeply, he taunted her, "You wanted excitement from me."

"Let me go or I shall hate you," she managed to whisper.

"That is the idea."

As he let her go, she retorted vehemently, "I shall go home in the morning, and I pray that I never see you again." She left hurriedly in a swish of silk skirts.

Derek had accomplished it, the dissolution of the infatuation. He reflected upon the incident, "Why do I feel so guilty, so tormented. I must not second guess myself. She persisted when she said that it was her wish to be in my arms. I will have many challenges before me in the days ahead. If I ever want Audra in the future, I will go after her, woo her. I am used to getting what I want in life. But for now, I cannot give her the false hope of a love union. I cannot promise her a courtship. It would not be fair to make her wait. It would be hard for us both."

Racing to her room, Audra threw herself on the bed and let the tears flow. Wallowing in self-pity, she did not go to the mess hall to dine for the evening meal. She felt too sick inside, and her head ached from crying.

Because of the turmoil of what she had just experienced she made a vow to herself that day, "I will never let Sergeant Derek Rands hurt me again."

An hour later, Miss Kirk heard a knock at her door. She bounded from her bed and wondered if it might be Derek, come to apologize. There stood the two prankster soldiers who had played the trick on her. Sheepishly and nervously, they expressed their regret, "Miss Kirk, please forgive us. We are very sorry that we deceived you. Please don't blame the Sarge. It was our fault, and we are ashamed of it. Because of our mischief making, the Sarge will no longer train us in the martial arts. I know that you don't like us much, but if we can ever be of service to you, please call on us. We want to make it up to you for what we did."

She gave them her prettiest smile. "Thank you for coming to see me. I do forgive you. Go in peace."

Derek recounted the prank and Audra's confession to Corporal Kenton Lott. He also confided to his friend, "I did not handle the situation delicately."

Going to the mess hall, Kenton brought Audra a plate of food. "Thank you for your kindness."

The corporal asked, "May I come in?" She nodded her assent. He gazed at her red eyes and attempted to console her, "Audra, I am sorry that you were hurt. This too will pass, and you will soon forget the occurrence."

"I am so embarrassed." And she tried to fight back the tears that trickled down her lashes.

Putting his arms around her, Kenton held her until she became calm. His nearness helped relieve some of her anxiety. She saw that he cared how she felt, and her attitude started to brighten up.

Finally, Kenton gave her a cocky grin. "Audra, I wish

that those young soldiers had played their trick on me. My response would have been totally opposite."

His words made her laugh. "I appreciate you, dear friend." After he left, Audra thought about Kenton's visit, "I have much more respect for him. Indeed, his attention to me in my time of misery was very flattering."

Being extremely tired from the events of the day, Audra retired early. She decided. "I will to go home to my family who loves me. My parents will surely comfort me in my anguish over the sergeant's cruelty. Derek certainly is not the ideal man that father envisioned. I have seen his dark side, and I hope to never encounter him again. It would be emotionally painful for me to see him, even on occasion. Also, I no longer want to serve the Apache on the reservation." Yet she remembered her father's words, 'Timing is one of the fundamentals of life. Take every opportunity that God gives you'.

Sleep was fretful for Audra; she tossed and turned.

The next morning, Audra was still discouraged. She rationalized, "I can come with my parents to the reservation in a more appropriate time. Maybe I can serve God in another way. Moreover, it appears that Agent Rands will not accept me anyway. It is done. I have made up my mind that I am going home. I will telegraph father to come and get me and not delay."

Vexed at being taken advantage of, Audra brooded, "I let myself become vulnerable to Derek. His inquiries had delved into my inward thoughts concerning him. His questions were but a pretense that humiliated me."

Packing her belongings, she was almost ready to leave

when a message came from Agent Rands. His note informed her, "Miss Kirk, I permit you to come to the reservation alone. I want to discuss some cultural conditions that you must observe."

She sent a reply message. "I thank you for your permission, but I am returning home."

Walking into the chaplain's office to talk to Derek, Garth Rands was wondering why Audra had changed her mind. He addressed his son, "I gave Miss Kirk her request to come and serve on the reservation."

He was visibly surprised. "What? You actually consented for her to come alone?"

"Yes, son, the Lord impressed upon me that she will be needed there. However, she no longer wishes to come and will return home."

Derek jumped up from his chair, knocking it over. "This is my fault." He stormed out of the office, slamming the door behind him.

He strode the distance of the compound to her room and knocked. "It's Sergeant Derek Rands. I must speak with you, Audra."

"I do not wish to speak to you. You mocked me with your questions. You let me ramble on, exposing my love for you, only to cast it away. Go, soldier, and pursue your fortune. I was wrong to think you were a man of character."

"Do not put me on a pedestal, Audra. Open the door, please."

But she persisted in inflaming herself. "No, I will not! I never want to see your loathsome face again!"

"Open this door, or I will kick it in." He waited, then he counted, "1,2,3."

Finally, she cracked the door and he barged in. "Sit down, please."

"No, I prefer to stand."

He ran his hands through his dark hair in frustration. Then he took a step and stood before her. "My father has granted you permission to go to the reservation. I forbid you going home."

She gazed at him fiercely. "How dare you tell me what to do! I demand that you leave this minute!"

"Audra, you are like Queen Esther, and you shall to come to the Apache nation for such a time as this. Do not let the incident between us keep you from your destiny."

Her eyes teared up. The words had fallen deeply into her spirit. Finally, she relented. "All right, I will go."

Suddenly like a flood, she felt joy rising within her, and she spoke up, "Indeed, I will go and serve the Apache nation. The idea is a little overwhelming, but I am dedicated."

Derek walked to the door and paused. "Audra, I am sorry that I hurt you. Please forgive me."

After he left, she fumed a little, "I resent that Derek barged in like he did. But I must remember that I, too, barged into the barracks with the intent of talking to him."

Though his son had already informed him, Audra went to tell Agent Rands of her decision. Garth Rands was still in the office, and he welcomed her in. With a broad smile, he spoke kindly to her, "Audra, it is my honor to take you to the Apache reservation. We must discuss some details.

You will live with Elena and I, and we will do our utmost to guide you. Elena is delighted to have you come. She always wanted a daughter."

She grinned at his statement. "It reminds me that my father always wanted a son. Sir, I appreciate being a guest in your home."

Her face beamed with contentment. Then the agent declared, "Audra, because you are unmarried, it is imperative that I hire a body guard to protect you. Chet is a young single man and a dedicated Christian. You must be respectful, but stay somewhat aloof, no close companionships with him. He will watch over you like a hawk and will be as fierce as a lion to protect you. As needed, he will interpret the Apache language for you. Listen to him and obey him. I have arranged with your father for his pay. Derek will come to teach him fighting techniques for your benefit."

"Agent Rands, I will be obedient according to your words."

Thereafter, he assumed a grave expression. "There are a few cultural rules of etiquette or warnings that you must observe. Never talk to an Indian man alone or even smile at him. You may interact with the children, but do not interfere with their work. Be careful not to criticize the women's domestic habits. Do not eat any of their food. I will inform them. If anyone asks you to borrow money, you must tell them that it is not permitted. Most could not pay it back which would put them under condemnation."

"Yes, sir, I will obey all of your rules. I am truly grateful to you for this opportunity."

"Miss Kirk, the younger women will embrace you and your ideas. Some of them want more education. Yet the older women may resent you. Remember that your love and humility is what will win the hearts of this tribal people. God resists the proud but gives grace to the humble."

Audra felt the magnitude of the gravity of being among the Indians. A young, white, woman would be quite a phenomenon on the Apache reservation.

5

All was still at the garrison on the night before the trip to the reservation. A knock at her door spurred Audra to her feet. "Mother, father, please come in."

"We came to pray with you and to see you off," responded her father with a sly grin. "I am sorry that we are unable to go with you."

Elizabeth tearfully murmured, "I prayed for your protection and for all of your needs to be met."

There was excitement in Audra's voice, "Thank you. I am full of expectation to be of service to the Apache."

They embraced their daughter and kissed her good bye.

To Audra's chagrin, Sergeant Derek Rands was in charge of the trip to the reservation. Also, Corporal Kenton Lott would travel with the entourage. The soldiers had a commission from Camp Cavalry for ten days for this endeavor. The soldiers would consult with the chief and visit the people. Derek spoke fluent Apache and could communicate with them. The two men would bunk in the Indian agency station.

With Miss Kirk by his side, Corporal Kenton Lott drove the wagon full of goods toward the Apache nation. He deftly managed a team of large Percheron work horses which would remain on the reservation for the Indians' use. It was a bumpy ride with continual jostling on mostly primitive, rutted roads. Though the journey seemed rough, Audra reveled in the trip.

As she sat next to Kenton, she found him to be extraordinary company. He was well educated and quite intellectual. He told her, "I accompanied my grandfather on an extended trip throughout Europe."

She beseeched him, "Please tell me about your travels. I am quite interested."

"All right, my lady, your wish is granted. Riding the Gondola boats of the canals of Venice in Italy is a scenic excursion. The Eiffel Tower in France was built in 1887 to celebrate the French Revolution. The Eltz castle in Germany has medieval charm."

"Europe is a fascinating place that I would like to visit someday. I hope the war does not destroy the historic land marks. I am enjoying your travelogue. It makes the time pass more quickly as our horses plod along this road to the reservation."

The corporal was very kind and attentive to Miss Kirk. "Here, take my canteen to drink more water." Removing his neckerchief, he requested, "Put this over your mouth to keep out the dust." As Audra grew weary and her eyes were blinking, Kenton encouraged her, "Rest your head against my shoulder."

When the wagon hit a bump, she fell forward, and Kenton grabbed her and pulled her back. He saved her from falling to the ground and under the wagon's wheels. After this incident, Audra scooted closer to him and locked her arm inside of his. "Excuse me, I am extremely tired from the heat and this rugged ride. I hardly slept the night before."

She was so bedraggled and drowsy that her head kept bobbing forward. Finally, Kenton put his arm around her and held her secure against his side.

Derek rode up on Rio and trotted next to the wagon. He frowned. "Is Audra ill?"

"No, but she is fatigued. May I stop and assist her to get inside of the back of the wagon to rest?"

"Yes, hand her down to me."

Audra felt like a wilted flower. Kenton helped her down to where Derek stood waiting. Instead of leading her to the back of the wagon, he picked her up and carried her. His strong arms were tight around her. She loathed for Derek to touch her, but she was too weak to struggle against him. On top of the wooden boxes in the wagon was a narrow pallet with a feather tick mattress. Audra laid down upon it, and within minutes, she was fast asleep. It was nightfall before she awoke to the smell of wood and smoke. The soldiers had made camp and were cooking food over a fire.

~~~~~~

The trio entered the reservation the next morning. As they neared the agency house, a pretty, dark-haired woman ran out to meet them. Elena Rands, Derek's mother, had been a Mexican beauty when she was younger. Still an attractive woman, her dark hair gleamed. She hugged and kissed both Derek and Audra. She shook hands with Kenton and also welcomed him.

A doting husband, Garth Rands showed Elena much af-
~~~~~~

fection. "My dear, you are the love of my life." He wrapped his arms around her and kissed her unashamedly.

Elena embraced her husband. "I have missed you, *mi amor*."

Garth introduced Audra to a young man, "This is Chet. He will be your body guard and interpreter."

"I am at your service, Miss."

"I am grateful for your help." Her smile was genuine.

The room for Audra was large and spacious. It was comfortable and bright with turquoise painted walls. There were also two other smaller rooms for her use. One was an examining room, and the other room would be used for supplies.

Kenton carried her trunks into her room and was very solicitous to her. "If you need anything, please come to me. I will try to get it for you. "

"That is very kind of you."

Derek also offered to assist her, "I also will be your body guard and servant. Your wish is my command."

"Thank you, sir." Audra was polite, but did not to look into his eyes. She was aloof towards him.

Elena and Audra established an immediate rapport. They visited and talked late into the evening. The agent's wife announced, "I have some unique plans just for the two of us."

"I will look forward to it!" Enthusiasm was in her voice.

~~~~~~

A rooster crowing in the distance woke Audra early the next morning. Yawning and stretching out her arms, she thought, "I don't care if it's early. I am so joyful to be on the reservation." She dressed and went outside to a rose garden
~~~~~~

that she had spied earlier. The dew on the red roses made them glitter in the sun.

Garth and Elena quickly observed Audra's cold and indifferent attitude toward Derek. It was obvious that she did not like him. The wife suggested to her husband, "You need to talk to Derek. If you have to talk to Audra, be gentle, she would be a stupendous daughter-in-law."

He rolled his eyes. "Oh my, woman, you only just met her."

"Audra is very special and worthy of our son!"

Seeking out his son that morning, Garth asked, "Derek, Miss Kirk has a smile for everyone but you. Why is that? What have you done?"

He appeared sheepish and related the incident of the young soldiers' trick. "Audra confessed her desire to be with me. It would have been very gratifying, indeed, but I could not let my mind wonder. My focus must be on my career. I am sorry to say that I did not act wisely or diplomatically. I certainly regret it."

"You need to talk to her, comfort her, get reconciliation. Audra is a mature young woman, but apparently, she has some hurt and bitterness toward you."

Walking into his mother's rose garden, Derek found Audra seated on a bench. She heard a footfall of boots come into the serene place. She tried to exit and hurry past the sergeant, but he blocked her way. "Audra, I need to talk to you. May I accompany you to the church where we will have privacy?"

"Say what you will here, and please be brief," she said sharply.

She glanced away from the soldier. The rose garden exuded peace and solitude, but when Derek entered, it became a hotbed of hostility for her.

"Please forgive me. My behavior toward you was irreproachable. I regret this breach between us."

"I have forgiven you, but I do have a question. Are you still laughing at me?"

"I never laughed at you!" He sighed in exasperation.

She looked up at Derek and bore her eyes into his. "I loved you."

He felt a twinge in his gut at her statement.

Audra again tried to brush past him, but he blocked her way. "You're going to listen to me, pretty woman." He gently took her arms to face him. She placed her palms against his chest, but he still held her. "That day, don't think I wasn't tempted to take you, to make you mine, even though I knew it was not the right thing to do. To marry you and partake of your beauty and innocence would have been very satisfying. It would also have been selfish on my part and unfair to you. Please, let us be on friendly terms."

"No. Let me go, and stay away from me! I loathe the very sight of you!"

Her tears wanted to come, but she would not cry in front of him. As she hurried from the rose garden, a thorn pierced her wrist, and the blood trickled down her arm. Though the thorn had hurt her, it did not compare to the pain that she felt inside. For Audra, the bright luster of the roses seemed to fade in the light of the conflict. She whispered to herself, "I made a vow that Derek will never hurt me again, and I intend to keep it."

The wedded pair saw Audra hurry to her room and heard her restrained sobs. Derek spoke of the encounter to his parents. "I am determined to make up for the hurt I have caused her."

The Rands wanted this conflict resolved, so they issued an invitation to Miss Kirk, "Please meet with us over tea in the parlor."

The agent placed his hand on hers. "Audra, with all kindness to you, we need to talk to you about Derek. I know that he has hurt you, but he has repented of it. To be content in life means to forgive others. It will give you peace in your heart."

Putting her arm around Audra, Elena expressed, "If you hold on to bitterness, my dear, it will only hurt you."

"I truly have forgiven Derek. I just do not want to be around him."

Furrowing his brow, Garth persuaded, "That will be impossible for the next few days. I have asked him to practice the Apache language with you. It will help you while you are here."

Elena pleaded, "Audra, I advise you to persevere while Derek is here. When he leaves, let him remember your sweetness. Do not discount the possibility that God may have a future for you two together."

It was the last thing that she wanted to hear, and she grimaced and pondered, "My parents' wish is for my union with Derek. Now Elena has expressed the same desire. Will she try to influence my life, too?" So, Audra prayed, "Lord, in Jesus name, I need your grace. My emotions are tangled and gnarled like the roots of an old tree. My feelings must line up with your will. I resolve to keep an attitude of civility."

~~~~~~~

An exceedingly large gathering of Indians came to the church meeting on Sunday morning. Many had risen early and walked two and three hours on a dusty road, carrying their babies. Some little children rode on burros. A few men drove ox carts or rode on horseback. The adults crowded together on wooden plank benches inside the church. The church was swelling to the point that the children had to sit on blankets on the floor. The news had circulated throughout the reservation that Audra, a doctor, had arrived. She would be the attraction and spectacle that many had come to see. Their anticipation was great, as many Indians had never seen a woman doctor. The people kept coming and coming for over an hour. Soon there was only a little standing room in the back of the large church.

Of all the Indians who had congregated, only one young lady greeted Audra warmly, "My name is Miriam, and I will assist you in any task. I will be your friend and helper during your stay here."

"That is very kind of you and a comfort to me." It was a unique first impression.

In the church yard, several women were preparing for the fellowship dinner in honor of Audra's arrival. Two large iron kettles, filled with goat stew, were simmering over an open fire. After the meeting, all of the benches would be brought out for seating for the congregation to eat their dinner.

Audra attempted to dress simply for the church meet-
~~~~~~~

ing. She wore a long dark green skirt with a jacket trimmed only with a black braid. Even in her plain attire, she looked stunning.

Elena advised her, "You may leave your long red hair in curls and not in a tight chignon. The Apache people must accept you as you are."

As she walked across the church yard, Derek came to greet her. Accompanying him was a young Indian man, his wife, and baby. He explained, "Audra, this family has walked for three hours and are eager to see you."

The young man, Reuben, petitioned, "Miss, I have had pain in my ear for several months. Would you please examine it?"

Since more Indians were still coming into the church, Derek suggested, "Let us all go inside the agency."

Audra brought out her black bag and reached for her otoscope. With the instrument, she peered into the Indian's ear. "Oh my, there is a dead insect in his ear, and it is in two pieces!"

Then she took long tweezers and retrieved the insect parts from the man's ear.

Reuben was very astonished and started to laugh. "I thank you ever so much!" He was amazed as he looked at the insect in his hand. Seeing it, his young wife began to wipe tears from her eyes.

At the church, Reuben began showing the pieces of the insect to everyone he met. "See this! See this! The lady doctor got them out of my ear!"

The Indians began to crowd around him and were talking

excitedly. A stir went throughout the church as the story reached the people of Reuben's good news and of how Audra had helped him.

The church meeting began with a time of worship. One fellow plucked the guitar while another man beat a hand-made drum. Miriam played hymns on an old, upright piano. Some songs were sung in their native tongue and others in English. Elena had translated Amazing Grace into the Apache language. The Indians liked it so much that they wanted to sing it every week.

The Indian children were quiet and respectful during the meeting. The mothers openly breast fed their babies, with their little heads occasionally popping up and looking around.

Garth Rands, who was also their pastor introduced Audra and admonished the Indians "My people, I want you to be respectful to Miss Kirk. Only seek help from her if you have a dire need, a wound, or severe pain. I warn you not to take advantage of her by coming for medical advice out of curiosity or for inconsequential things. Her medical supplies are limited."

Speaking a few phrases in the Apache language, Audra expressed, "I am happy to be here with you in the tribe." She played her mandolin and sang a hymn.

For Audra and Kenton, Garth informed them, "I will preach in the Apache tongue, and Derek will translate it so that you can understand the sermon. Also, I want the Indians to learn and use English."

Then he began his sermon, "It is important to have unity in the tribe and not to judge your neighbors."

The pastor gave an altar call for salvation and healing. Audra knelt at the altar to pray. When she arose from the altar steps, she sensed peace. She softly whispered a prayer, "I know that you, Lord, will give me grace to be near Derek these next few days. Thank you for Kenton's company. I am at ease when we are together."

Audra remarked to pastor-agent Rands, "Sir, you superbly delivered the message today."

A laugh escaped his lips. "If only two, old, snagged tooth women showed up, I would still preach the same."

During the fellowship time, Garth Rands was visiting with the Indian council leader. "Audra, these are my friends, William Satof and his son Joseph."

The councilman was cordial. "Welcome to the reservation, Miss Kirk. We appreciate your service to our tribe."

Joseph offered, "Please call on us for any need that you may have."

"I am grateful for your generosity." Her sincerity was apparent.

During the meal, Garth chatted with Audra, "William has much influence among the Apache. He and I work closely together with the chief to promote peace and prosperity in the tribe. William and his family are faithful to serve in the church. His son, Joseph, is the most prosperous man on the reservation. The young fellow has a very high work ethic. He will often labor tirelessly on his small ranch; he owns the largest herd of sheep and goats. He has built a log home with a wooden floor and also has constructed a stone fence corral. This Indian fellow habitually gives a large tithe of sheep and goats to the church. Joseph has accomplished much, but his character is that of a proud and stubborn man. His wife, Miriam, is a sweet-tempered young woman. Joseph esteems his wife and dotes on her. She reads the Bible to her family at night by the light of a kerosene lamp."

After the fellowship dinner, the Indians did not leave immediately to return to their homes but loitered in the church yard visiting. Audra was aware that everyone was staring at her. The Indian women were mostly shy and sober in facial expression. Some smelled of smoke from cooking over an open fire. It was a sharp contrast to her perfume. Audra boldly approached the women to visit. She greeted the women in their language. She smiled a lot, and they seemed to approve of her.

The little boys came up boldly to Miss Kirk, speaking in their language. They touched her with grimy hands. They were intrigued with this young woman with red hair. Derek and Kenton soon had a crowd of children around them. The soldiers would swing them around and lift them into the air. The little ones were laughing. It was great fun for them since it was not customary for the Indian parents to play with their children.

Audra summoned Kenton, "Would you please fetch the large trunk from my room. It is filled with rag dolls with yarn hair and wooden toys that my church collected for the children on the reservation."

It took four grown men to control a line to pass out the toys to the youngsters. After passing out the gifts, the children flocked to Audra. She hugged the little ones and asked their names. She giggled as she looked around at the five children who had encompassed her. There were two little ones sitting on her lap and three others with their arms around her.

A certain young woman, who was pregnant, approached Miss Kirk. "Lady doctor, will you birth my baby?"

With enthusiasm, Audra retorted, "Yes, I will deliver it. There will be a room for you in the Indian agency."

"My name is Sheyla, and I think my baby come soon. Thank you, Miss."

Chet, Audra's Indian body guard, was keen on the soldiers training him hand-to-hand combat.

Since Derek was acting as Audra's interpreter, the young man approached Kenton. "Sir, would you show me how to fight?"

Kenton studied him with a cocky grin. "You waste no time, do you?"

"No sir, I am eager for you to teach me."

"Let's find a place with less stones on the ground. Tell your friends to come and watch the mock fight."

The Indian quickly returned with a group of young men. Kenton admonished the seekers, "This training is for self-defense, not to be used in anger, vengeance, or violence."

The corporal snickered. "You won't mind a few bruises and a little soreness?"

They did not know what to expect, but they agreed, "We care not; we are ready."

The corporal motioned for Chet to 'attack' him, and Kenton grabbed the Indian by the shoulder and pulled him to the ground. Then another Indian came stealthily toward the soldier, and the corporal swirled and kicked him to the earth. The two Indian fellows were grinning, yet rubbing their arms. A crowd gathered and clapped. Kenton was a little stymied when all of the young men lined up to 'fight' him.

"Do all of you men want to hit the dust?" He gazed over the crowd.

A hefty fellow came forward in a mock attack. Kenton reached for him and flipped him into the air. The Indian men went wild with excitement, laughing and hollering. Derek came over to give his friend a break, and so the sergeant continued to demonstrate Kung Fu. He summoned two men to 'attack' him, and he took them both down. When the older men got in line to be thrown to the dirt, Derek called a halt, "The exhibition has ended. You mature men are more prone to be seriously hurt or to sustain broken bones."

The young Indian men followed the soldiers across the church yard, imploring them to train them some more, "We can come tomorrow, every day that you are here."

Finally, Derek addressed them, "If you men work hard during the week, we will teach you again on Sunday after the church meeting. Also, I want you to take time to pray and read Ephesians 6:10 in your Bible. I will preach on this scripture next Sunday. It basically says that we don't war against flesh and blood but against the powers of wickedness in high places. I can teach you how to fight, but the Holy Spirit will teach you how to have victory in life."

They nodded their assent, and Kenton asked them, "May I have permission to pray a blessing over your lives?" They immediately bowed their heads. "Lord, in Jesus name, I pray that you prosper my Indian brothers."

Upon their exit, each Indian man proceeded to say thank you and to shake hands with the soldiers.

Kenton commented to Derek, "If God can use Kung Fu to proclaim the gospel, here am I, use me."

6

It was almost dusk when a young boy rode into the agency on his pony. The boy found Derek and started talking to him excitedly in the Apache language, "My sister burned her hand in the fire, and she does not stop crying. Papa asks if the doctor lady can come help us."

Seeking Audra, the sergeant explained, "A little girl needs our help with a burn, but their house is not close by, and we will surely return after dark."

Her eyes were pleading. "Derek, I am extremely tired. The Indians came early, and we only just finished our consults. Could you not take the ointment and go yourself?"

He encouraged her, "Audra, I was impressed to fast and pray today. This is an unusual opportunity to minister to the child. Natan, the father, and his family keep to themselves. He does not bring them to the church because he is ashamed of his daughter's deafness and jabbering. They asked for you, and it is you they want. If you will take one step of faith, God will give you grace and strength."

"As you wish."

"I will saddle the horses while you prepare to leave."

Audra headed for her room to put on her riding skirt and

jacket. Then she remembered something, and murmured to herself, "There is a tiny doll in my trunk. The gift will be a pleasant distraction and will gain the child's trust." She quickly grabbed it.

It took almost an hour for them to travel to the hogan. There was only one candle for light in the small hut. A four-year-old girl, seated on her mother's lap, was whimpering.

Drawing near to the father, Derek asked? "What is her name, Natan?

"Her name is Leah."

Sitting next to the little girl, Audra presented the doll to her. The child was delighted and hugged it. Taking the youngster's grubby hand that was red and inflamed, Audra gently washed away the dirt with a bowl of water. Next came the ointment and bandage. Leah smiled at her bandage and seemed to be proud of it.

Focusing on the parents, Derek told them, "The Bible tells how Jesus healed a boy who was deaf and dumb."

He peered at Natan. "May we pray for Leah that God will heal her?"

The father nodded his assent.

So, Derek anointed the child's forehead with oil and then decreed, "Deaf and dumb spirit, I command you, come out of her in Jesus name."

Leah coughed and then twisted in her mother's lap. Thereafter, the sergeant stood behind the child and spoke into her ear, "Baby, baby."

The little girl quickly turned her head as if she had heard him. Derek brought her father up and told him, "Say the word 'baby'."

Leah tried to say what she had heard, "Baby."

The father said it again, and his daughter repeated it. The word was not perfectly pronounced, but they knew that Leah could hear.

Her older brother told her to say 'baby' and pointed to the doll. The little girl was starting to like all of the attention, waved her doll and again said, "baby."

Derek stood behind Leah and clapped his hands. The child turned her head around to look at him. The father fell to the floor. "Thank you, God, my little one can hear."

Audra contemplated the scene before her, "I have seen a few miraculous healings, but never anything like this." Her eyes beaded with tears.

Turning to Natan, Derek requested, "Please bring your little daughter to the church on Sunday and testify of God's healing power."

~~~~~~~

It was a late hour when the two companions finally departed the adobe house. The desert had turned cold. The narrow road appeared as a ribbon in the moonlight. Rio knew his way back to the agency and walked at a fast pace. Weariness set in for Audra. She felt weak and her body became like a rag doll. She leaned forward on her horse and started to fall when she caught herself.

Derek glimpsed that Audra was struggling to stay awake. He turned and grabbed the reins of her horse.

"What are you doing?" she gasped.

"You will ride with me on Rio."
~~~~~~~

"I certainly will not!

"Do not defy me. I will not let you be hurt." He lifted her to sit in his saddle, and then he sat behind her, holding the reins of Rio. He put his arms around her so that she would not fall from the horse.

"Do you like having your arms around me?" she challenged.

"I am carrying precious cargo. I cannot let anything happen to you." He snickered at the question.

Audra tried to sit upright in the saddle away from Derek, but it was not comfortable. Her back was hurting.

His words were soothing, "I will hold you and not let you fall. Relax, *chica,* you are in my care."

Her face showed that she resented Derek's nearness. It smacked of intimacy, but she was too tired to resist.

Finally, she quit fighting and began to yield in spite of herself. Audra shivered and made an effort to keep her teeth from chattering. She leaned against the soldier's chest and felt his warmth. Actually, it was comforting to rest against him. Derek felt the impact of her body next to his, but he did not pull away.

The swaying movement of the horse and the clip clop of its hooves lulled Audra into an uneasy sleep. When they neared the agency, the dogs began to bark and woke her.

Derek helped her down from Rio. "Let me take your arm so that you do not fall on the rocks ahead."

She jerked her arm away. "You do not have to coddle me like a lap kitten."

Then she took a step forward and did stumble on the

rocks. Derek reached out and caught her. Audra could see the smug look on his face in the moonlight.

"The next thing I know, you will be carrying me to the house."

With that dare, he swung her up into his arms and started striding toward the agency.

"Let me down!"

"It is with easy strength that I carry you." His voice was cocky, piercing the atmosphere.

"You are so arrogant!"

To balance herself, Audra put her arms around Derek's neck, and her head was near to his. She silently fretted, "I do not like this vulnerability, but I appreciate his concern for me".

At the door he released her, and then he was gone. After being held so close by the sergeant, sleep evaded Audra. She forgot how fatigued she was. She kept thinking about being held in Derek's arms and murmured to herself, "I have had more than my share of beaus, but none of them compares to this sergeant. I want an expression of love from him, however small, before he returns for duty to Camp Cavalry."

~~~~~~~

It was early in the day when councilman, William came to the agency to seek Audra. In the Apache tongue, he gave this account to Derek, "Miriam, my daughter-in-law, was stooped over pouring water from a pottery jug when my son's dog attacked her and bit her leg. This happened two days ago, and now she is in great pain and cannot walk. Joseph was not home at the time. He just returned this morning from a journey to buy sheep. I met him on his way to the agency to
~~~~~~~

seek medical aid for his wife. I told him that I would relay the message. Will you bring Miss Kirk to help her?"

"Yes, we are here to serve you."

William was in an antagonized mood. "Several days ago, their vicious dog bit my ankle, but my tall boots prevented any wound. My grandchildren, Isbede, eight, and Louis, five, are afraid of the dog and carry a stick with them. I told my son, Joseph, to destroy the dog. He assured me that he would, but as you see, he has disobeyed me."

"We will come this morning and tend to Miriam."

"Thank you, Sergeant Rands.

It was a long trek to Joseph's log cabin for the three companions. The excursion was difficult since they had to navigate around large rocks on the trail. The sun beat down upon them, and there was no cloud in sight. Only the cacti were a pleasant view in the arduous trip.

They arrived at Joseph's cabin by mid-morning. Kenton was hitching up the horses nearby when he heard Audra scream and saw her running. A dog was chasing her and barking. It was nipping at her heels and biting her long skirt. He ran to her and kicked at the dog. Then Derek rushed up, and the dog jumped up to seize him. He pulled out his pistol and fired. The menacing animal lay still on the ground.

Hurrying to Audra, Kenton took her into his arms. He was stroking her hair as she was breathing heavily and trembling. She jerked against him when Derek fired his gun. Kenton tightened his arms around her. "Are you hurt?"

She looked up into his handsome face. "No, just a little disconcerted. I appreciate your rescue."

Joseph and his children saw what had happened as they stood outside the door of their cabin. The Indian had a scowl on his face as he walked over to where his dead dog lay. He was visibly angry. "This was my guard dog that served me for many years, and you have killed him."

Making a fist, he brought back his arm to hit Derek, but the sergeant caught his arm and brought him to the ground; his face hit the dust. Then he helped the man up. "Joseph, this dog was a predator. My father, Agent Rands, will find a puppy for you to replace this despicable animal."

Nodding, Joseph seemed satisfied with that offer. Derek and Audra entered the cabin to be of help to Miriam. With only one window, it was somewhat dark inside, so Joseph lit candles. Miriam lay on a wooden bed with a feather tick mattress and her eyes were closed. The woman was obviously ill from infection, and her head was hot with fever. Her leg was wrapped tightly in a cloth towel. Derek held a flashlight as Audra put on her rubber gloves and removed the cloth. In her examination, she saw that Miriam's leg was red and swollen and oozing with infection.

Audra requested of him, "Please pray, I am concerned that she lay so still, obviously weak, and her head is hot with fever. What I am was about to do will be painful." Then she scraped off the dead, necrotic tissue down to the blood. The woman cried out in anguish, but it had to be done for healing to take place. Audra then applied ointment and bandaged her leg.

Miriam, who was usually healthy and vibrant, could only whisper, "I thank you."

Derek called Kenton to enter the cabin. Also, he asked Joseph and the children to stand next to Miriam's bed. Then he led the group to pray for the woman's healing.

As they were leaving, Audra touched Derek's arm. "May we return here in two days to change the bandage?"

"Yes, it will be done as you desire."

Then she turned to Kenton, "Thank you again for protecting me from the terror of the dog."

He chuckled as he teased her, "It's not every day that I get to hold a pretty girl in my arms; there are benefits of being your body guard."

When they returned to the agency, Audra told Elena what had happened with the dog and how Kenton and Derek had rescued her. She asked her sincerely, "Will there always be this much drama on the reservation?"

Elena her gave a knowing grin. "Wherever Derek goes, there seems to be drama. If anyone is in peril, he will save them. I have learned to trust the Lord for my son."

"I see the reality of it. The Lord uses these men to help those in need."

"My son, Derek and his companions, Matthew, and Kenton are highly disciplined soldiers. Their aim is to be qualified to fight and to win. They are a close-knit group, and where there is unity, there is power. These men often pray for divine appointments, and when they triumph, they give God the glory."

William visited his son, Joseph, a couple of days later. He had heard about the dog attacking Audra. "You have disobeyed me, my son. When your dog bit me, I told you to destroy it. Now your wife is suffering because you did not act. She might have died. Ignoring my counsel has hurt your reputation as a wise man. You must use wisdom if you are to sit on the council of the Apache someday."

"Yes, my father," he nodded in submission, but there was stubbornness in his eyes.

~~~~~~~

Putting her blanket over head to block out the sound of a rooster crowing, Audra went back to sleep. She was tired and thought that she might rest for the day. The previous day had been arduous as the Apache kept coming and coming for medical consults. A peaceful slumber had settled in when a knock came at her door.

"Good morning, Audra. It's Kenton. Rise and shine."

"Go away, please. It is barely light out."

"Today, Derek and I will go visit some of the Apache who live in the countryside. It is a long journey. We will leave in an hour. Do you want to come with us?"

"Only if you carry me to the table and spoon feed me my breakfast," she murmured.

Audra was in a daze as she dressed. Yawning, she took a step outside of her room. Hearing footsteps, suddenly strong hands were picking her up. Crying out in dismay, she found herself being carried in Kenton's arms. Glancing at his face, a cry erupted from her lips, "Sir, what are you doing?"

With a sly grin, he gazed at her. "I was just obeying your order." Then he gingerly let her down.

Giggling, she replied, "It was only an expression of how tired I am. Why did you wake me so early if we are not
~~~~~~~

leaving soon?"

"Don't all females need more time to get ready?"

The corporal exited and explained to Derek, "Audra is too fatigued to go on the day's journey."

The men were saddling their horses when she came out to meet them. They were surprised to see her donned in her riding skirt and clutching her doctor bag.

She peered at Kenton. "Corporal, would you please bring the saddle bag of medical supplies?"

"Yes, I will retrieve it now. By the way, you look pretty in the morning sun."

As he brought it to her, she whispered, "Will you try to sweet talk me, soldier? I will seek revenge on you for the rude awakening you gave me this morning." But her smile betrayed her words.

Kenton met her eyes and chuckled. "I can hardly wait."

~~~~~~~

The group visited several Apache families, and Audra administered medical assistance to those in need. It was late afternoon as the trio neared the agency on their return. They met two young Apache men on their ponies. Derek stopped to greet them and introduced his companions. The sergeant was acquainted with these two brothers known as Chago and Naiche.

"You are far from home, my friends. What brings you to the agency?"

Nudging his pony closer to Derek, Naiche spoke, "Our grandmother is very old. She wants to see the young lady doctor before she dies. Grandmother heard she is pretty
~~~~~~~

woman and help our people."

Chago leaned forward on his pony. "We come to take the doctor to our house tonight. We got blankets and made a bed for her to sleep. We bring her back here tomorrow." He then grabbed the reins of the bridle of Audra's horse as if to take her with them in that moment.

Responding quickly, Derek suggested, "My brothers, it is late. The journey to your home is far. Come and stay the night and eat supper with us. We will go early in the morning. Our prayer is that your grandmother will live to see Miss Kirk. God will surely give her this wish."

"No, we go now. Grandmother die soon." Derek's eyes hardened and he warned, "Chago, let go of the bridle."

He shook his head no and obstinately held on to the reins of Audra's bridle.

Anger flared up in Kenton, and he made his intention known, "Let me jerk the Indian off of his pony!"

The sergeant only grinned at his companion.

Derek did not want a confrontation, but he had no choice. He pulled his pistol from his holster. The Indian immediately dropped the reins and turned away in defeat.

"Come, my friends, we shall prepare a hot meal and a comfortable bed in the church for you."

They nodded their assent.

Agent Garth Rands welcomed the two young men and treated them with respect. He had the ability to make a person feel special and valuable.

The next morning, the party traveled to the adobe home where the grandmother lay on her deathbed. Chago and Naiche carried their grandmother out of the house and propped her up in a chair under a shade tree. Naiche pointed to the old woman. "This is our grandmother, Fairlight."

Audra greeted her in the Apache language, hugged her frail body, and kissed her wrinkled cheek. A smile broke out on the grandmother's toothless face. The old woman's composure became bright and alert since her desire to see Miss Kirk was being fulfilled. Audra sat close to her and held her hand. The stench of the old woman was in sharp contrast to the girl's perfume.

Fairlight studied her. "Young woman is so pretty. I could not think it, but I want so much to see her."

Kenton brought out the mandolin, and Audra sang a hymn in the Apache language. The old Indian lady tapped her finger to the music. As grandmother grew weary, the visitors made ready to depart.

In a hoarse voice, Fairlight murmured to Audra, "I so happy you come. Now I go to Jesus." And she closed her eyes.

Audra gently hugged her and whispered in her ear, "Goodbye, dear one."

Chago and Naiche carried their grandmother back into the adobe house. They were brushing back their tears. The young Indian men expressed, "We are grateful that you came here, and we are satisfied. Our grandmother has received her wish."

7

Sheyla was having labor pains and walked three miles in the hot noonday sun to the agency. Her little daughter, Cristina, was holding tightly to her mother's hand. Audra and the young woman had become friends since Sheyla had asked her to deliver her baby. A birthing room was prepared for her.

Late in the afternoon, Audra delivered a baby boy. He appeared to be healthy, or at least that is what they thought. They named him Thomas after his father. Audra stayed in the house and did not to go on calls so that she could monitor the baby carefully. The first day the baby was breast feeding and sleeping normally and had a couple of wet diapers.

But by the next afternoon, the baby would not stop crying or suck at the breast. Audra was ringing her hands and pacing the floor. She called to Elena, "There is something wrong with the baby. He may have colic, but his little stomach is protruded, and there are no dirty diapers. His color is pale, not pink like before. Hurry and fetch Garth, Derek, and Kenton to come and pray."

When the men arrived, Audra spoke, "The baby may be constipated or something worse. If there is a blockage, and the bowel becomes impacted, it could be serious." They immediately began to pray over the child. Then she requested, "Go get Thomas and let me think about this."

The Indian father was found nearby and appeared anxious as he entered the room. Derek explained to the young man, "Thomas, your baby son is sick."

"I trust the doctor, and I pray to God for my son. I believe in Jesus. I do not worship Indian gods."

Audra began to scrub her hands and glove up. The baby's skin had felt hot to the touch. So, she coated a sterilized thermometer in ointment jelly and gently inserted it into the child's rectum. The baby screamed and Audra almost screamed, too. However, as she removed the instrument, the bowl emptied itself.

The infant cried until he was exhausted, and then he became calm at his mother's breast. Little Thomas slept for two hours and then was hungry. Everyone in the house was elated.

Seated at the bedside of Sheyla and her baby, Audra prayed until almost midnight. The baby was still whimpering. Finally, mother and baby slept, and she was nodding.

Derek entered the room. "Audra, you must rest."

"Yes, I am so tired, I feel weak."

When she stood up, she wobbled and grabbed the chair. Derek reached for her. Before she knew what was happening, she was in his strong arms.

As she began to protest, he demanded, "I will carry you to your bed."

His face was close to hers, and she felt the prickle of his beard on her cheek. He gently laid her on the bed, took off her boots, and helped her out of her jacket. When he left, Audra was so fatigued that she immediately dozed off.

Sleeping late the next morning, Audra dressed hurriedly and entered the dining room. Derek brought her a cup of hot tea and a plate of scrambled eggs.

She gazed up at him. "The baby?"

"In the middle of the night I heard him cry, but now he is breast feeding, and more dirty diapers."

As she sipped her tea, Audra was beaming. She observed that Derek was giving her a very appreciative look.

She gratefully acknowledged the breakfast that he had served her, "This is a lot of food and quite delicious. May I share it with you?"

"No, thank you. I must be going."

"Could you please stay a few minutes?" she smiled and flashed her eyelashes.

There was a twinkle in his eye and a coy grin touched his mouth. "Yes, Madame, anything you wish."

"Well, if that is the case, then I proclaim this a day of celebration!"

He snickered. "If you are interested, I will spend a little time with you today as your reward."

Audra was delighted. "Wonderful! Horseback riding and a picnic?"

"Yes, I will arrange for a basket to be prepared. You should rest. I will see you this afternoon."

"Thank you for the eggs and tea."

"*Para servirte*. In order to serve you." He walked to the door, and then glanced back at her. She met his eyes with an endearing smile.

Being alone with the sergeant brought a sense of excitement for Audra. She thought about her future, "I have more admiration for Derek now than ever. I want his love, white lace, and promises. Yet I must guard my heart. My vow keeps me in remembrance that he once rejected me."

Derek warned himself, "I am flattered that Audra wants to spend time with me. Yet I have to consider her requests carefully. As a soldier, I have a commission before me. I cannot not let himself be caught up in her whims."

~~~~~~~

When Audra checked on the baby, his skin was pink, his eyes were bright, and the fever had abated. Sheyla's face was glowing with contentment, and the child was peacefully breast feeding.

Congratulating Audra, Agent Rands resounded, "I am so glad I obeyed God when He impressed me to bring you to the reservation. It did not seem logical to me at the time."

"I am very happy to serve this people!"

The Apache chief came to visit Sheyla and his grandson. There was a rumor in the tribe that the baby was dying. The mother proudly held up her son to his grandfather. The baby's bright eyes glistened as the chief spoke to him, "My child, you will live and grow to become a strong man."

Elena tapped the chief on the shoulder. "Sir, Audra saved the baby's life."

The Apache leader was moved. "Miss Kirk I am much in your debt. You saved our little one. May our people always be yours."
~~~~~~~

"I am blessed to be here in the tribe."

Cristina, the little three-year-old sister, had stayed with the Rands during this time, and the child had thoroughly enjoyed the attention the group had bestowed on her. When Thomas came to fetch his family, Cristina did not run to her father. Instead, she ran to Derek for him to bounce her on his knee. The little girl was clinging to him as he left the house; she did not want to leave and go with her father. Garth Rands had often preached to the parents, admonishing them, "Show affection to your children and love them."

Although Thomas had arrived to take his family home, Audra was not ready for mother and baby to depart. She rationalized, "The husband might pressure his wife to work so that she has to neglect the baby."

Therefore, she sought to persuade him, "Thomas, the baby has gone through trauma and is weak. He needs special nurturing, and I want to monitor him for three more days. Furthermore, Sheyla is exhausted from the baby crying for two nights. As we are taking care of Cristina, surely you can fend for yourself for a few more days."

Resisting her advice, Thomas took a step forward. "No, I will take them with me now."

Audra raised her hand in protest. "You will not take them today. I forbid it!"

God must have given her the words as she scolded him in the Apache language. But the man was not convinced and started toward Sheyla's room. "I need wife at house."

Standing in the doorway, Audra blocked Thomas' entrance. She yelled to Elena, "Please, go and fetch Derek!"

Fortunately, the sergeant was close by and entered as the Indian was about to push past Audra. Seeing the conflict, Derek grabbed the man and pinned him against the wall.

The sergeant's expression hardened as he warned the Indian, "Thomas, Miss Kirk saved your baby's life. Is this your response for her help? Your family is being well cared for here. Is your selfishness going to put your baby in danger? You may visit your family, but you will not take them for three more days. If you are belligerent, you will deal with me. Do you understand me?"

"Yes sir, Sergeant Rands."

Thomas was ashamed and hung his head. He glanced at Audra. "I'm sorry, Miss."

When her husband left, Sheyla voiced her sentiment, "I am so relieved to have more time to care for my son."

~~~~~~~

That afternoon Derek took Audra to a secluded place with a few trees among the cactus for a picnic. For her to be alone with this man was an euphoric yet dangerous experience. She instructed herself, "Be careful not be infatuated with him again. The pain will be unbearable if he leaves with no commitment. Try to be detached and enjoy the day." It was not easy for her as she saw the desire in his eyes. When they talked, he gave her his full attention, and his gaze never left her. It was very satisfying. Yet she reminded herself, "Girl, you are here to serve the Apache, not to snag a husband."

Ten days had passed rapidly for Audra as she served the Apache on the reservation. The day came when the soldiers would be leaving early the next morning to resume their
~~~~~~~

commission at Camp Cavalry. They had been gone most of the day. As she waited for their return, Audra hoped, "If only Derek will speak of his love for me, for I am smitten again with the sergeant."

Arriving first, Kenton ate his supper, and expressed his gratitude to the Rands, "I have appreciated your generous hospitality here at the agency."

Audra walked from the dining room to accompany him as he was leaving. She touched his arm. "Kenton, I want to thank you for all of the favors that you did for me here on the reservation. You have been most gracious to me."

"It was my pleasure to assist you. You are a precious jewel. I will always be there to support you in any circumstance." He took her hand and kissed it.

"I am grateful for your kindness to me." Her smile was sweet. She reached up and brushed a kiss to his cheek. A revealing thought came to her. "I have grown quite fond of the corporal."

It was evening when Derek walked into the agency house. He was visibly tired from a long day in the saddle. Audra deferred her hunger in order to dine with him. The couple visited over their supper. Finally, he arose from the table. Derek gazed at the fair lady before him and suppressed the yearning that he felt for her. "Audra, I will leave tomorrow before you arise. So, I will tell you good bye at this time. I commend you on your service to the Apache. I have admired your ability and dedication. You are a remarkable woman. I will pray for you as you continue to serve the people here. I must now go and visit with my parents." He bowed, and then he left.

With devastation came tears. There were no words of love, nor any kiss or embrace. She was deeply hurt, and she looked again for her vow that she had cast away. Her thoughts were wild with anger and self-reproach. "Here I am, the fool again, spurned by the man I adored." Quickly wiping her eyes, she placed the vow back into her heart and seethed, "I will never be infatuated with Derek Rands again!"

The sergeant had hardly left the dining room when Elena entered and spoke to Audra, "My dear, would you please take this mended shirt to Kenton for his journey tomorrow? If he is asleep, hang it on the inside door knob for him to see it."

"Yes, I would be glad to."

Audra immediately thought, "This is my opportunity to play a prank on Kenton."

Previously, he had brashly awakened her early one morning from a restful sleep. Outraged and distressed over Derek's rebuff emboldened Audra to do something both rash and impertinent. She took a small cloth, folded it several times so that it was a thick square in her hand and soaked it in water so that it was still dripping. Then she walked to the soldiers' room on the far side of the agency, knocked on the door and called out, but there was no answer. She quietly opened the door and put the shirt in as directed. A light shone from a small candle, and Audra could see the corporal lying on his bed with his trousers on and a book at his side. His eyes were closed. Standing in the doorway, Audra took aim and threw the sopping wet cloth onto Kenton's bare chest. Leaving the door ajar, she hastily made her getaway.

Kenton woke up startled, jumped out of bed, and ran through the open door. He viewed Audra, scampering down the hall. He swiftly ran after her and caught her. She stifled a squeal as his arms came tightly around her.

In between giggles, Audra murmured, "Please, let me go." And she pushed her palms against his forearms.

"An apology first, Miss Kirk."

"No."

He turned her around to face him, and his lips met hers in a tantalizing kiss.

Finally, the corporal released her. "Audra, I am sorry if the kiss offended you."

In the dim light, he could see her coquettish grin. "It was quite diverting. I must go."

She barely reached her room when she met Derek. She glanced at him nonchalantly as he bid her good night.

Audra silently chastised herself, "What was I thinking? What if he had seen me a few minutes earlier?"

Bitter thoughts about Derek kept her awake, but sweet thoughts crowded in regarding Kenton.

~~~~~~~

The next morning, Audra was still reeling from Derek's rejection. She was miserable and wished to return home. She spoke of it to Elena, "I think that I may go back to Shiloh tomorrow."

The woman was adamant. "My dear, you must stay and finish the two remaining weeks of your commitment to the tribe. What has happened between you and Derek?"

Audra blinked back tears. "He has rejected me. I have
~~~~~~~

reconciled myself that a life with him will never be. He once told me that I would be a hindrance to his army career."

Taking her hand, Elena tried to convince her, "Do not give up, *mi hija*. (my daughter) You are young. Don't make any hasty decisions. Be careful not to commit to any of the aspiring doctors. Wait and see what happens concerning my son. You have your whole life before you. You do not want a life of regret, of what could have been."

At that moment, Garth walked into the room and saw Audra sitting on the floor with her head in Elena's lap. He noticed that the girl's eyes were red. There was tenderness in his voice, "What is your problem daughter?"

"When Derek left, it was perfectly clear. He does not want me."

The agent snickered. "From a man's perspective, I seriously doubt that."

"The bond between us is over. I truly desire to return home."

Garth frowned in disapproval. "It would be a great defeat if you were to leave now. I believe that God has much more for you to accomplish here on the reservation. You have gained the trust of the Apache, and they would be disheartened if you were to leave so soon."

Elena pleaded, "Audra, we love and esteem you. Please reconsider your decision to leave. Do not let your emotions keep you from your commitment to serve the Apache in these next few days. If you impulsively leave now, you may regret your decision for the rest of your life."

Her soothing words broke the despair that Audra felt,

and the young woman perked up. "Yes, I will stay and fulfill God's destiny for my life. I accept your counsel and encouragement. I do have integrity, and I will finish my service here. I must admit that a life with Derek may never come to pass. I will not grieve or cling to any hope of a union between us. My future husband will most likely be a doctor, and I am satisfied with that goal."

8

Before the church meeting began on Sunday, one of the Indian men came to confide in councilman, William. The man reported a rumor, "There will be a contest this afternoon for boys from the age of four to seven years to ride a sheep. The purpose is to increase the child's bravery."

Receiving permission to speak to the church, the councilman scowled in anger. "I sternly warn the fathers of this tribe not to partake in any sport where your sons will ride a sheep. The fathers should protect their children, not put them in harm's way. If any man puts his son on a sheep, I will personally horsewhip him."

As he peered out over the church group, the men stared straight ahead with stony looks on their faces. The fathers knew that the custom of their sons riding a sheep was forbidden on the reservation. The Apache council had prohibited and condemned such a practice.

After the benediction, Garth noticed that the Indians did not tarry to visit as was their usual tradition, but they hurried down the road. A large group of them traveled in the opposite direction of their homes. They gathered at Joseph's log cabin to witness the contest of riding a sheep. The Indian had tied up a sheep for the sport and announced, "My son, five-year-old Louis, will be the first contestant."

When Miriam saw what was about to transpire, she argued with him. "I forbid you to make our son ride a sheep!"

Ignoring her, he dragged Louis, kicking and crying toward the sheep which started to jump around. By this time, Miriam was in hysterics. She screamed and fought Joseph to let the boy go. The young wife grappled with her husband, and he shoved her back. Joseph did want to be humiliated in front of his friends. Therefore, he set Louis astride the ram. "Son, be brave and ride the sheep."

The boy tried to put his arms around the sheep's neck to hold on, but he could not. The ram's horns jutted backward from its head making it difficult for him to get a grip.

With the bystanders watching, Joseph released the sheep to run with Louis on its back. The father was holding the rope, but he was struggling to keep up with the sheep as it bolted away. The ram got tangled in the rope and stumbled, throwing the boy off to land in the dirt. The frightened animal in its frenzy trampled over the child's chest. Louis lay still on the ground, his head against a rock. Joseph and Miriam rushed to their son and found him unconscious. As the father carried the boy into the house, the mother was wailing and praying, "Oh Lord, in Jesus name, heal my son!"

Upon seeing the horrible accident, the Indian audience immediately scattered and hurried away.

Joseph yelled to a friend, "Hitch my horse to the wagon. I will take my son to the agency."

Louis was cradled in his mother's arms, and Isbede sat

close by whimpering. Joseph pressed his horse to gallop the distance to the agency. Garth, Elena, and Audra heard yelling and screaming outside of the agency house. They quickly opened the entry door as Joseph carried his son inside. Elena pointed to the exam room. They laid Louis on the bed, and he did not move.

Miriam beseeched Agent Rands to pray. "Yes, of course I will."

The trauma had left Louis in a state of unconsciousness. His head was swollen, and his breathing was shallow. Taking her stethoscope, Audra listened to his heart. Elena put her hand on the boy's chest to pray for him, but the woman immediately snatched it away. She turned to Audra, frightened and troubled. "Why is his heart beating so fast?"

"Because there is not enough oxygen getting to the brain. I must get an intravenous bottle started."

Garth called the family to pray at the child's bedside.

In deep anguish, Joseph blamed himself for his son's calamity. In his regret, he wept and murmured, "I pray to God that He will take my life if my son can live."

The agent responded, "No, Joseph that is not scriptural. Jesus made the sacrifice for our healing, not you. We prayed that your son will live and not die."

The man was not convinced. "I have repented of my sin, but I fear I will die soon. I do not deserve to live after what I have done."

"You need to stop this kind of talk, Joseph. You do not want those words to come to pass. The Lord forgives us of our wrongs. Our God is a good God, and He will honor our prayer. Stay in peace, my brother."

Joseph asked Miriam to take a walk with him. "My wife, please forgive me for hurting our son and for hurting you. I am sorry and ashamed of my horrid actions. I love you, Miriam."

She only nodded.

~~~~~~~

The following morning Louis lingered in unconsciousness. William, his grandfather, came to pray for his grandson. Thereafter, the council members took Joseph to a field, tied him to a tree, and horsewhipped him. William, the young man's father, delivered the first lash of five to his son's back.

The wounded Indian man had lain on the ground in his pain for some time before Agent Rands found him. He brought the fellow into the agency for Audra to tend his lacerations. In her examination, she found that Joseph's neck was severely swollen. Also, there was a pock mark below his chin as if a snake had bitten him. A high fever beset the Indian, possibly from the poison of a venomous snake. Audra now had two patients to monitor, so Elena assisted her in the vigil. Miriam did not leave the bedside of her son.

A friend of the family came to the agency to inquire about Louis. When the companion heard that Joseph had been bitten by a snake and lay with a fever, he reacted in astonishment. "Joseph was extremely fearful of snakes, and had spoken that someday he might die of snake bite."

When Agent Rands heard this testimony, he began to intercede for the young Indian man. The agent-pastor discerned, "Oh Lord, just like Job, what Joseph feared has come
~~~~~~~

upon him."

By late afternoon, the Indian's condition had grown worse. He was dizzy and his throat was sore and swollen; he could hardly swallow any liquid.

Garth entered his room and helped him to sit up in his bed. "Joseph, you have to be alert. I want you to repeat these words. Will you, do it?"

"Yes, Agent Rands," whispered the Indian.

"Lord, I repent of my fear of dying from snake bite. I cast my words down. I will live, in Jesus name."

Joseph murmured the prayer that the agent told him. By evening his fever was diminishing.

His son, Louis, was breathing easier, and his heart rate was nearing normal. However, he was not lucid, but delirious.

By the next day, Joseph, though weak, was well enough to go and see his son. The father leaned over and tenderly stroked his brow. "My son, I believe that the Lord wants you to live."

As the sun went down, Garth went to check on Louis. The parents, Audra, and Elena were gathered around the boy's bedside. A righteous indignation rose up in the agent-pastor. "Louis, if you can hear me, open your eyes!"

The child fluttered his eyes and opened them. He then closed them and lay very still. Holding her son's hand, Miriam tried to communicate, "Louis, this is mama. Can you hear me?"

"Mama, I'm so tired," the boy whispered.

The parents started to weep for joy and thanked the Lord for his mercy.

The remaining days on the reservation fell one over the other for Audra. The Indian consultations consisted mostly of women and children. The young women confided freely in Audra. Their spiritual problems were often greater than the physical ones. Chet interpreted, and everyone received prayer who came to the clinic.

In a large agency room, Audra and Elena began sewing lessons with the Indian women to make clothes for their children. Elena brought in her treadle sewing machine so that there were two available for the women.

The Apache ladies quickly learned to use the machines and utilized all of the bolts of fabric that Elizabeth had sent for them. A large table was set up to cut out the fabric. There was a 'beehive' of activity in the agency; it was like a factory sweat shop as the women sewed from early until late. It was exhausting for Audra and Elena as the Indian women constantly wanted their help. Babies crawling around and little children running about created pandemonium in the area. There was some jealousy and arguing among the women until Agent Rands entered the room.

He threatened, "I will put an end to this sewing project unless there is more peace here." After his warning, things settled down.

All in all, the enterprise was a tremendous blessing for the mothers and grandmothers who sewed new clothes for their children.

On the reservation, the child, Louis, rested at the agency for one week under Audra's supervision. He was then released to return home with restrictions. His recuperation was ongoing. The boy could walk a short distance but his chest would hurt if he tried to run.

Joseph addressed the church. "I ask for forgiveness for endangering children in the sport of riding a sheep." He then went to the altar to pray and confessed his sin of stubbornness.

~~~~~~~

The day before Audra's departure, her bodyguard, Chet, accompanied her to Joseph's home to say good-bye to the family. Louis had grown stronger, with much less pain in his torso.

In Miss Kirk's farewell, she embraced Miriam. Through her tears, her friend begged her, "Audra, please come to visit us in the future."

At the end of Audra's mission term at the Apache reservation, Daniel and Elizabeth traveled to the Indian agency to fetch their daughter. She was overjoyed to see them. They talked of the news of the town and of the ranch.

The Rands bragged, "Audra was quite dedicated as she served the indigenous people here."

Indian agent, Garth, gave the couple a tour of the agency and compound. The rancher viewed firsthand the agent's ingenuity and ability in his projects. "This is the church I built for the Apache to worship in. Since the Indians' livelihood is animal husbandry, I have helped them to develop their sheep and goat herds. Also, a worthwhile endeavor was to dig a deep well for each family. It was only by the Lord's power that I was able to make these accomplishments on the reservation."
~~~~~~~

Elena prepared a Mexican feast for their guests' supper. There was merriment at the table as the group discussed the aspects of life in the Apache nation. Audra shared some of her moments of living with the tribe. When the Kirks were ready to leave the reservation, a bond of friendship and respect had formed between the two families.

9

A dinner party at Shiloh was planned for Audra's homecoming. Matthew and Kenton were in attendance, but Derek was absent. His friends explained that the sergeant had an urgent counseling session.

All of the guests visited and mingled at the celebration. They were quite interested in Audra's experiences on the reservation. Daniel and Elizabeth noticed that Audra and Kenton, who were seated together, got along well. They talked and laughed and seemed to enjoy each other's company.

After the meal, Matthew asked Raquel to join him in the parlor. She was hardly seated when he was down on one knee in front of her and pulling out a small box from his pocket. The young woman was in awe as an emerald ring glittered before her.

The lieutenant looked up into her delicate face. "Raquel, you are the epitome of everything I desire. I promise to love and cherish you. It is my dream to ask you to become my wife."

She was overcome with emotion. "Yes, I commit my love and my life to you as my husband."

Her face glimmered as he put the ring on her finger.

Matthew's strong arms enclosed Raquel in a tender embrace and his lips found her willing mouth. She felt his passion as he kissed her. He held her tightly to his chest and whispered endearments into her ear. He entwined his hands in her hair and kissed her face. Raquel had never known such a feeling of elation as this. She wondered, "What will it be like to be married to a man of such dignity and strength of character?"

Matthew informed Daniel of his proposal, and the latter announced it to the visitors. "I am pleased to announce the engagement of my daughter, Raquel to Lieutenant Matthew James, a man after my own heart."

Everyone at the table applauded and made a toast. Audra was ecstatic and hugged her sister.

Daniel made another comment that made the friends laugh, "Now, only one daughter left to get married off. She certainly will not be an old maid."

~~~~~~~

At dusk all of the invited folk left the gathering, and the evening darkness descended upon the land. Suddenly, the dogs began barking outside and would not stop. An intruder had climbed over the entry gate. Daniel went to investigate and discovered that the unwelcome visitor was Wade Conner. He had hopped on a freight train and traveled to Columbus. He came to the ranch after dark, because he feared that the ranch hands would beat him and not let him enter. The dogs had Wade cornered against the patio wall. He was a *persona non grata* at the ranch, but Daniel allowed the young man to come into his office.

Wade wiped his sweaty palms on his pants and began
~~~~~~~

his plea, "Sir, I have a chance to buy more orange groves. The land for sale directly joins my property. It is a golden opportunity. In the future I want to be able to support my children. The bank will not lend me money. I have come to Shiloh in hopes that you might help me."

"How much do you want?"

"I need $500. I will pay you back when the crop is harvested. I have some money saved as I have worked seventy hours a week at other jobs. I promise not to remarry until the loan is repaid. Anyway, my possibilities are null in that area. My sister-in-law spread it around town that I am a deadbeat."

"I will pray about the matter of a loan."

"Sir, my friend in Columbus wrote to me that there is a rumor that Raquel is pregnant. I am overjoyed at the news. I want Raquel and I to be a family again. I desire to redeem myself as a loving husband and father. Would you speak a word in my behalf for reconciliation with her?"

"No, I will not. Raquel will marry Lieutenant Matthew James in one week. He is an honorable man and also has the means to provide a prosperous life for her and the children."

When Wade heard the news, he gave a deep sigh of defeat. "Could I speak to Raquel tomorrow? I want custody rights of my children. I regret that I gave up parental rights. I was under duress at the time. I hope court action will not be an option."

"A meeting can be arranged for tomorrow, Saturday, at 4:00 in the afternoon. There is a condition if I am to give you a loan. Some people may come to testify in Raquel's behalf, and you must stay until I dismiss the meeting."

"Yes, I will agree to it."

When Wade mentioned court action, Daniel immediately knew that he must act. He planned to contact his lawyer and others to come to the meeting.

Raquel voiced her dislike, "I dread a meeting with Wade. I had hoped that I might never see him again."

The next morning with her parents present, the lawyer advised Raquel, "Give monthly, supervised visits to Wade for the children. It will be difficult for a judge to award any custody rights of the children since their father signed an agreement. Also, request that Matthew James adopt Sofie and Andrew immediately after your marriage."

~~~~~~~

Coming to the meeting early, Wade planned to spend time with Sofie and Andrew. As he walked down the hall toward the nursery, he heard giggling and laughter. He peered into the open doorway. On the floor was a soldier on his hands and knees. Little Andrew was on top of the man's head and pulling his tie. Sofie was on his back spurring him with her heels, saying, "Giddyap, horse."

Their father quickly walked back down the hall so as not to be seen. He waited until the soldier exited the nursery. When Wade entered the room, Sofie and Andrew ran to Audra and her grandfather who were caring for them.

As he approached Dr. Kirk, Wade was in a sullen mood "Was that soldier Raquel's fiancé?"

"Yes, it was Lieutenant Matthew James. He serves at Camp Cavalry Columbus."

The young man turned to the children, "I have brought
~~~~~~~

gifts for you, a little rag doll for Sofie and a top for Andrew. Come to Papa." He held them out, but the children would not go to him. They turned their backs and clung to Audra and Dr. Kirk. After much coaching to no avail, the father finally walked to where his children were and handed them their presents. Andrew took the top, but Sofie pushed the doll to the floor. Their papa visited a short while with Dr. Kirk, but the children never left the safety of their protectors. Wade's composure was that of much regret as he left the nursery

The hour for the meeting had arrived. Wade nervously shifted in his chair, and appeared very displeased to see that other people had gathered in the parlor along with the family. Among them were the sheriff, Pablo, and Maria. Lieutenant Matthew James sat next to Raquel with Elizabeth and Audra on the other side.

Staring at Raquel, Wade saw how lovely she looked with her hair in long curls and wearing a fuchsia-colored dress. Remorse welled up within him. He grimaced and brooded about his past rebellion, "I recklessly threw away all that was good in my life. I have reaped what I sowed."

Seated next to Wade was Daniel as they faced this group. The lawyer was unable to attend the meeting, so Derek was chosen as moderator. After introductions were made, the sergeant asked Wade to speak.

In a condescending tone, he spoke, "I want custody rights of my children and for the baby to have my name. I am prepared to go to court."

Raquel retorted, "I offer you generous visitation privileges." Wade sneered at her remark.

Derek announced, "Certain witnesses have come to testify on Raquel's behalf. I decree that no one should interrupt the person speaking."

Riveting his eyes on the ex-husband, Matthew stated, "Sir, I will be diligent to care for Sofie and Andrew. I will love them as my own children."

Glaring at the soldier, anger and jealously arose in Wade as he viewed the emerald engagement ring on Raquel's finger.

Next in line to comment was the sheriff. "I will testify in court of Wade Conner's drunkenness and disorderly conduct."

Speaking Spanish, Derek interpreted for Pablo as he gave his account, "Wade sought to abandon his family and leave them destitute in his quest to go to California."

Wade began to fidget and squirm in his chair. He was filled with shame and embarrassment.

Called in to testify was one more witness who had been waiting in an outer room. Doreen was a dark-haired woman of about thirty years in age. She appeared haggard and tired with dark circles under her eyes. As she entered the parlor, Wade was aghast. He got up from his chair to leave, but Daniel quickly grabbed him and pulled him back down.

Then he murmured to the estranged young man, "Do you want your loan?"

So, Wade sat back down, leaned over, and put his head in his hands.

Nervously twisting her handkerchief, Doreen glanced at the group of witnesses; she appeared timid and afraid. The crowd seemed to scrutinize her. Hesitantly she began her testimony. "Wade flirted with me at the tavern. Because he said that he was not married, we spent some nights together. He told me that he had taken in a poor, pathetic, wretch of a woman upon whom he had pity. He promised to take me with him to California, but he lied."

Wiping her eyes, Doreen gazed at Raquel. "I am very sorry, Mrs. Conner. I did not know that Wade was married. I see that you are a fine lady. I will gladly come to the court and testify in your behalf."

Scowling, Wade declared vehemently, "I am not daunted by this array of witnesses against me! As for custody, I want Sofie and Andrew to spend a month with me each year in California!"

Raquel stood up and screamed at him, "No, I forbid it! Also, I will not put your name on the birth certificate as the baby's father! And there is nothing that you can do about it!"

He shouted back, "Then I will see you in court, Raquel!"

Sobbing, she began to walk toward the door. Elizabeth followed her and also Matthew. As the latter approached the door to exit, Wade accosted him, sticking his finger in the soldier's chest. "All you want is Raquel's ranch!"

Matthew grabbed Wade, threw him to the floor and held him there with his arms twisted behind him. With his knee in his back, the soldier scolded him, "You will be respectful to an officer in the U. S. Army."

The ex-husband cried out in pain, begging for release. He struggled to get free but could not. He did not know that Matthew was skilled in martial arts. None of the bystanders approached the captive to help him.

Finally Wade squeaked, "I regret my words, sir."

The lieutenant helped him up to which he walked away, rubbing his arms and shoulder. Then Wade sat down with his back to the group to wait for Daniel to verify if he would still get his loan.

Hurrying to Raquel's room, Matthew encountered his fiancée sitting on the settee next to her mother. The young woman was weeping uncontrollably. When he entered, Elizabeth left the room. Matthew sat down next to his beloved and cradled her in his embrace. Raquel clung to him. She found comfort and strength in his nearness. When she finally stopped crying, his chest was wet with her tears. He soothed her fears, "Raquel, we serve a God who cares for us, and He will help us to get through this crisis." The soldier gently stroked her hair. He lifted her chin and covered her face with kisses. Raquel quieted her troubled spirit and took solace in the man she loved.

In the parlor, right before the adjournment, Audra handed a note to Derek, "Please detain Doreen after the meeting. I have sympathy for the woman, and I want to talk to her. I request that you also be present."

When she received the note, the barfly raised her eyebrows in surprise that they would be interested in her and would want to speak to her.

Derek introduced himself, "I am an army chaplain, and this is Miss Kirk."

Smiling politely, Audra said to her, "Thank you for coming to testify for my sister, today."

"I was glad to help her, mam."

After a few minutes of small talk, Audra boldly asked, "Doreen, would you be interested to pray and invite Christ into your life?"

She shook her head. "I am too bad of a person to be converted. 'You can put lipstick on a pig, but it's still a pig.'"

With confidence, Derek explained, "Eternal life is a free gift by the blood of Jesus on the cross, God loves you, and he made the sacrifice so that you may enter heaven someday."

So, Doreen prayed, "Lord, come into my heart and be my Savior and forgive me of my sins. Jesus is the son of God. I believe that he died on the cross for my sins and rose again. Eternal life is mine. In Jesus name." Her tears fell to the floor.

Seeking further guidance for her, Derek recounted an occurrence in the Bible, "In a summary, Jesus confronted a mob who was about to stone a woman caught in adultery. Yet, he did not condemn her, but told her to go and sin no more."

In sincerity, Doreen declared, "I will not to go back to my corrupt, immoral life."

In compassion, Audra offered, "Here is a Bible, and I invite you to come with us to the church meeting on Sunday."

When Doreen left the Kirk ranch, a bright smile graced her face. She murmured to herself, "I now have a new hope in Christ. I came here sorrowful, but now I am leaving joyful."

~~~~~~~

At dusk, Matthew left Shiloh and returned to Camp Cavalry. Audra slept on the spare bed in her sister's room to be near her.

Raquel had refused supper and slept fretfully. She awoke with a start and called to Audra, "I had a terrible dream that
~~~~~~~

my children were in California with their father. In the dream, a step mother was taunting my little ones, and the woman's own children were bullying Sofie and Andrew." Then Raquel started crying and pacing the floor. Finally, she returned to bed, but insomnia set in, and her mind was churning with fear. Eventually she slept, but just after midnight, she felt sick with cramping. There was blood on her sheet.

Raquel screamed to Audra. "Hurry and get grandfather to come here!"

Racing down the hall to other side of the house, Audra pounded loudly on her grandfather's door. "It's Raquel! The baby is at risk!"

Running to Raquel's room, Dr. Kirk was only clad in his trousers with no shoes or shirt. He instructed his granddaughter, "My dear, lie quietly and do not move."

The commotion woke Daniel and Elizabeth, and they came quickly to the bedroom. They immediately began to pray, but it was too late. There was already much blood in their daughter's bed. Raquel had miscarried. She was but three months along. The family gathered around her and prayed for her to have peace in her spirit.

Dr. Kirk told her, "You must rest in bed for a few days, but you should return to full health."

Raquel rallied, "Though I have lost my baby, the turmoil is over, and I am comforted." The young woman was emotionally exhausted and finally slept

~~~~~~~

Early the next morning, Wade came to the ranch to obtain a promissory note and also to receive a bank draft to
~~~~~~~

purchase his land. When he entered Daniel's office, he sensed that something was wrong. Elizabeth was sitting close to her husband, and her eyes were red. The rancher's face was grim, and his mood was unfriendly.

As Daniel spoke, his steel gaze did not soften. "Here is a train ticket, Wade. You should not hop on a freight train with the amount of money you will carry."

"I am extremely grateful to you, sir. I have decided not to proceed with a court case against Raquel. I will accept the visitation privileges for Sofie and Andrew. I am convinced that the soldier will treat them well. I saw him entertaining the children in the nursery."

"It is with much sadness that I tell you this. Raquel miscarried the baby in the night."

With a look of horror, Wade dropped to the floor. On his knees, he cried out, "Oh God, please forgive me! I am to blame for losing my baby."

He wept, and his tears fell to the floor. Elizabeth left the office quickly so as not to be overcome with grief, and Daniel led the young man to the door. Wade left with money in his hand but bereft of his child.

~~~~~~~

Matthew came to visit Raquel in the evening. "How are you sweetheart?"

She smiled brightly. "I'm feeling much better." She was resting in her bed but sat up when he entered the room. Matthew leaned down to kiss her on the lips, and he lingered the kiss for a moment.

Physically and emotionally, Raquel recovered from her
~~~~~~~

miscarriage. The lieutenant called upon her often as she convalesced. It was a couple of days before the wedding, and Raquel had a topic of concern. One evening while Matthew was visiting her, she confessed her burden to him, "Grandfather Kirk has advised me to wait a short while before I give myself completely to you. I am very sorry for this. I want to please you, and I hope that you will not be disappointed."

Matthew grinned smugly. "Holding you in my arms in the night will be satisfying enough."

Drawing her close to his heart, he kissed her softly. She responded to his affection, nestled into his shoulder, and relaxed against him. As he held her, she rested, secure and peaceful.

On the day of the wedding Raquel looked radiant in the satin gown that her mother had fashioned. Her auburn hair was curled in a meticulous, elaborate manner. Audra, as maid of honor, appeared in an exquisite crimson silk gown. Her red hair and rosy cheeks illuminated her smile. Matthew chose Derek as his best man. The two soldiers stood tall and looked impressive in their army uniforms. Kenton seated the guests of family, friends, and soldiers that overflowed the church.

Walking down the church aisle, Raquel smiled like she was on a primrose path to happiness. Reverend Barr officiated, and the couple repeated the vows. Matthew kissed his bride with passion and tenderness. The bride and groom were applauded and were greeted by the well-wishers.

Audra took the sergeant's arm to walk back down the aisle to exit. And in that moment, she daydreamed, "I wish that this was my wedding. Of course, the groom would be

Derek."

As the guests threw flower petals in the church yard, one of Derek's soldier buddies made a remark to him, "Your wedding will be next, Sarge. Who could resist such a fancy lady as Miss Audra Kirk?"

Derek returned the comment with a sly grin. He approached the bride's maid and commented, "Audra, you have the appearance of royalty in that dress."

In a flirting manner, she replied, "I hope it bedazzles you."

"Yes, it does." But then he went to visit with friends.

10

In their parlor chatting, Elizabeth spoke in a serious tone, "Audra, while you were on the reservation, I observed something that you should know. Do you remember Penelope Adams?"

Audra snickered. "Yes, a cute, dark-haired girl and quite precocious."

"Even though Penelope is quite young, I noticed that she is an accomplished flirt. She sits in the front row when Derek is preaching and has been giving him a lot of attention. After the meeting, she seeks him out, flirting and laughing. Penelope fawns over him at every opportunity. She is like a butterfly on a string. It appears that she has set her heart on Derek for a husband."

"Really, I thought that she was interested in Kenton Lott and he in her. He is more her age."

"True, but it appears that Kenton may be Penelope's second choice. After the coquette leaves Derek, then she seeks out Kenton."

"Mother, Derek is aware that I have returned home to Columbus from the reservation, because father sent him a message. Yet almost two weeks have passed, and he has not called on me. The sergeant has been elusive regarding me. At the wedding, he only visited with me briefly. Maybe it's true that Penelope has captured his heart."

Elizabeth persuaded, "Do not give up, daughter, the sergeant may have been detained at the garrison."

Audra sighed, "I know that you and father adore Derek, but I must face the reality that he has shown no interest in me. I could love him, but the feeling is not mutual. I cannot continue to live in the hope that he will ever care for me. It is futile to entertain the possibility. It looks as though there will be no future for us together. We shall not mention his name again."

A few days after the wedding, an unexpected visitor appeared at the door of the Kirk family, Miss Penelope Adams. The young woman asked only to talk to Audra. She entered the parlor, her dark hair shining, and wearing a fashionable periwinkle dress.

The young lady entered the parlor and Audra welcomed her, "Please sit down, and I will bring tea."

"Thank you. I hear that you will soon attend the medical school in El Paso. Will you become a doctor?"

"Yes, I am looking forward to studying medicine."

"I bet there will be many handsome, aspiring doctors there."

"Yes, I am sure."

"Will there be any females amongst the male students?"

"I have heard that a young and pretty, blonde-haired nurse will also enroll. Her name is Lisette Galt."

"Therefore, you two women will have the pick of the

young doctors."

"I guess you could say that, but the man must be a Christian. I do not want to be unequally yoked with an unbeliever. A man's character is of utmost importance."

"Yes, I understand."

"You are very young, Penelope. Choose wisely, and seek God's will for a husband."

"I will. I chat with Sergeant Derek Rands after church. He came by to see me last week, and we had a wonderful conversation over tea and crumpets. I have invited him for supper tonight. I saw you conversing with him at the wedding. I am infatuated with Derek as he is with me. Do not try to steal him from me!"

Audra wrinkled up her nose in distaste. "Why should I care? He is of no concern to me."

"Good!"

Their visit ended amicably, but Audra questioned herself, "Has Derek forsaken me for this 'little thing'? Does this confirm that there will be no future for Derek and I? I will no longer dream or wish for it."

~~~~~~~

Though still residing at the tavern, Doreen began to pursue a new life. She attended church and was baptized. The congregation was surprised to see her, as they knew of her reputation in the town.

She confided to Audra, "I still feel guilty for my sordid past. I think of myself like that old saying, 'You can't make a silk purse out of a sow's ear'."

"My friend, there is no condemnation for those who are
~~~~~~~

in Christ Jesus. You are a new creature. Your old life has passed away without remembrance."

"Thank you for telling me that. It is exactly what I needed to hear today. I so wish to leave the tavern as a barmaid and find other work, maybe nursing."

Upon hearing this, Audra made a plea to her grandfather, "Would it be possible for Doreen to be an apprentice in our clinic? She is desperate to get out of tavern life."

He graciously accepted her request. "Yes, she can start any time. We both can mentor her."

The woman came the next day to the clinic. She quickly became skilled in the nursing profession.

One day as the two young ladies were working in the clinic, Doreen asked, "Miss Kirk, do you think that the Lord would give me a husband? My greatest wish is to marry and have children. The men and the soldiers who patronize the tavern despise me. They know of my bad reputation."

"Yes, God gives us the desires of our heart if we pray and ask him."

Dr. Kirk inquired for a nursing job for Doreen. An elderly couple, the Clarks, had solicited a caregiver. The husband had sustained a fall, and the wife was frail. Their son, a merchant, lived in another state. The son wanted his parents to come and live in an 'old folks' home near him, but they refused.

Receiving the job, Doreen went to live with the Clarks in their large, stately house. She was compassionate and patient toward the couple. The wedded pair quickly bonded with her and treated her like a daughter.

While visiting with Doreen at the Clark's home, Audra

was curious. "How has your life been since living here?"

"It is wonderful. The Clarks are very kind to me. They give me a generous wage. Since I have no expenses, I am able to save a large sum of money. My plan is that it will be my dowry when I am married."

"What is it like being a caregiver?"

Her friend was eager to report her nursing success, "I have established a regimen for the elderly couple. With a healthy diet, rest, and exercise, they have grown strong enough to walk down the street."

"You have become an esteemed nurse. Are there any challenges here?"

The young woman began to snicker. "The man and wife were hoarders. I am helping them to get rid of their junk. The mice problem was so bad in the home that I had to borrow a cat. Audra, I am so happy here. In growing up, I was unwanted and neglected. This couple now helps me with life skills. Mrs. Clark is instructing me in social etiquette and bookkeeping. Mr. Clark is teaching me self-defense; he gave me a rifle for target practice. They allow me to attend church, and I have time to read my Bible."

"You have adjusted well to this life."

She started laughing. "The Clarks see me as their student. It is their sense of purpose to educate me."

~~~~~~~

In California, Wade purchased the land that adjoined his own, and he harvested a profitable orange crop. He wanted to make good his promise to pay off his loan to Daniel Kirk. He also wanted to see his children. So, he took a train to
~~~~~~~

Columbus.

Returning from their honeymoon Matthew and Raquel, now lived in their own home on the ranch. For their father's visit, Raquel brought the children to Shiloh.

Wade was allowed to chat with his children in the nursery. "Papa has brought you some oranges." This time Sofie and Andrew came to their father to accept the gift of oranges. Yet they quickly ran back to their guardians, Elizabeth and a hired girl.

The ex-husband only had a glimpse of Raquel at the end of the hall to the nursery. He considered her fair to behold, and he sensed a stab in his gut of regret as his former wife hurried from view. He sadly reflected, "I am guilty for my selfishness and unfaithfulness. But I am determined to make a better life and never go back to the hateful man that I was."

Since his train would not arrive soon, Wade walked leisurely through the town, taking in the sights.

At the Clark home, Doreen was kneading bread dough when she heard a knock at their door. She parted the curtain at the parlor window and peered out to see who the visitor might be. She did not recognize the young man standing there. Yet, on closer inspection, Doreen was puzzled, "He looks similar to Wade Conner. But my memory of him was that of a man with greasy hair, a scruffy beard, and a foul smell from infrequent bathing. This fellow is well groomed, clean shaven, and wears a dark suit."

Shuffling down the hall to the vestibule, Mr. Clark opened the front door, and invited the man to come into the parlor. Doreen quickly removed her apron and came face to face with Wade Conner. Astonishment showed in her demeanor.

She introduced the man to the Clarks who were excited to have a visitor. Wade studied her with eyes of approval, "Miss Tate, I came by to see how you are. I hope that it is all right for me to inquire."

"Yes, I thank you for your concern, sir."

The Clarks were about to exit the room, but Doreen insisted, "Please stay and visit for a while."

The old couple was pleased when Wade also requested that they be part of the conversation, "Tell me about your life." Mr. Clark told some interesting stories about the past.

When the young man mentioned leaving, Mrs. Clark quickly asked? "Would you be able to stay for lunch?" She wanted him to stay longer since they seldom had guests.

"I accept your gracious invitation." He smiled as the couple exited to the kitchen.

Doreen tried to still her nervousness of being alone with Wade, "How are your crops in California?"

"My orange groves are prospering. I am in Columbus to visit my children. I hear that you are now a nurse."

"Yes, I assisted Dr. Kirk in his clinic to learn the trade. I must say that I hardly recognized you in a suit."

"The suit belonged to a widow's deceased husband. In the church, I do repairs for the widows. I have learned much about carpentry in this manner. It looks as if this house could use some upkeep."

"Yes, it was once a grand home, but it is now somewhat dilapidated. However, Mr. Clark recently replaced the roof and front porch"

Wade bit his lip. "Doreen, please forgive me for the past. I treated you badly ."

"Yes, of course, I forgive you." Her face warmed, and her gaze fell to the hem of her dress.

"You look rested and content. I don't deserve this request, but may I write to you in the future?"

"Possibly, you may. I will consider it and let you know."

When it was time for Wade to leave for his train, the Clarks expressed their delight for his visit. "We invite you to return to our home when you are in Columbus."

Doreen walked to the door with Wade, and he took her hand in his, "I am grateful for your forgiveness and for welcoming me. I bid you good day."

After Wade had left, Mr. Clark spoke to Doreen with a twinkle in his eyes, "You should marry that young man." She was speechless and her face was aghast.

~~~~~~~

At the garrison, Kenton consulted Derek, "My first allegiance is to you. You are my mentor. You have taught me the power of the scriptures, self-discipline, and integrity. Would you care if I were to call on Audra?"

"No, but remember that she will leave the area soon. Be careful not to set your heart on her."

So, Kenton met with Daniel and Elizabeth and boldly asked, "May I call on Audra during the coming days? I have much admiration for your daughter, and I am financially well fixed."

Looking at each other, the parents nodded. "Yes, if Audra is interested, we give you permission to come courting. She
~~~~~~~

will have almost two months to spend here at Shiloh before she leaves for medical school."

Thereafter, Kenton spoke of his good fortune to Derek and Matthew, "These past weeks, I have been calling on Audra. We have gone horseback riding and taken long walks. I find her to be smart, beautiful, and she shares my faith. We are very compatible, and we have the same outlook on life."

Then Derek warned, "Ken, you have only called on Audra a few times. You may be moving too fast in this romantic endeavor. I advise you to proceed with caution. I challenge you to pray and seek God's will if she is to be your life mate. When she attends medical school, she will be among gifted male students. Frankly, she will receive much attention from them."

"Thank you for your concern, but I cherish Audra. When I hold her and kiss her, it is almost paradise."

At that remark, Derek winced. Matthew could not restrain himself from chuckling, because he knew the feeling that his friend had described. "I would give you similar advice, Ken. Take a little time to pray and think things over. We do not want to see you hurt. What about the young lady from church, Penelope? You had been calling on her before Audra returned to Columbus."

"Penelope does not 'hold a candle' to Miss Kirk. I love Audra, and she has expressed her love to me. Her parents have given us their blessing. She has accepted a courtship with me that will culminate in marriage. I am ready to buy a ring and propose matrimony."

Commenting on his plan, Matthew was doubtful. "Won't

a long-distance courtship be hard?

"Not at all, my family live in El Paso where Audra will attend medical school. My grandparents have offered for her to live with them in their large home until I am discharged from the army. I can take the train to see her on weekends."

"Are you ready for the responsibility of a wife and baby on a soldier's pay?" Derek argued.

"Yes, I am. I have other means; a stipend from a trust fund is sent to me each month. I never imagined that I could win the heart of a young woman as fine and sweet as Audra. Of course, I invite you both to be in my wedding party. I believe that this courtship is right, but I will pray. I seriously do want the will of the Lord in the matter of a wife"

~~~~~~~

In the interest of his friend, Derek confided to Matthew, "I want to be sure that Kenton's courtship is not flawed." So, the sergeant went to Shiloh ranch

The sergeant voiced the motive of his coming. "I am here to see Audra, sir."

With a large smile, Daniel Kirk welcomed him, "I am glad to hear it. I have missed you, son." But the older man became quickly aware that the sergeant seemed to be in a serious mood.

Audra entered the parlor where Derek waited. He could not help but gaze at her beauty. She noted his eyes assessing her appearance.

The young lady greeted him cordially, "Good evening, sir."

"I will cut to the chase, Audra. I want to know what your
~~~~~~~

intentions are concerning Kenton Lott?"

She glared at him. "Is that so?"

He raised an eyebrow. "Kenton is young, and he is smitten with you."

"He is a year older than me."

"I would not be concerned if you really liked him."

"I do like him, and father approves of Kenton because the corporal reminds him of you."

That declaration sent a jolt to Derek's senses. For a moment, he said nothing, but seemed to be a little disconcerted. Yet he persisted in his debate, "Audra, you need to pray and hear from Lord about this courtship. You will be leaving soon, so I want you to tread lightly with Kenton. I know that he is pursuing you, but you need to slow it down."

Staring icily, Audra goaded him, "By the way, congratulations on your new love. Maybe you need to pull back on the reins. The girl is very young."

"What are you talking about?" He frowned and his face showed surprise.

"Penelope Adams paid me a visit. She declared that you and her are infatuated with each other." Then Audra grinned smugly. "She threatened me not to steal you from her."

Derek burst into laughter. "That deceitful, little liar! I will deal with her tawdry behavior. I did have tea with her family, but I do not accept their dinner invitations. Penelope comes up to me after church to flirt. She is like an annoying cat at my feet that I would like to kick away."

"Be gentle in speaking to her; she is only eighteen years old."

Then the sergeant appeared solemn. "Audra, be careful of the fascination that Kenton has for you."

She became inflamed. "I do not have to answer to you! I am not under your authority!"

He shrugged. "All right. It's your life." Then Derek snickered. "As an afterthought, how did you answer Penelope when she threatened you?"

"I told her this: for me, you are a *persona non grata.*"

With a bruised ego, he left, and Audra smiled that she had the last word.

Later on, when it was Derek's turn to preach at the church, Penelope came afterwards to flirt with him. She was fawning on him, picking off imaginary lent from his uniform. He stopped her and spoke frankly to her, "Penelope, your deceit and lies have come to my attention. On my part, there has never been an infatuation for you."

When she left him, she was dejected with tears in her eyes. She made her way to the altar to pray.

Then she found Audra, humbled herself, and apologized. "I am sorry for the words that I spoke to you. I was dumb and immature. Please forgive me. Will you still be a friend to me?"

"Of course, I will." And Audra hugged her.

After Derek's talk with Penelope, she was afraid of the sergeant and purposed to avoid him.

~~~~~~

At Shiloh, Audra mused, "I am in awe of my courtship with Kenton. I greatly admire and trust him. He is a man of high character and will be a most excellent husband. He is the ideal man: smart, confident, ambitious, and spiritual.
~~~~~~

I believe that, at last, I have found true love. I wonder if I could ever meet a man as noble as this soldier. When I am with him, it is like heaven on earth."

Yet as the days went by, she lamented, "As I become clingier to Kenton, he has become less attentive to me. I am worried that he has become distant. My heart is set on him for a mate."

Taking his companions' advice, Kenton prayed, "Lord, in Jesus name, is it your will that Audra become my wife? I ardently love her and want her by my side." After he prayed, he discerned that he must wait, and that she was not the appointed one.

One evening soon after the prayer, the couple was seated together on the loveseat in her parents' parlor. Audra gently touched Kenton's arm. "I am pleased that you are here tonight."

His reaction frightened her as he gazed back at her with troubled eyes, and he gave a deep sigh. "Audra, I prayed to the Lord and told Him that I love you ardently and want you for my wife. However, I received the answer that it is not His will for us to have a future together. I questioned my maker and pleaded with Him to give me the desire of my heart. It has been like a war within me, but it is futile to continue to struggle. My peace has left me. I am a soldier, and I understand obedience. I put off this conversation as long as I could, but it is the final countdown. You will travel to El Paso to attend the medical school in a few days"

Starting to tremble, Audra was dumbfounded. "I want to be with you as long as I live. Do you not love me?"

He took her hand and swallowed hard. "No, it's not that. We just have to follow God's will; it is the highest authority. It's my fault that I went chasing after you before consulting the Lord. I am sorry for that."

Tears of sorrow started to pummel down her face. "So, are we to part?"

Rubbing his brow with his hand, he replied, "I think that we must. I wish that circumstances were different, but they are not."

He grasped her into his arms, and she wept on his shoulder. When she looked up, there were tears in his eyes. He looked into her beautiful, tear-stained face. "You are very dear to me. I promise you that if you ever need me, I will come to you. I will never forsake you nor forget you."

When the corporal took her hand and kissed it, Audra's eyes begged him to stay. "I loathe leaving you, but I must. Dear, sweet Audra, goodbye."

Sobbing, she ran down the hall to her parents' sitting room. Her father and mother looked up abruptly from their reading.

Elizabeth's features showed distress, but Daniel reacted first. "Daughter, why all of these tears?"

Audra's lips quivered. "Kenton just told me that our courtship is over! He believes that I am not the one to be his wife. This is the worse anguish that I have ever experienced in my life! The weeks that we spent together were the most wonderful I have ever known. His love for me left me in awe. Now all I will have left is a memory. The fire of our love has turned into ashes."

Her father spoke in compassion, "My dear, you will get beyond this hurt. Do not grieve over the loss of your beau. You will have to let the peace of God reign in your life."

In a consoling tone, Elizabeth declared, "Do not be alarmed, my darling. The Lord has a destiny for you."

So, Audra left the room with her parents' comforting words.

Daniel turned to Elizabeth, "This parting is very sad news. We were both quite fond of Kenton and heartily approved of the match. However, now it's possible that Derek may still become our son-in-law."

11

It was hot day as Dr. Kirk made his way to Camp Cavalry to talk with Derek. He explained to the sergeant, "I have information that may be pertinent for the officers here. I recently conversed with the sheriff and local officials. They have noticed that various strange Mexicans have entered Columbus. They also commented that the friendly Mexicans have left the town. I conclude that the strange Mexicans could be Pancho Villa's spies to obtain information about the U.S. Army post and the town. I know that Pancho Villa's raiders from Chihuahua have recently besieged and plundered towns along the border of northern Mexico."

On the day of March 8, 1916, a report had come into Cavalry Camp from Juan Favela, the foreman of a ranch near the town of Palomas. Favela saw Villa and his army traveling north near the border. There had been other warnings so the report was not considered a threat. That same evening, Colonel Slocum, the commander of the 13th Cavalry garrison and several officers traveled thirty-one miles to Deming, New Mexico to watch a polo game.

As night approached, Derek called his companions to pray, and he warned them, "Comrades, Pancho Villa has been seen again along the border. I believe that we need to get ready to mobilize. I suggest that we sleep in our uniforms with our boots on. Prepare your saddle bags with ammo and food. Fill extra canteens with water. We will be the first to march out if there is an attack on Camp Cavalry."

Yet only a few of the soldiers heeded the word of caution and began to act accordingly. Derek and his companions made themselves ready for an attack, and they did not sleep easy that night. The atmosphere in the barracks was ominous with the threat of a clash with Villa's marauders

At dawn, the sound of gunfire awoke the enlisted men as the sudden realization came that that Pancho Villa's army had invaded Camp Cavalry. The soldiers of the thirteenth Cavalry Regiment could see that Columbus was on fire. The imminent danger had now arrived. Pancho Villa and his bandits made a bloody siege and pillaged the town of 400 citizens. They entered the houses stealing supplies and ammunition, shooting the residents, and then setting their homes on fire. It was a surprise attack, and they killed or wounded several citizens. The soldiers from the garrison rapidly began to mobilize. Villa's raid turned into a raging battle when they were resisted by the U. S. Cavalry.

The troops, under the command of Lieutenant John Lucas, fired upon the Villistas from the garrison with machine guns. Lieutenant James Castleman with a second division of U.S. soldiers made a counteroffensive. Lieutenant John Lucas, in charge of the machine gunnery, could not find his boots in the dark. So, he ran barefoot to the battle.

Daniel Kirk awoke before sunrise, preparing to sort some

steers for market. When he saw the smoke coming from Columbus, he alerted his household. Fortunately, Dr. Kirk had spent the night at the ranch and not at his clinic. The father, son, and ranch hands quickly saddled their horses and grabbed their pistols and rifles.

Begging to go with them, Audra started to saddle her horse. "Father, please, let me come. I may be able to help the wounded."

Finally, he submitted. "All right, stay behind us and wait outside the village! Do not fear to use your pistol if you have to."

At a fast gallop, the vigilante group hightailed it for the town. In the distance they saw the fracas and heard the gunshots of the attackers. Entering Columbus, they viewed bodies in the streets and several buildings in charred ruins. The group of men from the ranch chose an establishment, and from there, blasted the Villistas with their rifles.

Pancho Villa, cowardly did not engage in the attack, but watched the battle from the edge of the town. The invasion was a disaster for the Mexican guerrillas. Villa's rebels suffered enormous casualties and retreated back across the border to Mexico. When the attack occurred, Colonel Slocum, the commander of the garrison, returned from Deming more than hour after the Villistas had invaded. He ordered Major Frank Thompson and the regiment's third Squadron to pursue the invaders. They chased the bandits 15 miles beyond the border into Mexico in their attempt to seize Pancho Villa. The Villistas forfeited much of the weapons, horses, food, and supplies that they had stolen at Columbus. The U. S. troops levied some casualties on the desperados, but they had to disengage due to lack of water and ammunition. Their horses were exhausted, and they could not continue their pursuit. Though Pancho Villa escaped back into Mexico, the attack was a huge defeat for his army.

Villa's raiders were evil predators and caused death and destruction on the town of Columbus. There were a number of casualties. Eight civilians had died which included a pregnant woman. Two of the town's people were wounded. The losses in the U. S. Cavalry counted ten dead and eight wounded of the 350 soldiers stationed at the garrison.

Dr. Kirk and Audra were enlisted to help care for the wounded. Daniel assisted in carrying the victims on stretchers to the clinic and into the army infirmary. Elizabeth and the household workers loaded a wagon with food, blankets, and other supplies, and made their way to Columbus.

In the aftermath of the battle, Audra was anxious to check on Doreen. She discovered that her friend and the Clarks were safe, but Doreen was traumatized. The woman related her experience to Audra while wiping her eyes as she talked, "We were awakened in the night with someone pounding and jangling the outer door with the iron bars. They were Mexicans, yelling and cursing in Spanish. The robbers had climbed over the brick wall to break into our home. Mr. Clark had a strategy. He instructed me to get my Winchester repeating rifle and then to drag two of the tall, upholstered chairs to the foyer. I threw a lap robe over the chair bottoms. The chairs were placed together but with a crack in the middle for the rifle barrel. I got on my knees behind the chairs so as not to be seen. Mr. Clark turned on the porch light, and then slowly opened the interior wooden door with his back to the wall. When he signaled to me, I opened fire on a bunch of Villistas who were standing in front of the iron bars. I shot through the iron bars. They quickly fled away. I don't know if any of them were wounded."

Audra put her arm around Doreen who by this time was shaking and sobbing. "You were very brave. You did the right thing to defend your home."

"Trying to comfort me, Mr. Clark told me not to regret my actions. He believes that I may have saved the lives of some of the town's people and the soldiers."

"That is absolutely true."

Doreen sniffled into her handkerchief. Please pray for me that I will not have nightmares or tormenting thoughts."

~~~~~~~

Reports of some of the victims came into the town. At the Commercial Hotel the raiders killed three men. John Walker, who was recently wed, was seized from the embrace of his bride and murdered by the Villistas. His young wife was released by yelling "*Viva* Mexico!"

The wife of an army officer, Mrs. Smyser, heard pounding on their front door. She and her children climbed out a window, hid in the outhouse, and then ran through the cacti into the desert.

Mrs. Parks used her telephone switchboard to alert the people that Columbus was under siege. She received cuts from flying glass but lived through the attack.

Carrying her tiny baby, Mrs. Frost pulled her injured
~~~~~~~

husband into their car. They then drove to Deming and escaped from harm.

The Villistas captured a boy, Sam Ravel, fourteen years old. They yanked him out of his house, but he got free when his attackers were struck down by gun fire. Dressed only in his underwear, the boy fled into the dark, chilly desert.

Milton James swiftly took his pregnant wife from their home and hurried for the Hoover Hotel for safer protection. Before they could reach the hotel, the Villistas shot and murdered Mrs. James and her unborn baby.

Pancho Villa kidnapped a young American woman named Maud Wright who was living on a ranch in Mexico. The rebels ransacked the home and murdered her husband and another young man who was a visitor there. They tore her baby boy from her arms and left him in the care of a ranch hand. She was forced to travel with the renegade band one hundred miles through the mountains of Chihuahua. Grief stricken, Maud suffered extreme thirst and hunger. Water was scarce, and one time she was deprived of it for thirty-three hours. Her food was meat with hair on it, burned on one side and raw on the other. Her only covering in the cold mountains was a thin serape. Maud attempted to escape by untying a horse, but she was caught and brought back.

Fluent in Spanish, Mrs. Wright overheard a malicious plan. Villa declared "I am going to shoot up Columbus and make a torch of every man, woman, and child." She desperately wanted to warn the citizens of Columbus, but she was closely guarded. Pancho Villa did not wish to kill Maud but rather to let her faint from fatigue. When the Villistas retreated after the attack on Columbus, Maud was released, and she made her way into the town. Soon after, her baby boy was brought to her by the authority of Presidente Obregon from Mexico.

Villa's army received 190 casualties out of 484 men. Six Mexican guerrillas were captured and hanged. The bodies of the mortally wounded Villistas were strewn across the desert outside of Columbus. Many of them were 14 to16-year-old boys. Villa was an evil, mass murderer. His reputation was that he would murder on a whim. Villa, and his men killed many innocent people as they terrorized the towns and ranches along the border. Pancho Villa was a rapist, a kidnapper, and a defiler of women. He officially married 26 times. It is unknown how many of those unions were forced marriages.

President Wilson was angry that Pancho Villa had raided Columbus, New Mexico and had murdered 18 Americans. He commissioned General John Pershing to command a Punitive Expedition of 10,000 enlisted men to capture Villa and his guerrillas. The United States Army utilized airplanes for reconnaissance and mobilized trucks to deliver supplies to the troops. Villa and his men had a six-day head start before the U. S. soldiers arrived to pursue the desperados.

Entering the ranks of this army were Sergeant Derek Rands, Lieutenant Matthew James, and Corporal Kenton Lott; they would ride in the cavalry. Sergeant Rands was commissioned as a Spanish interpreter.

He also would aid the Apache scouts since he had lived on the Apache reservation for several years.

On the night before the troops would mobilize toward

Mexico, Derek went to Shiloh to see Audra. Luisa, the hired girl brought him to the parlor and summoned Miss Kirk.

"Good evening, Audra." His astute presence bore into the core of her being.

"What do you want, sir?"

"I know that you were hurt in the painful breakup with Kenton. I came to see how you are and to comfort you. I prayed for you." His face softened with compassion.

Her color rose. "I do not need your sympathy, nor do I want your pity."

Glaring, she accused him, "I adored Kenton, and he loved me. You did not approve and sought to separate us. How could you interfere like that?"

"No, that is not true, Audra. I accepted the honor of best man at his wedding. I only wanted the two of you to take more time in your courtship."

Her eyes were like darts directed toward Derek. "I regard you with utter contempt, so leave my presence!"

He stated quietly, "I am sorry you feel that way. I do care for you, Audra."

~~~~~~~

At dawn, Matthew prepared to leave for the garrison to join the Punitive Expedition with General Pershing's army. He walked with his wife, Raquel, his arm around her, to where his horse was waiting.

Her voice quavered, "I will pray for your protection and strength. Please come back to me, my love."

"As a soldier, I am aware of danger, I will stay alive. God is my protector. He will watch over my going out and my
~~~~~~~

coming in." He lifted her face to his. His confidence soothed her fears. "I love you, sweetheart," he murmured.

Raquel tilted her head up to reach his lips as he kissed her goodbye. Matthew held his wife close for a moment, and then loosed her embrace. He turned and mounted his horse and peered down at her as she gazed up at him. He then threw her a kiss and galloped away. She would not let herself cry until her husband was far into the distance.

12

Before boarding the train to El Paso, Audra hugged her parents and her sister. The conductor shouted, "All aboard!" Then the whistle sounded. She peered through the train window and waved until her family was out of sight. In the sway of the train, she daydreamed, "I have much anticipation of entering the hospital school. My past medical experience will help me to prosper in that arena."

On her arrival at the school, Audra was greeted by a nurse named Lisette Galt. The girl was tall with curly blonde hair and blue eyes. She was very fair with a beautiful face and figure. Her complexion radiated a peaches and cream aura. Lisette had been crowned Miss El Paso. She was about the same age as Audra. The nurse worked part time for Dr. Scott and would also attend the medical school.

She gave Audra a tour of the hospital, and the two young ladies immediately bonded.

Lisette was enthusiastic to make the new acquaintance. "Audra, I will help you in whatever you need here, and I will try to answer any questions that you may have. I play the organ at Christ church, and I invite you to come and worship with us."

"Thank you very much. I also am enraptured with music. Indeed, I will be in attendance."

As her new life began, Audra mused, "I am quite content to be here. My lodging in Miss Riley's mansion is quite comfortable. Lisette will be my confidante, and Ian will be my friend and ally."

Life was good, but her bliss did not last long. There were ten young men in the medical school, and only two women. Audra was unaware that the required dress was a white blouse and a long black skirt.

Consequently, she did not bring this uniform apparel with her. Therefore, Dr. Scott allowed her to wear a long white apron over her pretty dresses. Her elegant clothing made her beauty even more alluring. Many of the young male students were very bold in vying for her affection. Two of them had a tussle and a scuffle over who would sit by her. A number of the young men told Audra how pretty and smart she was. They complimented her on her red hair and ivory skin. One male student gave her the accolade of being a flawless beauty. Another man called her the Princess of the Kingdom. Various men brought her fruit and sweet cakes. They sent her flowers with love notes and sonnets. Several of the fellows invited her to dine and to attend the theater. As politely as she could, she declined most of the invitations. Nevertheless, she was inundated with male attention. It was overwhelming being the 'celebrity' in the class.

Audra confided to Lisette, "I was in love with a soldier named Kenton, but he spurned me. I will be leery in making any serious attachment this year."

The nurse, Lisette, also experienced much attention from the male students. She felt like a gazelle, running. Several of the upcoming doctors were chasing after her, seeking her attention. The men in the school nicknamed her the Regal Countess. One medical student was so smitten with the nurse that he hired a lackey to bring a white horse to the school. When Lisette went out to see the animal, the fellow declared, "Someday I will carry you away on it." The entire class enjoyed the spectacle. She was impressed with the token of adoration but not moved by it.

Notwithstanding all of the male students' overtures of endearment toward Audra, Ian began to claim her as his sweetheart. It perturbed and irritated her that he was trying to be possessive. The first week of class was barely over when Ian approached her about a courtship. He boldly stated, "Audra, I plan to travel to Columbus next weekend to ask your father's permission to court you."

"My father would never agree to your petition for a courtship! He only allowed you to visit us because you accompanied my mother's friend on her trip to the ranch. Father has searched for a husband for me, and he has found one. His name is Sergeant Derek Rands, a chaplain at Camp Cavalry.

"What are your feelings for this soldier?"

"I have no interest him. I find him arrogant."

"What are his intentions toward you?"

"That remains to be seen. Sergeant Rands is presently in Mexico on an expedition to capture Pancho Villa."

"When he returns, then I guess that I will have to fight him for you. If he comes around here, I will surely threaten him to keep his distance from you."

Audra began to giggle and then to snicker. "Derek would take you down in two seconds. He is highly skilled in combat fighting."

Ian was indignant. "Wait a minute, Missy. In the nursing home where I work, I often pick up a 200-pound man from his bed and place him in his chair. Every day I run a mile to this hospital and another mile to work in the old folks' home."

"I know that you are very strong, but you would be no match for Sergeant Rands. You would be quickly defeated and extremely embarrassed if you ever tangled with him."

"We shall see about that."

Coaxing, he persisted, "Audra, we could keep our courtship a secret. I am serious about my affection for you. Together, we would certainly make a team of distinguished doctors. Gorgeous girl, I make a decent wage, and I desire to escort you to the finest restaurants in El Paso. My father is the director of the nursing home, and I schedule my work hours at my discretion."

"I appreciate your thoughtfulness, but I cannot. We must continue only as friends."

"Friends now, but not for long!" he declared smugly.

Seeing that Audra did not give Ian the attention he craved, he perceived it as rejection. His male ego was wounded, and he began to be bitter towards her. He was jealous of other medical students who befriended her.

Therefore, Ian began to taunt Miss Kirk. Often before class, he would announce, "Here comes the Sanctified Woman."

His sarcastic teasing annoyed her, and she developed an

intense dislike for the man. Though it was difficult, she tried not to gratify his taunts with a response. She would not sit near him or go on rounds with him to consult with patients in the hospital.

When Ian realized that Audra had forsaken him, he turned his attention in pursuit of Lisette. He often teased the nurse and tried to flirt with her. Sometimes he would bring her a card or candy, and he sent flowers to her nurse's desk. Yet she was wary of his trifling.

As a skilled nurse, Lisette exhibited wisdom beyond her age. She was also talented in music and would sometimes sing hymns to the patients of which Dr. Scott approved. On one occasion, Ian heard her singing to a patient. When she left the patient's room, he halted her. "Would you sing at the old folks' home where I work?"

"Well, yes I could, early evening on Tuesday."

"That would be wonderful."

So, at the nursing home, Lisette played the piano and sang hymns. The residents were most favorable to her performance. Many of the elderly begged her to come and talk with them. After the program, Ian took her to the dairy bar for ice cream. Thereafter, the old people began to ask for Lisette; so, she went often to sing for them. The medical student repeatedly asked her to dine out with him or to attend the theater. But she was hesitant to accept his invitations.

Ian also targeted a nurse's aide named Cora to flirt with. The girl was very young and impressionable. She had just graduated from secondary school. He gloated when she would blush from his flattery and teasing.

Concerned for Cora, Audra warned her, "Dear girl, with all respect to you, be cautious of Ian and his lecherous ways. I do not want to see you hurt."

"You just want him for yourself!"

"No, I don't care for him, but I do care about you." So, Audra left the girl to her own devices.

13

In northern Mexico, the U. S. troops were traveling up mountains on treacherous trails. Their quest was to capture the thief and murderer, Pancho Villa. Many times, the procession was held up to move rock slides and debris. If it rained, the horses often stumbled on the slippery, rocky path. On one occasion, Rizana, the Apache scout, was at the head of the column with Derek. Soldiers, Matthew and Kenton were following close behind. Derek could see that the Indian was traveling too close to the precipice of the mountain.

"Rizana!" shouted Derek in Apache, "Move away from the edge of the cliff!"

But the Indian scout ignored his warning and horse and rider continued to pick their way up the trail close to the side of the mountain drop off. Rizana was a stubborn, proud Apache who gloried in his appointment as a scout for General Pershing's army.

Suddenly, Rizana's horse lost its footing. "Jump, Rizana!" yelled Derek.

The Indian jumped just as his horse slid down to a lower embankment of the mountain. The bewildered animal was stranded and nervously tried to climb the steep wall of mud and rock only to fall back down.

The procession halted in the dilemma. "Get some harness and ropes from the pack mules!" ordered Derek. The soldiers lowered Rizana to the embankment to calm his panicky horse.

The colonel in charge rode up to where the column had stopped and the accident occurred. The officer surveyed the scene. "Put a bullet in the animal and let's keep moving. This is an arduous journey."

"Sir, if you will give me a half hour, I will do the engineering and rescue this steed. We are already low on horses."

The colonel threw up his hands disgusted as he looked at the cliff and steep slope. "I say, it is impossible and a lost cause."

Undaunted, Derek was persuasive, "Sir, my horse and the horses of James and Lott have the strength to pull this horse to the top. They are trained to pull heavy loads. You have witnessed how our horses have moved large rocks off the trail."

Finally, the officer permitted it, "All right, I'll give you a half hour. Take the men you need and then try to catch up with the corps."

Mobilizing the soldiers, Derek obtained harnesses and ropes from the pack mules. Other troopers chopped down trees to build an apparatus to winch the horse to the surface. Rizana put the harness on his horse. The soldier team had lifted Rizana's horse almost to the top of the cliff when some leather straps of the harness broke, and the horse tumbled back down the embankment. The horse, in agitation, began to thrash against the remaining harness and ropes.

"Rizana, get a blindfold on that horse!" yelled Derek to the Indian. The Apache took off his shirt to use as a blindfold for his horse, and the animal immediately calmed down. The soldiers threw down more harness, and the next attempt to elevate the horse was successful. There was much excitement as the feat was accomplished. The soldiers who witnessed the task were amazed at Derek's engineering ability, and they commended him, "Excellent work, Sergeant."

He commented, "God gave me the wisdom and grace to do it."

Rizana, who usually exhibited a rather cocky attitude, was meek and humbled by the whole ordeal. Within less than an hour they had rescued the Indian's horse and were back on the trail.

14

While living at the mansion, Audra discovered that the widow, Miss Jenny Riley, was a retired nurse and that she had two passions in life. She put much energy into a young ladies' Bible study and also a Christian orphanage.

The widow explained to Miss Kirk, "I host a luncheon for young mothers each week in my large, spacious dining room. Ladies from the church prepare a delicious meal for the mothers, and others supervise a nursery for the children. The nursery is set up with beds, rocking chairs, and toys. The ministry outreach has been quite popular and keeps growing in number. I invite you to attend if you ever have a day off from the school."

"It sounds marvelous."

Miss Jenny had another invitation for Audra. "My dear, tomorrow is Saturday. Please go with me to a Christian orphanage run by Curtis and Patricia Allen. They are a couple in age of about fifty years. Mr. Allen works six days a week in a lead mine so that they can support five orphans. Their own children are grown and married. Curtis' mother, Grace, also lives with them and helps care for the children."

"It sounds like fun."

At the orphanage, Audra quickly noticed that the children were loved and well cared for. The widow brought cupcakes for the children. Lisette met them at the home with a bag of apples. Four little boys, who craved attention, ran to the visitors to be hugged and kissed. The guests played games with the youngsters, and there was much laughter.

Audra was particularly drawn to a beautiful baby girl. The adorable child was a year old with dark hair and dark eyes. She immediately picked up the baby, Gabriela, and held her on her lap. The child's mother, a young Mexican woman, was in union with a man who had deserted them. The mother decided to put the baby up for adoption with the hope of a better chance to find a husband.

~~~~~~~

At the medical school, several men in the class persevered in giving Audra their attention, but she put them off.

There was only one male student that she was slightly attracted to, and that was Joshua Corbin. He was tall and good looking with blonde hair and blue eyes. He exhibited an air of a wealthy aristocrat. Becoming friends, he was attentive to Audra but with a cool reserve. Now that the romantic relationship with Kenton had ended, she decided to accept Joshua's invitations. She questioned herself, "Might this man be the mate that God has willed for me?"

~~~~~~~

There was an influenza epidemic in El Paso, and the hospital was full of patients. The students were extremely busy caring for the sick. Dr. Scott was pressed to the point of being overwhelmed with so many cases. Therefore, he assigned Dr. Carlton to teach the students in their afternoon class. The doctor read to them from the text book and avoided answering their questions.

After the class, the students went as a group to Dr. Scott's office. They threatened, "We will boycott the class if Dr. Carlton continues to teach it."

Joshua suggested, "Let Audra teach us. She has the ability."

But she had another idea. "Dr. Scott, sir, you are well acquainted with the reputation of my grandfather, Dr. Kirk. You both have been friends for many years. Presently, my grandfather has a brilliant intern who is finishing his internship. If that man could take the Columbus practice, would you be interested in asking grandfather to teach the class for a few weeks?"

Dr. Scott gave a sigh of relief. "It would be of great benefit if the doctor could be an interim instructor. I will telegraph him this afternoon."

The doctor received an immediate answer from Dr. Kirk, "I will take the next train to El Paso and will be there tomorrow to teach the afternoon class."

Audra was elated that she would soon see her grandfather. Previously, she had expressed to her grandfather a wish for him to meet the widow, Jenny Riley. He had postponed the meeting, saying that he was not ready for the encounter. Of course, now he would have to become acquainted with his granddaughter's benefactor.

Arriving home that day, Audra raced up the mansion steps. She found the woman and asked her to sit down for some good news.

She clasped her hands together in delight. "Miss Jenny, I already told you that my grandfather is a doctor and a widower. Well, he will come to visit us tomorrow!"

When she announced this, the dear lady started chattering excitedly, "I have to buy a new dress. This house must be sparkling clean. Audra, will you help me to look pretty for Dr. Kirk?"

"Yes, of course. You are an attractive woman. However, I do have some beauty tips for you. We will go through your closet and get rid of your old dresses. The young mothers may use them for fabric to sew clothes for their children.

"Yes, I would be glad to do that." Her manner was positive.

"Your silver, wavy hair becomes you, but I suggest that you have it cut and styled. Eliminate the 'old maid' bun."

"I totally agree."

When Audra came home from the hospital the next day, she hardly recognized Miss Jenny. She looked ten years younger. She was wearing a new dress, and her silver hair was styled. "Miss Jenny, you look elegant!"

"Thank you. I feel pretty! Audra, I want to tell you this. After my husband passed away, suitors came flocking. I quickly realized that none of them were interested in me personally. They were only interested in my money. I had given up the idea that I would ever marry again."

~~~~~~~

Arriving at the hospital school, Dr. Kirk delivered the lecture in the afternoon class. The students were enthusiastic
~~~~~~~

about his presentation. He told of some of his experiences and answered all of their questions in detail.

The carriage came to take them from the hospital to the mansion in the late afternoon. The doctor greeted Jenny Riley with a box of chocolates, and he seemed to be impressed with her appearance. Audra served the supper so that her elders could visit over tea. She retired to her room early in order to give Miss Jenny and her grandfather privacy to become acquainted.

Dr. Kirk and Jenny got on well together and chatted for a couple of hours. Grandfather, as the honored guest, was to spend the night in the east bedroom. The following day was Saturday. The widow and the doctor spent the day together walking through the neighborhood and visiting in the parlor. They seemed to enjoy many topics of conversation. Audra and her grandfather played a couple of games of checkers, and she won them all.

He snickered. "I think I was too distracted."

Room and board at the hotel were arranged for Dr. Kirk, since Dr. Scott had asked him to continue teaching at the hospital for an indefinite period of time. At the school it was very enjoyable for Audra to have her grandfather go on rounds with her in the hospital and on consults in the clinic. She was always alert to learn from his medical expertise.

15

Derek and his two friends had read about King David's mighty men in the Bible. King David had three soldiers who had unusual courage and strength. The names of these mighty warriors were Josheb-Basshebeth, Eleazar, and Shammah. These soldiers stood their ground and struck down the enemy in separate battles. They fought the Philistines with King David, and through them, the Lord brought about great victories for Israel. These ancient heroes became the ideal for Sergeant Rands, Lieutenant James, and Corporal Lott.

On the Punitive Expedition trail with General Pershing, the army continued their search for Pancho Villa. However, in the mountains of Mexico, the villain and his followers were elusive. Yet the soldiers pushed on month after month seeking to capture the murderers. On a rare occasion, the three companions would practice sparring, using Kung Fu in the rugged terrain. It was an intriguing display of macho strength.

Corporal Kenton Lott bragged to some of the soldiers that Sergeant Derek Rands could win over any man in the whole army in hand-to-hand combat, "Sergeant Rands has no rival, no equal. No man can stand against him."

The troopers were incredulous. "How can that be? There are ten thousand men on this expedition!"

Kenton asserted, "I tell you the truth; he is intrepid, but of course no one is invincible but God."

So, this group of soldiers implored Derek, "Demonstrate to us your fighting prowess."

"All right, bring me two volunteers."

They were very impressed when Derek took down two men at a time when they made a mock attack upon him. Seeing the sergeant's capability and strength, these enlisted men asked Derek if they could set up an arm-wrestling contest as a diversion?"

"Yes, I will agree to it, but limit the number of competitors."

The soldiers lined up to match their strength with Derek. Several tried to arm wrestle with him, but none could beat him. The men were amazed at his power and might to defeat all of those who competed.

Some of the soldiers had criticized Derek because he preached to them on Sundays. They knew that he was a chaplain, and they nicknamed him, the preacher. After the arm-wrestling contests, many of the soldiers had greater respect for Derek. The attendance to his Bible meetings increased significantly.

This same group of soldiers saw a chance to profit on Derek's physical ability. They inquired, "Would you enter into a combat fight with a prize for the winner and with bets on the side. It would not be a boxing or wrestling match but hand to hand combat?"

Derek agreed to their request. "I will only accept if I am allowed to use martial arts."

They asked around in the regiment for who would be a worthy opponent. A soldier spoke up, "There is a major whose nickname is Bucky. He is big and tall with a rough and tough manner. The man has a reputation for brawling and fighting and has often boasted of his past experience in this area."

When they approached Bucky to be the challenger, they informed him, "Sergeant Rands will fight using his martial arts background. Is this acceptable?" he replied, "Of course, and I will fight this chaplain. I am keen on winning the prize money."

The organizers watched each day for the right place and time to hold this combat competition. They saw their opportunity on a particular day of rest for the regiment. The army had camped in a clearing with a hill on one side. The news went out that the contest would be that afternoon. Several soldiers cleared the trees on the hill with axes to make a crude amphitheater for seating. The bets were collected, both for Derek and for Bucky to win. Excitement was in the air as the soldiers started seating themselves on the hill. They seemed anxious to see this spectacle of strength and cunning. Two referees were appointed, both of whom were officers with the major.

Derek had the utmost confidence and was not nervous. He knew that he would win the contest because of his training. However, he pondered, "I am cautious that I might really hurt the major. I will wear my tightly laced moccasins to give myself agility of movement. Also, it will be less painful for Bucky than if I kick the man with clunky, army boots."

The major boasted to his comrades, "This contest will be a 'piece of cake' for me. A chaplain could not be physically strong. With my background of fist fighting, I believe that I will easily win over Sergeant Rands."

The announcer yelled out the names of the opponents, "The sergeant, known as the preacher, versus the major, known as Bucky."

As the two contestants entered the 'ring', the soldiers began to cheer. Many more soldiers cheered for the major than for the sergeant. The majority of the soldiers thought that Bucky would be the victor. Derek looked up the hill, and he was astonished to see a huge crowd of men sitting close together. It seemed to be an event of the century.

The referee called for the fight to begin. The men circled each other, prancing around in their primitive arena. Derek wanted to get this fight over quickly, but he knew that the soldiers had come for a show. He motioned for the major to come and attack him, and Bucky took the bait. As the major lunged for him, Derek grabbed him and did a scissors throw, hurling the big man into the air. Bucky hit the ground hard and lay there moaning. The crowd roared and cheered. The soldiers had never seen anyone fight with the Kung Fu method. Derek allowed time for officer to get up from the dirt and rocks where he lay. The major was feeling pain and began to fear. He did not want to 'bite the dust' again. However, he had to continue the fight or else he would be deemed a coward. Angrily, Bucky put up his fists and cursed his opponent. Derek made a flying, spinning wheel kick and kicked the major in the head with the heel of his foot. The major felt the impact, lost his balance, and dropped to his knees. The military audience went wild with clapping and shouting

One soldier yelled out, "Do it again, Sarge!" Derek's response was to salute the men. Again, the sergeant waited for the major to get up. His adversary seemed a little disoriented, but eventually, he regained his composure. Derek decided to change strategy to give the officer a little chance to recover. It seemed as though Bucky was chasing him around the ring, trying to punch him. Suddenly Derek stopped, grabbed the man's arm and pulled him to the ground. Then he placed his knee in the man's back and held his arms tightly so that the major could not move. The sergeant's mighty physical strength had overpowered this giant of a man.

The referee began the ten-count: ten, nine, eight. On seven, Derek released his grip on the big soldier, and the major struggled to his feet. Bucky's nose was bleeding where he had collided with a rock on the ground. The referee called time out. The major's coaches told him to move faster and more precisely. He was sweating profusely and drank much water. As Derek approached his coaches, Lieutenant James and Corporal Lott were grinning with their thumbs up.

When the contestants entered the 'ring' again, the troopers were screaming and whistling. It was like a roar in this mountain setting. Bucky began throwing punches, but he was slow, and the sergeant blocked everyone. This was not Derek's style of fighting, so he whirled around and kicked his opponent with such force that the major again fell to the earth. Derek pounced upon him to hold him down. The sergeant could see that the major was breathing heavily and at the point of exhaustion. This time Derek did not let his opponent get up.

The referee counted to ten, and then finally lifted Derek's arm to proclaim him the winner. "I present to you the champion, the preacher."

The soldiers yelled, "Hip, hip, hurray."

A group of soldiers ran down from the hill. They picked up Derek and put him on their shoulders. They paraded him around their 'arena' whooping and hollering.

Matthew James and Kenton Lott congratulated their friend, "Well done. We knew that you would be victorious."

He responded, "Either of you could have easily won the fight."

Derek approached the major to shake hands with him, but the latter only scowled and refused. Then Bucky threatened the sergeant with revenge. "Watch your back. I will get even with you."

The soldier group that organized the fight began to sort out the bets. Lieutenant Matthew James and Corporal Kenton Lott stood by to monitor the disbursements. The sun had gone down when the two companions returned to their tent. They were gleeful about their winnings, $300 for Derek and $100 for each of them.

However, when they opened the tent flap, the two friends were dismayed to see their champion sitting on his cot with his head in his hands. They rushed to him and questioned, "What is wrong, are you hurt?"

They knew that Bucky was not able to touch him and were puzzled at this dilemma.

Derek began to sob with sighs and groans. "I never should have thrown Bucky with the scissor method. It was a difficult maneuver since he is a big and tall man. If he fell awry, he could have broken his neck. I used the fancy, spinning wheel kick to kick him in the head which I did not plan to do. It was all part of the show, and it was dangerous. My lack of wisdom could have caused a tragedy. I am deeply repentant, and I have prayed for forgiveness. My friends, be extremely careful using Kung Fu in any fight."

~~~~~~~

The next day at dusk, Derek was walking to his tent. Matthew and Kenton had already retired for the night. He sensed that someone was following him. A young recruit was almost at his heels when Derek whirled around and grabbed him by the shirt. "What do you want, soldier?"

"I need to speak to you privately."

"Yes, come into the tent." And he closed the flap behind them.

"Sir, I came to warn you. I overheard a conversation that Bucky and some of his comrades will come at midnight to harm you. He seeks to avenge his loss in the combat fight. He will bring about five men with him. They plan to give you a bloody beating."

The sergeant furrowed his brow. "I thank you for this warning, soldier. I pray that God will recompense you for your kindness. You may take your leave."

Waking Matthew and Kenton, Derek told them about the
~~~~~~~

information from the young soldier. The companions dressed with their boots on, grabbed their guns, and sat on their cots until almost midnight. They prayed that a fight could be avoided. It was a full moon, and all of the surroundings were highly visible. At midnight, the three soldiers moved to the edge of the tent opening when they heard footsteps outside. Bucky opened the tent flap and was accosted by Derek who put his pistol to the major's throat. Matthew and Kenton suddenly burst from the tent flashing their guns.

They yelled to the soldiers who were with Bucky, "Retreat, men, go back to your tents before you get hurt!"

The soldiers who came with the major immediately turned and fled for their lives. They feared dire consequences. Bucky began to beg with words tumbling out, "Please do not use your gun. I am married with children to support. I had no cause for vengeance. You won the fight fair and square. I regret my action tonight. If you will release me, I will never bother you again. Please sir, I plead for my life."

"Major, I have two witnesses here. If I report this incident, you will be court martialed, but I grant you mercy."

Derek lowered his pistol, and Bucky turned and ran as fast as he could.

Facing his comrades, the sergeant quoted from Isaiah 54:17, "No weapon forged against you will prevail, and you will refute every tongue that accuses you."

In harmony they nodded in agreement. The rest of the night was peaceful, and the three soldiers slept without fear.

~~~~~~~

In the ensuing days of the Punitive Expedition, the major
~~~~~~~

was respectful to Derek and would greet him in passing. The militia was moving out in their continued search for Villa and his evil band. The cavalry was picking their way through the mountains when a halt was called. The major had slid off his saddle and hit the dirt. The officer was sick with dysentery. The soldiers riding near him tried to get him back on his horse, but he fell in a heap to the ground. Finally, they threw him over his saddle on his stomach with head hanging down. He moaned in pain. The soldiers were tying him to his saddle when Derek arrived.

"Untie him," he ordered. "The major can ride with me. Rio can support both of us. Hand me his canteen. The man must keep drinking water."

So, the soldiers placed the ailing man on Rio with Derek seated behind, supporting him with his arms around him. The sergeant put the canteen to Bucky's mouth, and he was able to drink a little water. The major's trousers were soiled from the diarrhea and the smell was pungent. Derek prayed, "Lord, in Jesus name, let this officer recover from his infirmity and not become dehydrated."

Lieutenant James and Corporal Lott took turns with Derek in transporting the ailing officer. They kept giving him water to drink throughout the day.

The major was weak and spiking a fever by the time the cavalry met up with the truck caravan in the evening. Derek and his comrades carried Bucky to the medic's tent. The medic administered medicine to the ill man and ordered him to bed rest.

The next morning when Derek checked on the major,

the officer was feeling better and his fever had abated. "I understand that I owe my life to you and your companions. I am deeply thankful to you. You dared to help me even after I meant to do you harm."

Derek smiled. "Though it was not that easy, God helped us to manage your care."

The major grimaced and struggled to control his emotions. "My gratitude is indeed great to all of you. I did not deserve your kindness."

Within a few days, Bucky recovered and was back on duty in the regiment. The major then recruited the soldiers under his command to attend Derek's gospel meetings.

16

After serving in the Punitive Expedition with General Pershing, Derek, Matthew, and Kenton arrived back to Camp Cavalry in Columbus, New Mexico. The army had searched for Pancho Villa and his marauding band of Villistas for nine months in Mexico but did not encounter them. The mountains were difficult for the recruits to traverse. Even the Apache scouts were sometimes perplexed in finding Villa's trail. The Mexican government was exasperated with U. S troops marching through their country and was threatening war. So, President Wilson ended the Punitive Expedition in 1917.

Leaving the reservation, Derek's parents, Garth and Elena Rands met their son at the train station in Columbus. It was a glorious homecoming.

He confided to his parents, "I no longer consider attending a military law school. The Lord has impressed me that I will have more influence in the kingdom of God as a chaplain and a preacher. My perspective on my career goal has changed. I still want to be commander of an army garrison, but I have committed it to the Lord to open that door for me. I will again preach at gospel meetings at the garrison and also at the church in Columbus."

Nodding, they responded, "Your ministry here is important. We support your decision, son."

The Rands later traveled on to the Kirks' ranch to visit and impart news of the Apache nation.

From El Paso, Kenton's parents came to greet their son. Through the 'grapevine', Penelope had heard that Audra and Kenton were no longer in a courtship. She inquired of the arrival date of the soldiers' homecoming, and she came to the station to meet Kenton. He did not embrace her, but only politely acknowledged her.

At the train station, Raquel looked for Matthew, and she ran towards him. He clutched her to his chest and held her tight. After being separated for many months, he kissed her thoroughly. The joy that they shared was exuberant. Matthew picked up Sofie and Andrew and held them. The children were excited to see their daddy. They clung to him and refused to be put down. Matthew had given his resignation to the army, and in a few months, he would manage the cattle ranch. He would focus his life on providing for his wife and family.

Derek was nearby and when he saw the love reunion of Matthew and his family, it stuck in his memory. As he thought about his friend's life, a sense of loneliness came over him.

~~~~~~~

Matthew had two weeks of furlough before returning to his duties at the garrison. He and Raquel had been separated for several months because of the Punitive Expedition. Therefore, the lieutenant planned some special outings in order to attest to his love and affection for his wife.

On one particular afternoon, he proposed, "Let's go horse-
~~~~~~~

back riding on the range today. Maria is always ready to watch the children; she dotes on Sofie and Andrew."

So, the arrangements for child care were made. When the older woman entered the main house, the children ran and took her hand to play games.

It was a cool, cloudy day, perfect for an excursion. Matthew saddled their horses to ride on the ranch's pasture lands. As they trotted along, they met Pablo, and greeted him, "*Buenos días, amigo.*" (Good morning, friend).

He spoke to them in Spanish, "Hello, I am checking the heifers that will soon give birth to baby calves." Pablo was keen on his work in cattle husbandry.

Raquel and Matthew leisurely rode a short distance until their horses trotted up a hill. They could see far below into the valley. There was a scene that greatly disturbed them. Three strange men were herding steers away from the ranch's property.

The husband whispered to his wife, "They are rustling our cattle. Go and find Pablo."

As the soldier reached for his rifle, she begged him, "Please come with me."

"Do as I say, darling, I will not allow thieves to steal our cattle."

The distressed young woman turned her horse and raced away in a gallop to find Pablo.

Matthew tied his horse to a tree at a distance. Then he chose a large rock to hide behind and began firing his Winchester repeating rifle in the direction of the rustlers. In the U. S. Army cavalry, the lieutenant had much skill as a sharp shooter. He trained new recruits in marksmanship. In this instance, the soldier did not want to wound or kill the perpetrators, but to scare them away.

The rustlers were taken by surprise when they heard the gunshots. The male trio decided to flee.

Finding Pablo, Raquel yelled, "Come quickly, rustlers are on the south range!"

The ranch worker spurred his horse towards the indicated direction. When Pablo reached the area of the incursion, he also fired his rifle as the rustlers fled away.

Not hearing any more gun shots, Raquel warily rode to where Matthew and Pablo were located. She dismounted and ran into her husband's arms. The young wife clung to him. "I thank God that you are alive. Nothing compares to your love," she murmured.

Matthew lifted her up and pressed a kiss to her lips. "My love knows no bounds where you are concerned, my darling." He removed a leather glove and stroked her cheek with his fingers.

The cattle were easily rounded up into the ranch's pastureland. The barbed wire fence had been cut, so the two men set themselves to repair the break. Then the wedded pair continued on with their diversion, riding their horses into the valley and beyond.

At sundown, the couple prepared a special supper for Pablo and Maria for their help.

Before the meal, Matthew prayed, "Thank you, Lord God for your protection today and for the plan of the enemy to be defeated. Amen"

17

A couple of days had passed since the expedition had ended, and Derek had a desire to visit Audra. Since he had a furlough, he left on the train for El Paso. He had not seen or heard from her since right before he left on the Punitive Expedition. He walked from the train station to Jenny Riley's mansion where Audra was lodging. From a distance, he could see the white pillars of the porch gleaming in the afternoon sun.

Derek introduced himself to Jenny Riley and informed her that he had come to visit Audra Kirk. The widow prepared tea, and the two visited while seated on the porch swing. They both were interested in history.

Miss Jenny asked the sergeant, "Would you be able to stay for supper this evening? My deceased husband was in the military for a time, and I have an affinity for soldiers."

"Yes, that is very kind of you."

Offering to do any repairs while waiting for Audra, he fixed the faucet, replaced a broken door hinge, and swept the large front porch.

Miss Jenny wondered, "Is this Audra's beau? I am quite impressed with this tall, handsome soldier."

Riding in the carriage from the school, Audra pondered her dilemma "I have no food for supper and no money. Furthermore, Grandfather has returned to Columbus for the weekend. I do not want to spend the money I saved for the orphans, nor do I want to ask Miss Jenny for help. I have a lot of funds in my savings account in Columbus, but I cannot access them here. Why hasn't father sent me money? Is he angry that I mentioned Joshua as a beau? Whatever the reason, my parents will visit me soon."

Contemplating this situation, she opened the front door and came face to face with Sergeant Derek Rands standing in the foyer. With an admiring smile, he scrutinized her figure in the emerald dress. With a bouquet of violets in hand, he greeted her cordially, "Good afternoon, Audra."

Her surprise was evident on her pretty face. She looked away to dismiss the anger of his presence, but it was still there. "Sir, you are not welcome here, take your leave."

"Audra, it is my endeavor to make amends for the past. Please take these flowers as a peace offering and forget your animosity."

"No, I have forgiven you, but I don't ever want to see your cocky face again."

"I have notes for you from the Apache people, and a card from your parents."

"You may give them to me and then take your exit, sir."

"My father wrote the messages in the Apache language as they were dictated to him. I will need to translate them for you."

"I do not want you to translate them. I want you to depart

now, or I shall call the deputy."

"On what charges?"

"On charges of stalking and harassment!" She clenched her fists in fury.

Grinning, Derek was undaunted at her threat. Yet the atmosphere was thick with her hostility.

At that moment, Miss Jenny entered the foyer. She was in a jovial mood and in high spirits because Derek was her guest and new friend.

"Audra, dear, I have prepared a delicious meal for you and Sergeant Rands. You can rest and enjoy your supper after a long day. I will put these lovely violets is a vase for you."

Fully aware that Derek had charmed the widow and gained her trust, Audra could do nothing less than to graciously accept. "That is most kind of you, Miss Jenny."

Actually, the meal was a pleasant experience. The widow had prepared baked chicken and dressing, cranberry sauce, homemade bread, and pound cake. Audra was annoyed but determined to be civil to Derek in front of Miss Jenny.

As they chatted, the soldier seemed interested in her medical experiences. "How was your day at the hospital?"

"It was busy; I helped Dr. Scott deliver a baby girl. What is your news?"

"The Punitive Expedition to capture Pancho Villa was not successful, but the Lord will take His vengeance. I have decided to remain at Camp Cavalry and not seek to join General Pershing in Washington D.C. Besides my military service, Reverend Barr has invited me to continue preaching in the church in Columbus."

This news was a little disconcerting for Audra, for now he would be near her family. She thought, "I know only too well how much father loves Derek and wants him to be his son-in-law."

Miss Jenny beamed throughout the supper as the couple complimented her on her cuisine.

Audra almost choked on her cranberries when she announced, "Derek will be spending the night in the east bedroom." The lady also commented, "I have cake ready for tomorrow's trip to the orphanage."

Then she turned to Derek. "Son, would you be able to accompany us to visit the orphans?"

He quickly voiced his assent, "Yes, I would be very glad to meet the orphans."

Audra sighed at the present scenario and considered, "Derek has weaseled his way back into my life. First supper, then staying the night, and now he is going to the orphanage with us. However, I know that he has an affinity for children. I remember his affection and attention to Cristina, the little Apache girl."

Still seated at the table, Miss Jenny asked Derek to read a Scripture. She brought out her old Bible. He read Psalm 73:28, "But for me it is good to be near God. I have made the Sovereign Lord my refuge; I will tell of all your deeds." He expounded, "The topic is to stay close to God and to live under his protection."

When everything was cleared away from the supper, Derek suggested, "Would you ladies be interested in a game of Rummy?"

An enthusiast for card games, Miss Jenny retorted, "It sounds like a good time. I will get the cards and meet you in the parlor."

When Audra entered the parlor, her beauty was illuminated by a fire that crackled in the hearthside.

After the card game, Derek translated the letters from the Apache, Audra was filled with awe that they all missed her and wanted her to come back to visit. Councilman William sent her a long note of gratitude.

Alone in her room, she opened the letter from her parents.

Dearest Audra,

We miss you and plan to come soon. Raquel and Matthew are very compatible in their marriage. They send greetings. Matthew has legally adopted Sofie and Andrew. The children are quite content with the love and attention their daddy gives them. The ranch is prospering. Your father and I had an enjoyable visit with Derek and the Rands. We are praying for you, daughter.

Love,

Mother and Father

The letter was a blessing, but they sent no money. She would have to inquire tomorrow among the ladies in the neighborhood to see if they needed any household help.

Knocking on her door, Miss Jenny asked, "May I come in, dear, to talk for a few minutes? I am troubled. Why are you so cold and callous toward Sergeant Rands? He clearly adores you. His eyes are always on you. I am a good judge of character, and he is an honorable man."

Audra looked a little forlorn but began to explain, "Miss

Jenny, I once was smitten by him, but he rejected me." She recalled the vow that she had made to herself. So, she disclosed to the widow the painful incident at Camp Cavalry.

Miss Jenny shared her wisdom, "When you think about it, he did not reject you forever, it was a matter of timing."

"He did not tell me that he loved me or ask me to wait for him when he left the reservation. He did not call on me when I returned home. I had given up on ever having a life with him."

"I am older and have more life experience. I understand his motives. He did not know what his future plans would be. Waiting can be hard. You are young and beautiful. You had goals and challenges facing you: serving on the reservation, and then attending the hospital school. It is unwise to make a promise that one might not be able to keep." Then Jenny Riley grinned. "I believe that it would take a strong-willed man to say no to you, Audra."

With those thoughts in her head, Audra retired for the night. "Is it time for the vow to be unveiled and cast down?"

The next morning, Audra awoke to the bells in the town. Today they would visit the orphanage and play games with the children. It was always a special time for her. Derek, Audra, and Miss Jenny took a carriage to the Christian orphanage run by Curtis and Patricia Allen. As the visitors entered the home, the children ran to see what was in the basket that Derek carried. The children looked forward to the treats of cake and fruit. Lisette also entered the home, and the boys grabbed her hands for her to play with them.

Patricia Allen introduced the children, "This is Timothy,

four years, Caleb, five years, Ethan, six years, Jake, eight years, and baby Gabriela, one year."

Audra immediately picked up the baby to hold her. She had not seen the boy, Jake, before today and thought it strange that he huddled in a corner with a sullen look on his face. When she approached to speak to him, he snarled at her.

Inquiring about the boy, Patricia described their dilemma, "Jake is eight years old and his dad left him with the sheriff at the jail a few days ago. The father solemnly promised that he would come back for his son in one month. Jake has been a terror for us and the children. He fights with the little boys and hurts them. You will see the bruises on their arms. He has broken toys, and he wrote on the walls of his room. We took him to church for prayer, but he kicked the pastor and threw such a temper tantrum that we had bring him home. The boy is intelligent and can read, but he is so angry that we cannot keep him. We contacted the Children Welfare Department, but they have ignored us. We plan to take Jake to the sheriff's office today. My husband, Curtis, wants to wait, but Mrs. Allen and I can no longer tolerate his belligerent behavior. Audra, would you please help us and go with us to the jail? The little boys must go in order to show their bruises. We have an appointment with the sheriff this afternoon."

"Yes, I will go with you."

"If the sheriff refuses to take the boy, then I will take the baby and go to my sister's house. Grace will take the little boys and go to her daughter's home. Curtis will have to deal with Jake by himself. We have made him aware of our plans. We are desperate!"

The younger boys were climbing all over Derek as he would lift them in the air and set them back down. He tried to draw Jake out to play a game, but the boy refused. Finally, he grabbed the boy and was carrying him around. He lifted him in the air and played arm wrestle with him. Before long, the two were playing ball. Audra and Lisette played London Bridges with the little boys. Patricia and Mrs. Grace Allen were amazed that Derek had broken through Jake's hard 'shell'. The children listened attentively as Derek told them a Bible story about Noah and the ark. Jake sidled up next to the soldier to listen to the story.

The three visitors played games with the children until refreshments were served. Audra was holding the baby, Gabriela, stroking her hair and talking to her. She loved the baby and would have liked to adopt her. However, when she had mentioned adoption to Joshua, he was vehemently opposed to it. She had invited him to come with her to the orphanage, but his excuse was that he had to work.

It was almost time for the visitors to leave when Patricia asked Derek if she could speak to him privately, "Sir, would you be able to take Jake with you? When he was with you today, we saw a glimmer of peace and happiness in him that we have not seen. I can call the Children's Welfare Department. On our recommendation, they will surely approve you to take immediate custody."

"Mrs. Allen, I am soldier at Camp Cavalry. I cannot be responsible for a child."

Patricia sighed sadly. "Then we must take him to the sheriff this afternoon."

"Madam, would you like for me to inquire among my church members if they would be interested in adopting any of these children?"

"Yes, that would be marvelous. Though Curtis is a good father, he works long hours. The little boys want their own daddy. I will get the contact information of the Children Welfare Department for you."

As the group announced their departure, Jake started clinging to Derek. "Please take me with you. I'll be good. I wanna go with you." And he repeated it over and over.

Leaning down, Derek took Jake's shoulders. "Jake, I am a soldier. I live at an army post. I cannot care for you. Your dad promised to come back for you. You must wait for him here."

Jake clung to the soldier's leg, crying all the way to the street. A carriage was waiting at the curb for the visitors. Patricia and Mrs. Allen together had to drag the boy back to the house. It was an emotional scene. As the group rode back to the mansion, Miss Jenny sat in silence. A tear dropped onto Audra's cheek. The scene with Jake reminded her of the encounter at Camp Cavalry with Derek, "Take me; I want to be with you." But he did not.

~~~~~~~

Derek would have to leave soon for Columbus. He was scheduled to preach the Sunday morning meeting to the soldiers at the garrison. He expressed his gratitude to Miss Jenny and tried to give her money but she refused. She quoted from the Bible, "Whoever welcomes a righteous person, will receive a righteous person's reward." Matthew 10:41.

The sergeant left an envelope with her to give to Audra
~~~~~~~

later.

Before leaving for the train, Derek sought out Audra. He had long been attracted to her but had not wanted romance to hinder the advancement of his military career. Yet now, he was determined to pursue her and end his lonely life.

"Audra, may I come to call on you? I resisted my attraction for you in the past, but now is the time to declare my affection for you."

Her eyes expressed bewilderment at his boldness. "I am all astonishment, but you are too late. I have a beau."

"I don't care. I want to spend time with you."

"No, I could never love you, nor will I give you an opportunity to hurt me again."

"I am asking you to pray, Audra. I know that you desired to be with me in Columbus. But think about it, you could not have attended the hospital school with a baby on your lap."

Seeing that he was serious, there was a sting in her words, "I did not know your character then. The façade of the man was all that I saw. You could not tempt me to ever care for you again. Go soldier, and earn your promotion. I warn you. My wish is to never see you again. If you return here, I will get an order of protection against you."

"I will be back to claim you as my bride."

Audra raised her hand to slap his face, but he grabbed her hand, put it to his lips, and kissed it. She quickly snatched her hand away.

"There is one more thing that I want to tell you, Audra. You are more alluring and desirable than I ever remembered. Until later, I will see you in my dreams. Adieu."

Shaken by Derek's amorous declaration, she brooded, "His rejection is vivid in my mind. I made my vow, and I will spurn him. It irritates me that he is so cocky and sure that he can win my heart. Yet, there is a nagging doubt in my spirit, and it haunts me. I am friendly with Joshua. Yet, I doubt his ability as a doctor since he is almost failing the course. I was impressed with Ian, until he began to taunt me. Now Derek has come back to declare his intentions. I see this quandary as quite confusing. I must make the right decision. It is a lifetime choice."

With a smile, Miss Jenny invited Audra to have tea in the parlor. She handed Derek's letter to her. Audra felt that the letter was heavy. When she opened it, to her surprise, ten silver dollars scattered to the floor. It was so unexpected.

Dear Audra,

It was marvelous to see you again. I prayed for you when I was on the expedition to capture Pancho Villa. Please take some of the money for treats for the orphans. The rest of the money is for you. I want you to have it. I adore you.

Forever,

Derek

Surprise overtook Audra at Derek's expression of adoration, but his pretty words did not convince her to trust him. However, she was impressed by his generosity. She thanked God for this provision. Now she had money for food and would not have to seek a job doing housework.

That afternoon Audra dreaded going with the Allens to the sheriff's office, but she knew that she must support her friends. A carriage took her to the orphanage, and the group walked to the sheriff's office. Only Mrs. Grace Allen stayed back to care for baby Gabriela.

Sheriff Dale Fraser was surprised to see an entourage of adults and children enter his office. The sheriff was a friendly sort of man about fifty years of age. He was respected for his astute ability at law enforcement.

While Audra waited with the children, the Allens talked privately with the sheriff, "Jake hurts the little boys. We are leaving Jake at the jail with you. We will advise the Children Welfare Department of his status."

The sheriff did not protest their decision. He wanted an interview. He called in the little boys first, "Boys, would you please answer some questions for me?" His kindness was evident.

The boys chimed in, "We sure will."

"Where did you get those bruises?" The sheriff pointed to their arms.

They all answered at once, "Jake hits us. We don't like him. He hurts us."

"You said, Jake hits you?" He inquired again.

"Yeah, we don't like to play with him," retorted Nathan.

"Do you like your mama?"

"Yeah, she read us Bible stories and kiss us good night," stated Charles.

"Is your papa good to you?

"Yeah, he takes us fishin, and he plays ball with us." answered Nathan enthusiastically.

"What about your grandma?"

"She makes us pies. Grandma smack our hands if we are naughty, but it don't hurt," piped up four- year- old Timothy, and he showed the sheriff as he smacked his hand.

Sheriff Fraser chuckled and tried hard not to laugh. "I think you boys have a pretty good life."

The sheriff talked to Jake privately. "Young man, how would you like to come and live with me? You could be my helper at the jail. My son, Carl, is sixteen and he would like a little brother. What do you say?"

"Oh yeah, I'd like to stay with you."

"You would have to behave and obey my wife."

"I'll be real good."

18

As the school term went on, Ian seemed to become friendlier with Lisette. Audra was concerned that the nurse might succumb to his charm. She had witnessed that he was definitely a 'skirt chaser'. As she entered the vestibule of the hospital one morning, she heard a man and woman talking and laughing in the adjoining hall. It was Ian's deep voice and the nurse, Lisette.

Ian was flirting with her, "Where have you been all of my life, sunshine?"

"Right here waiting for you."

"You are looking quite well today, Miss Nurse."

"You are welcome to look."

Breaking out into hilarious laughter, he retorted, "Miss Lisette, as you are a skilled nurse, may I make an appointment with you?"

"Are you sick?"

"Yes, I am lovesick for you."

With a coquettish grin, she replied, "You should be a comedian in Vaudeville."

As Audra peered around the corner, she saw Ian touching Lisette's hair and face. Aghast at the scene, she contemplated,

"It appears that there is an infatuation between the two. Ian has a reputation of a veritable flirt, and Lisette might not be able to trust him in a future marriage. There would be no tolerating his philandering."

Therefore, Audra sought to forewarn her friend and invited her to dine at the mansion. The two young ladies chatted throughout the evening. "Lisette, do not be deceived by Ian's flattery. He will walk down the street and flirt with every girl that he meets. It gratifies his male ego. Keep up your guard at his pretense of affection. Simply put, he is a Romeo and a lecher."

Lisette began to brag on him, "On occasion, I play the piano and sing at the nursing home where Ian works. I have noticed that the elderly immediately perk up when he is around. He teases the men and women and makes them laugh. The residents often ask for him when they are in pain, and he hugs and comforts them. The old people in the in the nursing facility adore him."

"Yes, he has some exemplary qualities, but not as a husband."

"I would like to give him a chance. It is diverting to be with Ian. Life would be a comedy with him. Wherever he goes, he exudes joy. He has been very solicitous to the patients at the hospital. I admire his friendliness and affection for people. He has hinted that we would be very compatible as a medical team. I believe that he will become an extremely popular doctor. We will be attending the theater together this weekend."

Shaking her head in dismay, Audra retorted vehemently, "Oh, no, do not trust his intentions! My advice to you is to run; run hard and fast away from him! Do not be naïve. Do you want me to spell infidelity and heartache for you? That is where you are headed. Pray for the will of the Lord. Choosing a mate is serious business."

"I already accepted the invitation, but I will pray."

Lisette thoughts were imposing, "Ian might declare his love to me if I give him some encouragement. I fancy the idea that he could be my future husband. Yet after Audra's warning, I am fearful, and my prayer has been made."

Attending the theater, Ian and Lisette viewed a live stage show. The play depicted a period piece set in the 1700s. The plot consisted of a swashbuckling melodrama that included a sword fight.

At the end of the evening when Ian returned Lisette to her door, he leaned in close to kiss her goodnight. "Lisette, I have tasted of the sweetest of loves, but you are the sweetest of all."

The young lady was offended by Ian's impertinence in kissing her. She thought about the statement that he had made. It was supposed to be a compliment, but it made her wonder of how many loves he had known.

~~~~~~~

The Kirks planned to visit their daughter in El Paso. A major reason for their coming was to meet her beau, Joshua. She had invited him to come and have supper with them. As a devoted daughter, she had great anticipation of her parents' visit. The day had come for their arrival on the train, early Friday evening. A carriage had been arranged to pick them
~~~~~~~

up from the station. Miss Jenny prepared a sumptuous meal of roast lamb, vegetables, and strawberries with shortcake. The sun had gone down when Audra heard a knock at the door. Like a little child waiting for the ice cream wagon, she ran to open it. There stood her mother with a soldier at her side. It was Derek Rands, and Audra was almost speechless. The shock was evident on her pretty face.

"Where is father?"

Elizabeth Kirk grimaced. "Your father had urgent business at the ranch. Right before our departure, a bull escaped from the corral. It was creating havoc and terrorizing the ranch hands. It was impossible for your father to leave. He inquired if Derek could accompany me. I am here because of his kindness."

Hugging her mother, Audra exclaimed, "I am so happy to see you! But of course, I miss father. Good evening, Sergeant Rands. Thank you for traveling with my mother."

Derek smiled as he surveyed her beauty. "You look lovely, Audra."

Their dinner guest, Joshua, arrived on time, dressed in an expensive, tailored suit. Introductions were made, and the group commenced to the elegant dining room. The brilliant chandelier twinkled overhead, and the big room was warmed with a fire. Audra was seated between Joshua and Derek. Joshua was witty and charming, and his manners were impeccable. He made it a point to visit with Elizabeth.

He bragged on Audra, "Mrs. Kirk, your daughter is superior to everyone in the school."

"I appreciate the compliment. What is your family's background, Joshua?"

"My home is New York, and my family are all doctors and engineers."

Since Derek made an effort to be friendly, the medical student was not intimidated by his presence.

At the end of the evening, Joshua thanked the hostess and bid all a good night.

In her upstairs room, Audra and her mother visited over tea. Elizabeth handed her daughter two envelopes. One contained money and the other a card from Raquel. "I'm sorry the money is so late in coming, an oversight on my part."

Audra took out several bills. "I am very grateful for your support."

"It is a joy to bless you."

The daughter took a moment to read Raquel's card while her mother sipped her tea.

Dearest Audra,

It is so marvelous being married to Matthew. I am glad I listened to you regarding him. My husband exhibits his love and devotion to me. The children run to him when he comes home in the evening. He hugs and kisses them, and then it is my turn. My life has gone from one extreme to another: from animosity to affection, from poor to prosperous, and from belittled to bliss. Oh sister, I pray that someday you will be as happy as I am. I miss you. Please come and visit us soon.

Much love,

Raquel

Audra commented explicitly, "I am thrilled for my sister

and Matthew's union! Raquel's letter exudes marital felicity."

Elizabeth remarked, "We thank God that Raquel is now married to Lieutenant James. He is a prince of a husband. It is so wonderful to see her happy again after so many years of sorrow."

The mother broached the subject of her daughter's relationship with Joshua. "Audra, do you intend to accept a courtship with Joshua? How well do you know this young man? Do you love him?"

"I do not know the answer to those questions yet. Joshua is very sweet to me."

"My dear, you know how your father and I feel about Derek. He has asked our permission to court you, and we have given it. Could you not give him a chance?"

"I don't think so. I don't trust him."

"I am asking you to please not elope with Joshua. It is my dream for you to have a traditional wedding. My parents could not afford one for me, and my mother always regretted it."

"May I elope with Derek?" Audra teased.

"A very emphatic yes!" Both mother and daughter laughed.

Then Elizabeth sighed in exasperation, and her demeanor grew forlorn. "After your breakup with Kenton, your father and I had hoped that you and Derek might marry." She grabbed her handkerchief and cried a little. She appeared to have lost her most prized possession.

"Mother, Derek is an admirable man, but you and father have almost made an idol of him. He is a mortal, not a god!"

Making one last attempt, she persuaded, "Be very careful who you choose, Audra. There is an old proverb, 'You made your bed, now lie in it.' It means this: you made your decision, now accept the consequence. Your father and I saw the reality of this proverb with your sister, Raquel. She chose amiss and suffered the result in her marriage with Wade."

"Mother, be at peace. I have made no decision. God will surely direct me."

"Audra, before we retire for the night, I have a favor to ask. Would you please inquire at the hotel for rooms for our family who will attend your graduation. Even though it is a few months away, a group will come."

"Of course, Mother, Good night."

Trying to sleep, Audra fretted, "Unbeknownst to anyone, I am still clinging to my vow. It is a secret, hidden deep within my soul. Yet the vow is like a veil covering my face so that I cannot see or think clearly. However, I am determined that the veil will not be pierced or my vow forsaken."

The next morning as Miss Jenny prepared a basket of goodies for the orphan children, she casually mentioned, "Audra, I may sell this mansion in the future. The young ladies' group has grown and will soon move to the church. As Derek has a furlough, he has agreed to help me refurbish this big house and get it ready for sale. He will be staying on here. I have perceived that the soldier explains scripture quite superbly. So, I have asked him to teach the Bible study here next week. Furthermore, I contacted the pastor and told him about this young chaplain. The pastor has invited Derek to preach at the mid -week service."

Her eyes widened and fear rose up within Audra. "This is a lot of news. You have put much trust in a man of whom you only recently met."

The widow saw her reaction. "My dear, do not be preoccupied. I will not let the mansion be sold until you have finished your school. I am not sure of my future, but God has assured me that he has a plan. And yes, I am impressed with Derek. I prayed before I made these decisions."

Sighing in exasperation, Audra thought about the situation, "I am not worried about having a place to stay, but of being near Derek for the next two weeks. My plan will be to ignore the man, stay in my room and study when he is around. I resolve myself not to succumb to the soldier's charm."

An entourage from the mansion including Lisette traveled to the orphanage the next day. It was a joyous time for everyone. Derek told the children a Bible story about Jesus healing ten lepers. Derek took note that Audra held baby Gabriela while Lisette sang songs with the children.

Patricia Allen told Audra, "This adorable child, Gabriela, has been in our home for six months. I am concerned that she has not yet been adopted."

The group returned to the mansion; mother and daughter said their goodbyes, but the sergeant lingered.

Audra spoke first, "Derek, please do not come to call on me again. I know that you have an engagement to speak at the church next week, but in the meantime, you can get a room at the hotel. Miss Jenny can find a carpenter to restore her mansion. Furthermore, I may accept a courtship with Joshua in the future."

"How will your father feel about it?"

"He will be irate."

"And your mother?"

"She is already piqued." To which he snickered.

Then Derek boldly proclaimed, "I want you, and I have prayed for you!" His aspect was earnest as he fixed his gaze on the young lady who stood before him. "Audra, there's no wall I won't kick down, no mountain I won't climb up, coming after you!"

"Very well spoken, soldier, but to no avail."

For Audra, Derek's words kept coming back and churning in her mind. "How can I withstand a man of such determination? It is frightening yet exciting. However, my memory remains of how he hurt me."

~~~~~~~

On the train ride back to Columbus, Derek stared straight ahead in a melancholy mood. He questioned himself? "Am I making an obsession of Audra? Would there not be another woman that I could be happy with? Yet, she is the vision of everything that I desire. As a man, I have gotten everything I ever wanted in life until now. However, I am not afraid though the competition looks ominous. What about the baby, Gabriela? I could use her as a pawn and suggest that we adopt her. Audra clearly adores the darling child. It is quite agreeable for me to be a father to the baby. The adoption idea might tempt her to accept my proposal. It would be like dangling a carrot in front of a donkey. Would it be manipulation or just leverage? I am in a battle for the fair maiden's heart. I will travail in prayer for the wife that I seek."
~~~~~~~

Elizabeth Kirk had no peace of mind either and fretted, "As parents, we know that we must let our daughter choose a husband. Yet we love Derek and want him to be our son-in-law. It is hard for us to let go of that wish. We earnestly prayed for a union between Audra and Derek. But in the end, we have to trust God."

~~~~~~~

The sun was glistening on the dew of the grass on this bright Sunday morning. A horse and carriage could be heard as it passed by on the brick street. Audra and Miss Jenny walked to the church which was near the down town area. After the meeting ended, Audra went to the altar to pray. "Lord, I am acquainted with Joshua only from the school; please show me his true character. In Jesus name."

As the new week began, Derek returned to resume his labor on the mansion. He painted a room, repaired the stairway, cleaned the chandelier, and cut firewood. Jenny Riley was exuberant for all that the soldier had accomplished in the house.

As a courtesy, the sergeant arranged for lodging at the hotel during his stay in El Paso.

When Audra returned at the end of the day from her class, Derek was waiting for her. He gave her an admiring glance. "Miss Kirk, I would like to invite you to dine with me at Las Flores Restaurant this evening."

"I thank you, sir, but I need to study." She quickly climbed the stairs to her room.

After a couple of hours, Audra came downstairs and ate the plate of supper that was left for her. Derek spied her
~~~~~~~

and asked, "Would you care to go for a walk through the neighborhood with me?"

"Well, I guess, it is pleasant weather this evening." She almost declined, but her desire for fresh air overcame her dislike of being near him.

Under the street light, Audra expressed, "I want to thank you for the money that you so graciously gave to me. It was very generous of you, and at the time I desperately needed it. I will reimburse you."

He shook his head. "No, you will not repay me. It was my wish. I care about you."

Thinking about the offer, her resolve was firm. "I would never want to be indebted to him."

As they walked, she noticed that he was very attentive to her and showed interest in the regimen of her life at the hospital. She found herself telling him about the patients that she had treated that day, "There are challenges and rewards working in the clinics."

Being a good listener, he retorted, 'I am interested to learn about the medicines and procedures that are used in medical science."

As they entered the house after the walk, Derek asked her about something that had been on his mind for some time, "Audra, did you receive my letters that I wrote to you while I was on the Punitive Expedition in Mexico?"

Meeting his eyes with a stare of indifference, she answered, "Yes, my mother informed me of them. I told her to burn them unopened."

The evening's atmosphere of courtesy and civility turned

into ice and alienation. So, they parted company, Derek rebuffed with a grimaced expression on his face. As to Audra's rejection, he steeled himself, "I have never walked away from a battle yet. I will win her heart."

At the mansion, the day came for Derek to teach the young ladies' Bible study. The women were so inspired that they extended an invitation, "Would you come back and teach us again next week?"

"Since I have one more week of furlough, yes, I receive your request."

The next day was the mid-week Bible meeting to be held at Christ Church. Many people were in attendance since the ladies in the Bible study had spread the word to come and hear this young chaplain preach.

Derek expounded on the scripture of Luke 12:32. 'Do not be afraid little flock, for your Father has been pleased to give you the kingdom.' He stressed, "It is God's will to give us the kingdom: prosperity, health, and success in life. We take the kingdom of heaven by faith, and faith comes by reading God's word."

The congregation's response to his message was very positive.

Previously, Audra had told Miss Jenny about how Derek had prayed for a little deaf girl on the Apache reservation and how the child was miraculously healed. The widow, in turn, recounted this incident to the pastor. Hearing this amazing testimony, the pastor and the elders met and contacted Derek. "Would you be interested to conduct a healing meeting at a Sunday service at the church?"

"I would be honored to pray for the sick." So, he graciously accepted their petition.

~~~~~~~

Returning to the post, Derek preached to the soldiers on Sunday morning and also went to visit with the Kirks. Daniel relished the fact that the soldier would be near Audra and encouraged the sergeant, "Son, don't give up in your pursuit of Audra."

With a sly grin, he replied, "She is a prize worth fighting for."

On Sunday afternoon, Derek traveled from Columbus back to El Paso on the train. He was returning for another week to finish his work on the mansion and to minister at the church. On arrival at the train station, he purchased a newspaper. The weather was overcast with drizzling rain. It would be a good day to stay in and read. Audra had gone out, and Jenny Riley rested in the afternoon. Therefore, Derek took his key and entered the mansion. All was quiet in the house as he walked into the parlor. He chose an upholstered velvet Victorian chair to relax in and to read his paper. He leaned back in the comfort of the chair and started reading the world news. As he was flipping through the pages of the newspaper, he came across an ad. It read: Miracle Healing Meeting at Christ Church. Bring the lame, the blind, the deaf, and the sick. Chaplain Derek Rands is coming to town.

Derek jerked himself out of his chair. He carefully read the ad again. He thought about the action of the elders, "How could those men do this to me? This is my first healing meeting. However, I see that they have exhibited their faith. Ex-
~~~~~~~

plicitly, I am aware that God is the healer. I am only the instrument that He will use."

As the week progressed, Derek continued his labor on the mansion. Miss Jenny was quite content to have him help her with the repairs and bestowed much favor upon him. "Derek, here is check with a bonus for your work so far."

He objected, "This is an extremely large amount; you are much too generous towards me."

Her eyes twinkled. "As I have no children, I would like for you to be my Godson."

"Yes, I would be honored." His smile was charming.

As an heiress, the lady also lavished her valuable heirlooms upon Audra. "My dear I want you to have this box of jewelry."

When Audra looked at the selection, she exclaimed, "These pieces are lovely and valuable! Should you not keep them in the family?"

"No, my nephew assumes that he will inherit the Riley estate. We raised him as our own son. Yet he has not visited me for several years. He lives in an eastern state and only sends a card at Christmas."

During the week, Audra tried to avoid being near Derek. He, on the on the other hand, was very solicitous towards her. Miss Jenny enjoyed playing board games in the evenings. Therefore, to please the dear lady, Audra would join in the games with Derek attending. During those events, she perceived that he kept his gaze upon her the entire time. She stiffened from the glint in his eye. Finally, she said to him, "Do you delight in constantly staring at me?"

A coy grin touched his lips. "As a matter of fact, I do. It is exceedingly more entertaining than the game."

In spite of herself, Audra blushed and gave him a coquettish smile for the compliment. As an afterthought, she scolded herself, "Do not be vulnerable to this man's charisma."

On Saturday morning, a group of four adults journeyed to the orphanage to bring treats to the children. Derek told a Bible story of how Jesus used a boy's lunch of bread and fishes to feed five thousand people. The children listened attentively to the story, and even little Gabriela sat quietly on Audra's lap. It was a merry time amusing the children.

Mrs. Allen gave the visitors a report from Sheriff Dale Fraser. "Jake adjusted well in the sheriff's family. The sheriff's wife, Veronica, is a strict disciplinarian. Yet, she was kind and loving towards Jake. Carl enjoyed having a little 'brother', and often played ball with the child. The boy stayed with the sheriff and his family for two weeks. Jake's father kept his promise, returned for his son, and it was a happy reunion."

In the afternoon, Derek went to the church to pray with the elders for the healing meeting that would occur the next day. They voiced their agreement with the sergeant, "God does not put sickness on people to teach them something; God's perfect will is to heal the sick and afflicted."

On Sunday morning, Christ church was filled to overflowing with a full balcony and with people standing in the back. The ushers were hard pressed to find seating for the crowd that had come to the healing meeting. The children congregated in the church basement to hear Bible stories, play games, and have treats. There was excitement and anticipation in the atmosphere of the church.

Derek read the scripture, Isaiah 53:5, "But he was pierced for our transgressions, he was crushed for our iniquities; the punishment that brought us peace was on him and by his wounds we are healed." The sergeant proclaimed, "This scripture declares that healing is part of Jesus redemption for mankind."

At the end of the message, Derek looked out over the people who had congregated. "Is there anyone sick in this place?" He had to say it. They advertised it.

Then he felt impressed to speak these words, "The first man who stands up is healed."

Two men immediately stood up. The chaplain requested of the older gentleman, "Come to the altar."

The man came forward, and Derek asked him, "What is wrong with you?"

"I have arthritis in my hands."

The sergeant took the gnarled hands into his own. They felt like sticks. With authority he commanded, "Arthritis, come out of him in Jesus name!"

When he released the man's hands, they were perfectly straight. The healed man was so excited that he walked up and down the aisles showing people his hands. "Look at that, look at that, I can flex my fingers!"

Then the younger man came forward for prayer.

Derek inquired, "What do you need prayer for?"

"I am a lineman for the county. I was working on a power pole. Lightning struck me, killed me, but when I fell to the ground, the jolt revived me. My heart is fluttered. The doctors say that I'll never work again."

"Well, Doctor Jesus is here to heal your heart!"

After Derek prayed for him, the man slumped forward. The ushers were nearby to assist him. With his hand on his heart, he was overcome with emotion. Finally, the lineman spoke in a tearful, husky voice, "The heart palpitations have stopped. My pain is gone!"

Those seated in the church began to clap and praise God.

Many more people came to the altar for prayer for healing. One woman suffered from migraines. After prayer, the pain in her head subsided. A young couple came who were childless and wanted prayer to have a baby.

The healing meeting lasted into the afternoon. All who came to the altar received prayer. No one was turned away. Some returned to thank Derek, but he would only tell them, "Give the glory to God."

Returning to the mansion after the meeting, Audra had a greater awe for the power and love of God. She was also humbled in her spirit with a different opinion of the chaplain. She reflected on the day's occurrences, "Who is this soldier that ministers so mightily for the Lord? My attitude toward Derek has been haughty and scornful. Though I still do not trust him, from now on I will be civil towards him."

After retrieving his belongings, Derek had to hurry in order to catch the afternoon train to Columbus. His furlough had ended. Tears clouded Miss Jenny's eyes as she hugged him. "Please, keep in touch, son. I now have a telephone." And he nodded.

Audra walked with Derek to the curb where the carriage

awaited. "Have a safe trip." He kissed her hand, but this time she did not snatch it away. So, he bid her goodbye.

19

It was a crisp spring morning as Audra walked into the hospital. Dr. Scott called to Lisette, "Quickly alert the medical students to meet me in the emergency room for an observation. A man has been carried in with a gunshot wound in his shoulder. The bullet has to be removed immediately."

Lisette brought in the tray of instruments. Before Dr. Scott could make the extraction, another nurse requested to see him. "A child had just entered the hospital with an asthma attack; Dr. Kirk has another case."

Dr. Scott was about to hurry from the room, when he glanced at Audra. "Can you extract the bullet?"

"Yes, I certainly can; I have assisted my grandfather in doing this procedure."

She studied the instrument tray and turned to Lisette. "I need the long tweezers. These are too short."

Racing down the hall, Lisette went to fetch the required instrument. Then Dr. Carlton strode into the room and announced, "I will do the surgery to remove the bullet."

Directing his gaze to the doctor, Joshua corrected him, "No, Dr. Scott has already authorized Audra to do the extraction."

As Dr. Carlton walked toward the instrument tray, Joshua blocked his way. Then the other students started to protest and crowded the doctor back. At that moment Lisette burst into the room with the long tweezers.

Praying softly, Audra whispered, "Lord, in Jesus name, help me to extract this bullet."

With steady hands, she did the surgery, locating the bullet, and finally, lifting it out. She breathed a sigh of relief.

The medical students murmured their congratulations.

But she shook her head. "This outcome is due to God's grace."

Later, Joshua and Audra made their rounds together in the hospital. They attended to some patients with flu-like symptoms. They were relaxing after lunch before their lecture would begin with Dr. Kirk.

Ian was visiting with a group of his friends. "Men, do you want to see The Sanctified Woman get angry?"

"Oh, yeah!" they all chimed in, rubbing their hands together, and grinning in glee when Ian approached Audra. "Miss Kirk, a little bird told me that I will make love to you very soon."

He said it with impudence, and his friends began to chuckle. Hardly thinking, Audra slapped him hard on the face. The sound was like a mirror that was cracked with a hammer. The laughter and uproar of the men rippled throughout the room. The hilarity stopped abruptly when Joshua shoved Ian up against the wall. The anger in his eyes showed that he meant harm.

"Peace, man, it was only a joke." Ian backed away, his

hands in the air.

"You have gone too far. Go and apologize to Audra!"

"I don't think so."

"Then we will finish this outside."

Then three other students joined Joshua. "We will come with you, too."

Ian realized very quickly that he was going to get a beating. "All right, men if that's what you want."

He walked up to Audra and saw a tear in her eye. "I am sorry that I insulted you. Please forgive me."

A few minutes later Dr. Kirk entered the lecture room. He noticed the red mark on Ian's cheek. "What happened to your face, son?"

The students burst into laughter, and one student piped up, "He got slapped."Ian looked down and put his hand over his brow.

Dr. Kirk snickered. "I'm sorry I missed the drama. We will cover the digestive system today."

At the end of the lecture, a student asked Dr. Kirk, "What is the major advice that you would give us as we pursue a career in medicine?"

The doctor did not hesitate to answer, "The very best counsel that I would give you is to pray for God's wisdom in diagnosis and treatment."

After the lecture, Joshua asked Audra, "May I come to the mansion in this evening to speak to you privately?"

"Yes, that would be fine, around 7:00."

~~~~~~~

Joshua arrived after sundown. The couple sat on the
~~~~~~~

porch swing and talked. Suddenly, his expression became serious. "Audra, I love you most ardently, and I want to marry you. We could be together now if we eloped. I will have money next week for a ring. I am sure that Miss Jenny would let us live in the mansion with her."

Audra's brows pinched. "Are you crazy? We have to finish the hospital school. Isn't that your goal?"

The young man became persuasive. "Yes, I am a little crazy. I am besotted with you, and I want you with me. I will work hard and provide a good living for us."

"I am flattered, but the timing is not right."

He pleaded, "I want you for my wife. It is hard waiting."

"I cannot even consider it now!" She was adamant.

He studied her. "I need to know this. If we marry, will you go anywhere with me to live?"

"Well, yes, I believe it is the wife's duty."

"By the way what is your relationship with that soldier?"

"He is my father's friend."

"Is this what this conversation is about, Sergeant Rands?"

"No. It's just that I am so in love with you. I will not let any soldier come between us."

"Joshua, I do care for you. Yet I do not want to elope."

He leaned in to kiss her, but she pulled back.

Audra had an afterthought about Joshua's proposal, "I am quite vexed and irritated that he asked me to elope. He did not consider that I might want a traditional wedding. I resent this pressure. But as I think about it, I now see how I had put pressure on Derek to marry me at Camp Cavalry."

~~~~~~~
~~~~~~~

The church bells began to peal out the start of a new day on Sunday morning Audra decided to leave early and stop by the Jorn Hotel and Boarding House. She would check on the room request for her mother. Her grandfather and Jenny would meet her at the church later.

She hoped that she might see Joshua. He had told her that he worked the desk on Sundays. As she entered the hotel, she saw an elderly woman sitting at the front desk.

The old lady had been reading her Bible and looked up when Audra came into view. She greeted her cordially, "Good morning, Miss, I am Mrs. Jorn, the mother of the hotel's owner. May I help you?"

"Hello, I am Audra Kirk. I am inquiring about rooms for my family, who will be coming to the hospital school graduation."

"We have several rooms, and they are upstairs if you wish to see them."

"Thank you. Does Joshua Corbin work here?"

"Yes, but never on Sunday mornings. I am here every Sunday. I cannot climb the steps of the church. Therefore, I watch the desk and read my Bible. It is my way of worship."

"Does Joshua work on Saturdays?"

"Yes, but only in the afternoon."

"I see. Thank you."

"Is he a friend of yours?" Audra noticed that she frowned as if she disliked the man.

"Yes, he is."

"I will show you to the stairway. The Commons room

and the men's rooms are to the left. The guest rooms are on the right."

Audra made her way up the stairs. The guest rooms were clean and well furnished. Out of curiosity, she opened the door of the Commons. It reeked of liquor. Empty whisky bottles and decks of cards were lying about on the tables. As she walked further into the room, she heard someone snoring. To her horror, she saw Joshua lying on the floor.

"O God, this is my answer," she whispered to herself.

Hurrying down the stairs, she missed a step and almost fell headlong. She bid Mrs. Jorn a good day as she sped past her desk. When she reached the outside, she saw a bench and sat down there, her head in her hands. Though tearful, she considered, "It is a divine appointment to find out Joshua's true character."

Despairing over what she had just seen, suddenly a medical student came out of the hotel door whistling. He was on his way to church. But when he spied Audra weeping, he hurried to her.

"Audra, what brings you here? Why are you crying?"

She looked up. "I just saw Joshua lying on the Commons floor."

Showing a chagrined aspect, he soothed, "Oh, no, I am so sorry."

"Why did you not tell me about him?" she accused.

"I am not a snitch. Besides, I believe that you now have made your decision in his regard."

"Yes, I have. This explains his bloodshot eyes and headaches in the school. Does Joshua ever study?"

He chuckled. "His medical books are under his bed. He spends much time reading engineering manuals. After the hospital school ends, he plans to attend an engineering college in New York City. He has not been happy here."

It dawned on Audra that Joshua did not disclose that he planned to take her to New York if they married. She tried to control her anger at his deception.

She sighed sorrowfully. "I am truly grateful for your friendship."

The young man arose from the bench. "Come, let us walk to church. It is getting late. The meeting will start soon."

Vexed and hurt, Audra knew that she must forgive Joshua for his deceitfulness. After the benediction, she went to pray and left all of her anger and pain at the altar. A sense of peace come over her, and she almost danced down the street. Her answer had come. In a moment of time, she had been set free from a bad infatuation.

Later in the afternoon Joshua encountered Mrs. Jorn in the hotel lobby. "Your friend, Miss Kirk, came to the hotel this morning and asked about you."

"What did you tell her?"

"I told her that you do not work on Sunday mornings."

Joshua's face turned ashen in color. "I am sorry that I missed her. I was preoccupied."

In a panic Joshua bounded up the stairs to his room. He quickly dressed in his suit. Nervously, he thought, "I must go and see Audra. What will be her reaction to my lies? I am fearful and sick at my stomach."

When Joshua arrived at the mansion, Audra came to the

door. She did not invite him in nor did she come out to the porch. She would only allow him to speak to her through the screen door.

"Audra, I am terribly sorry that I lied to you. Please forgive me. I intended to go with you to church and to the orphanage. I was just not able to."

"Why was that?"

When he hesitated, Audra took a bold stance. "Joshua, I saw you lying on the Commons floor."

"Old lady Jorn ratted me out, didn't she?"

"No, I was only checking on future lodging for my family."

"Sweetheart, please give me another chance. Don't let this isolated incident end our love."

"No, there will be no more chances."

He was wiping his eyes and his nose with his handkerchief. "Darling, please listen. I was going to leave the medical school, but I stayed because of my love for you. I never wanted to be a doctor. It was my father's wish, and I have been depressed. I have a failing grade, my money is gambled away, and I have been drinking liquor. I need your help to overcome this addiction. I promise I will change."

To Audra, Joshua's character reminded her of a chocolate Easter egg. It was attractive and sweet on the outside, but hollow on the inside with no self-discipline or integrity.

The young lady placed her hands on her hips. "I suggest that you go the altar at church and pray. Joshua, I do forgive you. However, from now on at the school, do not sit by me or talk to me. I will no longer go on rounds with you in the hospital."

"My lamb, I love you, and I want you as my wife."

"My answer is no. I will not be drawn into your realm of chaos. I wish the best for you in life."

Audra closed the door. She would have no pity on the man. Joshua left in desolation.

~~~~~~~

It was the end of the day at the hospital. The medical students were leaving to go home. As a charge nurse, Lisette's schedule was longer than that of the aides and the students. The young woman was in a patient's room when she saw Ian and Cora walk towards the back exit of the hospital. The nurse decided to follow them. She entered the storage room and peered out the window.

In the hospital yard, there stood Ian and Cora underneath a tree in a clinch embrace. He was caressing her and kissing her on the lips.

Lisette gasped and watched the lustful scene for a couple of minutes as tears fell from her lashes down to her cheeks. She hurried to the rest room to splash water on her face before returning to her nurse's station.

When Lisette later left the hospital, she went straight to the mansion to see Audra. Her friend sensed that something was wrong when she saw Lisette's red eyes. She invited her to sit down and brought her a cup of tea.

The nurse recounted what she had witnessed with Ian and Cora. "You were explicitly correct in your alert about Ian's character. I am so glad that I kept myself guarded. In this disclosure, God has protected me."
~~~~~~~

Audra was sympathetic. “Lisette, you prayed, and you still have your dignity.”

20

In Columbus, Elizabeth immediately sent Derek's letters that Audra had requested. The mother hoped that they might spark a romance between her daughter and the soldier. There were three letters, and Audra marveled as she read them. In the first letter Derek basically wrote, "I admired your dedication and service on the Apache reservation. You were marvelous in your care of this tribal people." In the second letter, he said, "I prayed for you in the breakup with Kenton. I know that you were hurt when the liaison ended." In the third letter, Derek asked, "Would you wait for me and not enter into a courtship with a medical student? I want a conversation with you about a future together."

Audra's mind was churning, "I cannot stop thinking about these letters. His words have gripped me to the core of my being."

Lisette sought out her friend on her break in the hospital. "Audra, I am impressed in my acquaintance with Sergeant Rands. You told me of your past experience with him, but maybe you should reconsider your attitude toward him."

"I have adjusted my opinion of him. His letters sent from Mexico have made a deep impression on me."

"By the way. Does he have a brother?"

"No, but wait, I just had a thought. Derek has a soldier buddy. Would you be interested to meet Kenton?"

Her friend was quizzical. "Your former beau? Yes, I would be thrilled to meet him. You have told me how much you esteem that soldier."

"We need to pray, because Kenton is currently calling on a young woman named Penelope in Columbus."

"Yes, amen! That relationship is subject to change according to the will of God."

Letting her imagination run wild, Audra squealed, "Lisette, you are a queen, you shall win over Penelope and capture the soldier's heart!"

Laughter filled the atmosphere. "This is uncanny."

"Incidentally, Lisette, did you hear about the announcement for the hospital's auxiliary charity ball?"

"Yes, I want to attend but not with Ian. I have been avoiding him."

"Here are my plans. I will invite Raquel and Matthew to spend the weekend and attend the ball. I am also inclined to send an invitation to Derek, too. He expressed a desire to spend time with me. It is perfect timing for you to meet Kenton. If Penelope cannot come, then I will ask him to escort you to the ball."

"It sounds terrific!"

"As an auxiliary member, Miss Jenny has tickets to sell for the ball. For each five tickets sold, a gratis one is given to the seller. Let's go through the neighborhood tomorrow selling tickets. I am sure we can successfully get six gratis tickets for the ball."

"Count me in. Making sales is one of my talents."

~~~~~~~

When Kenton went to call on Penelope, he was a in a jovial mood. "My dear girl, how would you like to go to a ball?"

"A ball, sounds delightful."

"It is a hospital charity ball to be held in El Paso in two weeks. Audra has tickets for us and also for Derek, Matthew, and Raquel. We will travel by train for the ball to be held on Saturday night. Our lodging will be in Miss Jenny Riley's mansion, and we shall return to Columbus on Sunday."

Penelope instantly became solemn. "Ken, I appreciate your thoughtfulness, but I think that I must decline the invitation. I would be uncomfortable seeing you stare at Audra."

He furrowed his brow in anger. "So that's how you feel?"

"Yes, I could not stand any pretense in the air. She appeared very contrite when you ended your courtship with her. Do you still love her?"

"I will always care for Audra. We shall continue as friends, that is all. Penelope, your jealousy and suspicious mind is a stumbling block to any future for us. Good night." He turned on his heel and stalked to the door.

Later, Penelope scolded herself, "I have been impudent and immature for not accepting Kenton's invitation. I feared that he might spurn me and go back to Audra. Yet after considerable thought, I think that it would be a mistake for me to lose the good will of this noble man."

Sending a message to Kenton, she wrote, "I have changed my mind, and I do wish to be your guest at the ball."
~~~~~~~

To her regret was his reply, "I already have an escort for the ball."

The young lady fretted, "I will be more respectful to the corporal in the future. Another decision I will make is to be more discreet in flirting with men. It has caused me problems in the past and even more recently. As a teller at the bank, the manager cautioned me to not be overly friendly with the male clients."

Penelope could be compared to a cat, always looking for a strategic and cozy place to settle in. She already had her eyes on a young rancher who was a patron of the bank. She would come to his side, purr, and then dig her claws in until she captured her prey. If any man would drop her, just like a cat, she would always land on her feet.

~~~~~~~

Prancing into the hospital, Audra hurried to Lisette's desk, "Dear friend, I have wonderful news! Raquel, Matthew, and Derek are pleased to attend the ball. Furthermore, Kenton sent a note that he indeed is delighted to be your escort! Equally gratifying is that the group from Columbus are welcome stay at the mansion. Also, Dr. Kirk and Miss Jenny have offered to prepare food for us. It will be a festive occasion!"

Eyes sparkling, Lisette retorted, "I am excited at the prospect of meeting the corporal."

It was early morning and no one was around so Audra took her friend's hands, and they danced down the hall. Lisette started singing, "A dainty countess goes to a fancy ball and meets a handsome soldier. She's going to dance all night and win his heart. Yes, the magic of this fairy tale is a
~~~~~~~

dream that will prevail."

Giggling, Audra spoke, "Your lyrics are poetic."

Giving her a cunning grin, the blonde belle retorted, "When the ball is over, the lyrics may be a reality."

Lisette had tried to be elusive concerning Ian, but he seemed not to notice. Seated at her nurse's station, Lisette saw him approaching. "My lovely nurse, I have missed chatting with you. My father, as director at the nursing home, had a problem. A disgruntled employee quit, and I had to work extra hours. I am sorry that it is late notice, but would you accompany me to the charity ball next weekend?"

"I offer my regrets. I already have an escort for the ball." Her eyes then focused on her record keeping.

Arguing, he demanded, "Make an excuse and cancel. I anticipated that we would attend together."

"I certainly shall not."

Then he scowled. "Lisette, I thought that we had an understanding between us."

"You did not inform me of any understanding. Excuse me; I must take the vital signs of a patient." She hurried down the hall, and Ian left vastly annoyed.

Dr. Scott called Audra and Lisette to come to his office. "Ladies, I excuse you from attending the school tomorrow which is Friday. I know that you plan to help decorate the Opera House for the event."

"That would be wonderful! Thank you very much." The young ladies were quite pleased.

The organizers had worked decorating the Opera House the previous night. Audra inquired of the committee, "What is the work plan for tomorrow?"

They replied, "Everything is complete." The girls clapped their hands to be able to spend extra time with their friends.

~~~~~~

At Camp Cavalry, the three soldiers had been granted a leave. Traveling on the train, Kenton mentioned to Derek that he would be escorting Lisette. "Do you know anything about this nurse?"

Grinning slyly, Derek replied, "Yes, I have met her on a few occasions. She is a musician at Christ church. Lisette is a beauty queen. The medical students call her The Regal Countess. Her elegance compares to that of Audra's."

"Really, how fortunate I am, but don't make me crazy. Pretty is as pretty does."

The sergeant snickered. "Brother, you seriously need to pray. Lisette is worthy of your attention, and she lives in your home town of El Paso, how convenient for you."

"You have convinced me. I will pray."

Then Kenton questioned his friend, "I am curious. Would you happen to know what accolade the medical students give Audra?"

"I have heard that they call her the Princess of the Kingdom."

He nodded and chuckled. "That figures rightly."

Derek peered at him warily. "Do not go back to thinking about her, my friend. Do you want more anguish and anxiety?"

"No, I do not"

So, the group from Columbus arrived in El Paso on Thurs-
~~~~~~

day evening. Dr. Kirk arranged for a motorcar to transport them to the mansion. The guests were introduced. Raquel hugged both her sister and Lisette. Kenton brought a box of chocolates for the group. Derek greeted Audra with a bouquet of flowers.

Nervousness fluttered inside of Lisette about being in the presence of a stranger for the entire weekend. However, when she met Kenton, his friendliness put her at ease. She began to explore the prospect of what it could mean to spend time with the soldier. Lisette would be residing at the mansion for three days with the other guests.

Everyone enjoyed a savory evening meal in the mansion's dining room. The conversation was lively with talking and laughing. The men discussed the war that was raging in Europe. They listened to the latest news on the radio in the evening.

Derek peered at Audra, "Thank you for inviting me to the ball."

Smiling, she commented, "We will have a marvelous time."

Kenton was attentive to Lisette who sat next to him. As the corporal gazed at her, he stated, "I could not have imagined how beautiful you are."

Her smile was gracious. "Your remark is flattering."

As they sat around the table, Matthew turned to the sergeant. "Derek, tell us about your experience at the train station in Columbus."

"In the distance, I saw an elderly woman hurrying to catch the train as it was about to depart. She could not run fast so

I waited for her. The train started to move and she fell on the entry steps. I swiftly picked her up and carried her onto the train. If she had fallen to the tracks, it could have been fatal. As I searched for a seat for her, she was sniffling and clinging to me. When we exited in El Paso, she stuck a coin in my pocket and hurried off before I could return it to her."

"What is the coin worth?"

Derek retrieved the coin from his pocket and handed it to Kenton. "A $50 gold piece! I'd say that you were at the right place at the right time for the best deal."

Reaching out his hand, Matthew viewed the coin. "What do you plan to do with it? Do you have anything in mind?"

"I plan to buy something very special."

Grinning slyly, Matthew and Kenton both glanced at Audra, and her cheeks blushed pink.

Miss Jenny relished the chance to host the young people. She had prepared guest rooms for them. Matthew and Raquel were lodged next to the upstairs parlor where they could relax and chat. It was a welcome break away from the demands of their children. It was the first time that Kenton had seen Audra since he had returned from the Punitive Expedition. As she was showing him to his room, he nervously broached the subject of their breakup, "Audra, I hope that you do not hate me. My love for you was genuine."

She gave him a dainty smile. "Kenton, I was in love with you. Now we must not speak of it. We shall remain as friends."

"My sentiments entirely. I appreciate your generosity of spirit."

Before retiring for the night, Raquel brought out a large

satchel. In it were three flamenco dresses for the ladies to wear to the ball. As a surprise for Lisette, Elizabeth had sewn a lavender flamenco dress for the young nurse, her size being similar to that of Audra's. A note, 'Enjoy your gift' was pinned to the dress.

Lisette clapped her hands in glee. "How wonderful is your mother to me! I could not afford to buy a fancy dress. In my family are younger siblings, and I work to pay for my medical school tuition."

The visitors slept late the next morning and awoke to the smell of quiche and waffles. There was a holiday aura in the mansion. After the breakfast, Matthew gave a devotion and prayer for the day.

The sun was shining, so a game of croquet was suggested. The yard was decorated with spring flowers and everyone enjoyed the competition.

After the lunch, Kenton inquired of Lisette, "Would you be interested to see our family business? My grandfather and father run a lumber yard here in El Paso. My army service is up in three months. I will not re-enlist, but will help manage this business."

"Yes. It sounds very interesting!" Her enthusiasm was genuine.

Inside the mansion, Derek challenged Audra to a game of chess, but she was distracted and disinterested. Finally, she brought out the checker board. "What is your bet?"

He suggested, "You will spend another weekend with me."

Giving him a scheming look, she agreed, "All right. This is

my bet. At bedtime, you will carry me up the spiral staircase to my room, then you will go downstairs to bring me a glass of milk upstairs, then you will return the glass downstairs to the kitchen."

As she continued to speak, he began to snicker. "After that, you will enter the children's play room and find a nursery rhyme book. You will bring it upstairs and read it to me, and then." At that point Audra hesitated.

So, Derek finished the sentence, "And then I will kiss you good night."

She gave him an amused glance. "You wish."

Derek won the game, and then remarked, "I will also give you your bet as a consolation prize."

But she objected, "Oh no, my bet was not a serious one. It was only a yarn to be funny, to see your reaction, and to make you laugh. I knew that you would win the checker game since you are more skilled than I."

"I took it seriously, and I shall perform it to the last detail."

"We shall see about that."

All of the young people took a rest in the hot afternoon. It was refreshing to relax within the cool mansion walls. During the leisure time, Audra told Lisette and her sister about the bet; they thought it was hilarious.

~~~~~~~

In the early evening, Kenton and Lisette bicycled to her home. She wanted him to meet her family. Her father, Seth Galt, worked in a coal mine, and her mother, Kate, was employed at a glove factory. Lisette had a brother in high school and a sister in grade school. Kenton and Mr. Galt visited while
~~~~~~~

the mother and her daughter served the supper. Lisette's father was witty and especially enjoyed telling jokes.

Mr. Galt passed the fried chicken to Kenton, and the soldier took a piece. The father urged, "Take another piece. Would like a neck or did you get enough of that last night?"

The younger brother burst out laughing, and his mother rolled her eyes.

Lisette's color rose. "Daddy, you are embarrassing me."

Grinning, Kenton sided with the father. "It was all in good humor."

Sticking the fork into the bread to the hilt, Mr. Galt then passed the plate to Kenton. When the corporal picked up the fork, three slices of bread came with it.

The father chuckled. "I see that you like bread."

The little sister began to giggle and could hardly eat her supper. Her brother started to crunch ice of which his father disapproved. "Son, stop, you will hurt your teeth. Besides, you sound like a hog eating peach seeds."

At that comment, Lisette felt like crawling under the table.

Later, Mr. Galt spoke privately to Kenton, "If you want to marry my sweet, pretty gal, come and consult me."

"Thank you, sir. Your daughter is like a precious jewel."

The day was ending, and all of the couples including Dr. Kirk and Miss Jenny were gathered in the parlor visiting. Suddenly, Raquel made an announcement, "It's time for Audra's consolation prize. Let the show go on!" Then she started to giggle. "We are anxious to see Derek carry her up the spiral staircase. I have been waiting for this moment all evening."

Surprised at the comment, Audra glared at her sister.

Then Derek came forward and dictated to her, "Put your arms around my neck and hold on tight."

Looking around, all eyes were upon her. They were all nodding for her to do it. So, she agreed. He picked her up and carried her up the long, winding staircase. It seemed an easy task for him. Then he entered her room and gingerly let her down. Downstairs, the audience was laughing to the point of pandemonium. Derek came downstairs, poured a glass of milk and took it back upstairs. The soldier saluted as he walked past the onlookers. Then he came downstairs to the playroom to find a nursery rhyme book and took it upstairs.

Audra was seated in a chair, and Derek stood before her and pretended to read from the book.

The Soldier and the Lady

A soldier on horseback traveled down a road.
He met a fair lady walking to her abode.
Upon seeing the soldier come,
The maid turned on her heel to run.
Gently he called to her, "Do not flee, come ride with me."
The soldier came near, and the maid did not fear.
An arranged marriage would be her fate,
If very soon she did not escape.
The soldier placed her into his care.
The two did make a handsome pair.
At the journey's end, would they decide to part?
The fellow inquired of the fair lady's heart.
Though I am a soldier and you are a lady,
Would you marry me and have my baby?

He had scarcely bended his knee,
When she quickly accepted his plea.
So, the soldier took the maid as his wife,
And ever after they lived a merry life.

When Derek ended the nursery rhyme, Audra gazed at him in awe. "Did you just make that up, ad lib?"

"No, I wrote it during the rest time." He held up the paper from the book.

"May I please keep it?"

"Yes, my lady, I composed it for you. To finish the prize, will there be a kiss good night?"

"Well, yes, after such a romantic gesture."

Walking up to her, he lifted her chin and lowered his head to place a kiss on her soft cheek.

Her mood was capricious. "The poem was creative, but the kiss was lackluster."

So, Derek stepped forward and his arms encircled Audra drawing her to his chest. He found her lips, and the kiss sent a tremor through her. He appeared smug. "Did that satisfy you or do you want another?"

"No."

"No, you are not satisfied?"

"I mean yes."

"Yes, you want another?"

She began to giggle. "Quit teasing me. Good night, soldier."

"Goodnight sweetheart." He turned and then he left.

Alone in her room, Audra mulled over her circumstances, "If Derek wants to pursue me, then I will flirt and lead him on.

I will let him dangle just as did to me. In the end, if I decide to reject him, then my revenge will be sweet."

On Saturday, the guests were preparing to leave for the evening's entertainment. Audra inquired of Lisette, "Have you seen the love birds, Matthew and Raquel?"

"Raquel has some pressing duties; she is ironing her husband's shirt."

Amused, Audra shook her head. "Lisette, where did you get your wit?"

"My dad."

The couples entered the Opera House for the event of the charity ball. Their group of six people was ushered to a round table. Matthew pulled Raquel's chair close to his so that he could rest his arm around her. The young ladies, dressed in their flamenco dresses, were the adulation of many onlookers.

Soon after they were seated, Lisette turned to Kenton. "Sir, would you please do me a favor? Ask me to reserve every dance for you."

"It would be my utmost pleasure."

"If any man would ask me to dance, then will you answer for me?

"Yes, I certainly will."

She seemed worried. "There is a medical student that has been stalking me. I never allowed Ian to call on me. He is a womanizer. However, I did play the piano and sing a few times at the old folks' home where he works. As a reward, the nursing home gave us tickets for the theater. I attended the event with him, which was a mistake on my part. Since then, I have been receiving his unwanted attention. If he persists, I will call the deputy."

Kenton frowned. "I will keep you in my care."

Her smile was sweet. "Thank you."

At the ball, the orchestra was stupendous and even touted violins. The musicians played popular songs of the day and many old favorites. Matthew held Raquel close in the waltz.

Derek offered his hand to Audra, "Shall we dance?"

"I guess I will not be too nervous in your arms to dance."

"Someday you will be well used to being in my embrace." She perceived that his character was very cocky. However, Audra had a perpetual smile on her face as she whirled with Derek.

All of the couples were enjoying the occasion, but Lisette was especially happy to be accompanied by Kenton. Her feet rose to dance, and her heart was singing. Her bliss was interrupted when she viewed Ian approaching their table. The girl slipped her hand under Kenton's, and he enclosed his fingers around hers.

Ian extended his hand to her. "Miss Galt, may I have this dance or possibly the next one?"

Answering for her, Kenton spoke up, "Sorry, sir, I am Lisette's escort, and I have reserved all of her dances for the evening."

Ian was visibly angry. "Listen, army boy! Lisette is my girl, and I will fight you for her."

"Shall we step outside? I warn you. I am trained in combat."

But Ian boldly proclaimed, "I'll take the challenge!" He wanted to impress Lisette, and he smirked when he saw the soldier holding the young lady's hand.

Removing his suit coat, Kenton followed Ian outside to the yard of the Opera House.

Lisette directed a fearful gaze to Derek and Matthew and made a desperate plea, "Aren't you going to support your friend?"

Derek grinned smugly. "Kenton does not need our help."

Then Lisette raced to the outer door. She had barely opened it when she viewed an incredulous scene before her. Ian bounded toward the corporal with both fists up ready to punch him out. However, Kenton spun around swiftly and kicked him to the ground. Ian lay there for a moment trying to regain his bearings. He realized that defeat was inevitable, and he did not want to suffer any more pain.

Approaching the man, Kenton helped him up. In a low, brittle voice, Ian murmured, "My apologies, sir."

The corporal only nodded. The fight was over in less than five minutes. As Kenton walked back toward the Opera House, Lisette ran to him, and he grasped her hands into his.

When the band took a break, the couples visited around the table. With a dainty smile, Lisette raised her finger to speak. "I have a confession to make, and I want everyone to hear it." Then she peered at her escort. "Kenton, I wish to tell you that I am attracted to you, because you remind me of my first husband."

He was astonished. "What? You had a husband?"

"Oh, I've never been married."

"I don't get it." He appeared puzzled.

Matthew started to laugh, and then Derek chuckled. "It's

a joke, man. You are to be her first husband."

Wondering at Lisette's boldness, Raquel and Audra became tickled and tee-heed.

Kenton snickered. "Did your father tell you that joke?"

Giggling, Lisette nodded. "How did you guess?"

The corporal's eyes pierced those of Lisette's as he continued the charade. "Shall I ask for your hand?"

"No, your proposal would be a farce."

The young people danced until the orchestra stopped playing.

At the ball's end, Lisette flashed her eyelashes at Kenton. "You were a very snazzy escort this evening."

"I enjoyed it immensely. I find you most intriguing, Lisette."

~~~~~~~

The weekend had ended, and the group said their farewells before leaving for the train station to return to Columbus. They expressed their gratitude to Dr. Kirk and Jenny for their hospitality. The visitors secretly hung a hammock in the mansion's patio as a hostess gift.

Derek wanted to take Audra into his arms and kiss her good bye, but he dared not. She had been charming and polite, but her attitude toward him was rather sassy and nonchalant. He kissed her hand, and expressed, "It was a delight to spend time with you."

"You were good company, Sergeant."

Kenton was effusive in his adieu to Lisette. "I was told that you were the epitome of beauty, but I could scarcely imagine it until I saw you with my own eyes."
~~~~~~~

"That is a compliment that I will always remember."

"May I call on you again? Is next weekend a possibility?"

"Yes, I will be waiting for your return."

"Lisette, in a couple of weeks my parents and I will attend the rodeo and Wild West Show in Santa Fe. It's an excursion that begins on Friday and ends on Monday, which is a holiday. We will travel by train and stay overnight with friends. Would you come with me?"

Her eyes twinkled. "I would very much like to go with you. It sounds wonderful, but I am scheduled to work that weekend and the holiday. I will try to find someone to trade with me or to take my place."

"I will see you soon." The soldier lightly embraced the nurse and brushed his lips to her cheek.

When the visitors had departed, Lisette confided to Audra, "I can hardly comprehend the joy that I am feeling after being with Kenton for the weekend."

Smiling, Audra nodded. "I had an inkling that there would be an attraction, like the force of magnets."

With enthusiasm, she replied, "I can hardly wait to see what the future holds for us."

~~~~~~~

On Sunday evening, Ian went to Lisette's home. She came to the door and met him on the porch. He greeted her, "May we talk?"

She nodded in the affirmative. "Yes."

"I guess I am not invited in."

"No."

"Lisette, I adore you. Please tell me what I have done to
~~~~~~~

offend you, and how I can fix it."

"I saw you and Cora under the tree behind the hospital."

He swallowed hard. "Cora was distraught; I was comforting her. She got a little carried away, that's all."

Lisette shook her head. "No, it was not like that. You took advantage of that young girl. She is barely out of secondary school."

With lament, he sighed, "Please forgive me. I am very sorry for my indiscretion and lack of wisdom. It will never happen again. Lisette, I am in love with you, and I want us to be together."

"Ian, there is a nursery rhyme that says, 'Humpty Dumpty sat on a wall and had a great fall. All the king's horses and all the king's men couldn't put Humpty back together again'. There is nothing you can do to restore our relationship. I am moving on to greener pastures."

The young man argued, "I can give you a better life than that soldier."

"A life of fidelity and trust is what I want. Good evening."

His pleading was futile. So, Ian went away exceedingly sorrowful.

21

It was a misty morning as Dr. Kirk and Jenny Riley made ready to travel to Columbus for a few days to visit the ranch. Since the doctor had arrived in El Paso, the two adults had been constant companions. The dear lady was bedazzled with Dr. Richard Kirk, and she catered to his every whim. The doctor, in turn, reciprocated his attention to the lovely woman.

Furthermore, the widow had been extremely happy to have Audra live with her. She adored her and ultimately desired to be a part of the Kirk family.

Miss Jenny was fluttering around making arrangements to depart. "Audra, the regular scheduled Bible study is tomorrow; Miss Molly will be in charge. Here is money for any expenses at the mansion.

"I will take care of everything. Have an enjoyable time at the ranch."

"I bought a fancy dress for the occasion. I hope it's not too extravagant."

Dr. Kirk prayed for their trip, and the couple hugged Audra goodbye.

The day turned dreary and the rain pelted down as Audra

entered the hospital. She found Lisette at her station. "Will you attend the rodeo with Kenton this weekend? Here is a riding skirt for you, and Miss Jenny sent western boots for you to try. If they fit, they are yours."

Lisette gave her a bedraggled, sad stare. "Thank you, but I cannot go. None of the nurses will trade weekends with me, especially since there is a holiday. I am sorely disappointed."

"Do not fear, sister dear, your best friend is here. I will work the weekend and the holiday for you."

"You are making me laugh with your rhyme. If you are serious, we must ask Dr. Scott today as I am his primary nurse. Please go on rounds with us this morning."

At the end of the consultations, the girls explained their scheme to the doctor. He did not hesitate to give them their petition.

Lisette was exuberant. "Audra, it will only take a little time to train you for my job. I am extremely grateful to you."

"I am ready. I always say, if you help others, God will help you."

Headed to the afternoon class, Audra contemplated Ian's taunts, "If he tries to tease me again, I have in mind a change of strategy for his shenanigans."

Before the class commenced, Ian walked up to her with a group of students following him.

"Oh no, here he comes." Exasperation clouded her face.

Ian got down on one knee and looked up at Audra. He lifted up a tiny metal ring from a box of Cracker Jack Carmel corn. "Miss Audra, I, your humble servant, am madly in love with you. Would you accept my proposal of marriage?

I promise to make you a most happy Sanctified Woman."

The students in the background were snickering and waiting for her reply.

She nodded and smiled sweetly. "Well, yes. How could I refuse such a cavalier proposal?"

Then she reached for the ring and put it on her little finger. The atmosphere was filled with applause and whistles. A fellow yelled out, "Jolly good, Miss Kirk!"

Since Audra had played along with his joke, Ian made an effort to befriend her. His plea was sincere, "May there be a reconciliation between us?"

"Of course, I would be glad for it."

Dr. Scott walked in to give the lecture in the class as Dr. Kirk was out of town. The doctor had watched Ian's charade. He could not help but chuckle.

As the class ended, Dr. Scott announced, "Students, tomorrow, you will observe an amputation of a man's foot in the operating theater. The man is diabetic, and his foot is black and gangrenous. It is imperative to amputate it."

~~~~~~~

Early the next morning, after consulting with patients on their rounds, the students were eager to watch the amputation surgery. However, Dr. Carlton came into the operating theater and announced, "Dr. Scott is delivering twin babies and will not be in the operating theater this morning. Dr. Kirk is out of town on business."

Then he surprised the class. "Miss Kirk, come forward. I assign you to do the amputation this morning. You may choose a student to help you."
~~~~~~~

Astounded, Audra grabbed her chair. She dropped her notebook and pen to the floor as she assessed this unforeseen event. She went forward to speak to Dr. Carlton privately, "Am I to assist you in this operation?"

"No, you are to perform it."

"Sir, may I study the patient's case, review the instruments, supplies, and scrub up?"

"No, only put on your gloves and apron. The orderly will bring the man in shortly."

"This is beyond my present knowledge and practice. I came to observe this surgery, not to perform it."

Dr. Carlton scowled disdainfully and turned to the class, "Miss Kirk has declined. Would any other student be interested in performing this surgery? The experience could be invaluable."

None of the students volunteered. Even Ian looked away. Then Dr. Carlton informed the orderly to bring the patient on the gurney into the operating theater. The students began to watch the grueling operation. After making the incision, Audra noticed that Dr. Carlton's hands were shaking, and he was perspiring profusely.

So, she spoke to Ian seated beside her, "Come on, we must assist the doctor."

They immediately went to help with the surgery. As they hurried, Joshua had already left his seat and had walked to the gurney.

"Students, take over, I feel light headed!" Dr. Carlton commanded. A student brought him a chair, and he sat down and slumped over with his head in his hands. Then he began having dry heaves.

Another student called out, "I'll get some wet cloths for the doctor!"

Dr. Scott did not come immediately as he was detained. The patient before them was sedated, so the students had to continue with the surgery. Joshua took over and performed the surgery. Audra and Ian assisted him. The minutes passed as Joshua worked on the patient. The others hovered close by. The patient was losing a lot of blood, and Audra prayed that the man would survive the ordeal. Dr Scott had received word to go directly to the operating theater. He arrived as Joshua was suturing the incision.

The doctor examined the patient. "I am satisfied with this surgery."

The amputation ended, and Audra bandaged the stump.

Dr. Carlton was feeling a little better, so some students helped him up from his chair. Dr. Scott talked with him briefly and told him, "Come to my office as soon as possible."

The doctor had acted insubordinately, trying to do the surgery when Dr. Scott had told him that he, himself, would perform it a little later in the morning.

As the students began to exit, Dr. Carlton threatened Audra, "Miss Kirk, a word with you. Don't ever disobey me again. When I give you a task, you will do it immediately, or I will have you dismissed from this hospital school. There will be no recourse for you."

God gave Audra the courage to speak, "Sir, the surgery went well. It was a comfort knowing that you were close by."

"Thank you."

Audra pondered, "Dr. Carlton chose to humiliate me in front of the class. Was it not unfair? The doctor usually asked me to assist him. I supported him more than all of the other students. I sutured wounds, recorded notes, and cleaned up after the male students left. In the past, Dr. Carlton seemed to appreciate my help and expertise. How could he treat me in such a manner? No, I will not submit to self-pity or judgment. Despite the persecution, my choice is to forgive."

Joshua approached Audra as she was leaving the operating theater. "Why didn't you accept Dr. Carlton's challenge when he first called on you?" His question had a condemning tone.

"It was obvious. I had no advance notice to prepare. Why didn't you volunteer?"

"You're the 'Miss Know It All' in the class."

"Are those the words of a gentleman?"

He suddenly became contrite. "No, they are not. Please forgive me for my rudeness. I guess I still feel the sting of losing you. Thank you for assisting me today."

"Of course. I congratulate you on your skill in the surgery."

"I appreciate your comment."

With that retort, Audra hurried to leave. In the doorway, Ian was waiting for her. He frowned after hearing Joshua's insult.

Taking her hand, he spoke sternly, "If he ever talks to you that way again, he will answer to me."

She smiled up at him. "Thank you for caring."

His eyes hardened. "Audra, did Dr. Carlton threaten you?

I could tell he was chastising you."

"Yes, but please, do not dwell on it, my friend."

He covered her small hand with his large one. "You will soon forget this incident, Audra. You have an ally in me. I will always be by your side when you need me."

Taking his hand, she replied, "Your words are comforting to me."

Shaken and depleted emotionally, Audra made her way to Lisette's nurse station. She told her friend about the events of the amputation surgery. Lisette had been assisting Dr. Scott with the delivery of the babies during the time of the surgery.

Audra gave a deep sigh. "Lisette, Dr. Carlton has threatened to dismiss me from the medical school."

"I assure you; Dr. Scott will not let that happen."

In the afternoon, Dr. Scott called the students into his office to discuss the amputation. The patient was recovering. The doctor congratulated Joshua, Audra, and Ian on the excellence of their surgical skills. One thing perturbed Audra; Dr. Scott did not mention anything about Dr. Carlton being insubordinate. She had seen Dr. Carlton making his rounds in the hospital, and he acted like all was well.

~~~~~~~

Returning to El Paso, Dr. Kirk and Miss Jenny arrived on the late afternoon train. When they entered the mansion, they both were in an animated mood.

With a twinkle in his eye, Dr. Kirk announced, "Jenny and I eloped last weekend." The doctor held up his wife's hand with the gold band.

Audra was ecstatic. "How wonderful! I had a hunch that
~~~~~~~

you two would make the perfect couple."

Giggling, Jenny told her, "My fancy dress that I wore at the ceremony was the 'icing' on the cake."

Dr. Kirk was exuberant. "We will have a reception later to celebrate with friends and family in Columbus."

After hearing details of their elopement, Audra excused herself, "I think that I will skip supper and rest. She dragged her feet up the stairs like a wooden marionette and lay on her bed to pray. She deliberated about the events of her life and then fretted, "It's rather late, and it appears that Derek will not come. Maybe he has been put off by meeting Joshua. He does not know that my infatuation has ended with the medical student. It has been a sad day for me with the encounter at the operating theater, and now perhaps I have lost the man who loves me. Maybe the decision has already been made on his part."

Hearing voices downstairs, Audra awoke from her sleep. She thought to herself, "Who could be coming at this time of the evening?"

Then came a knock at her door. It was Jenny speaking, "My dear, someone has come to see you. Dress tastefully."

Mysteriously, she did not wait to tell her who it was. Audra combed her long curls, quickly dressed in her burgundy satin skirt with matching brocade jacket, and made her way to the parlor.

She was surprised to see Derek putting a log on the fire since the weather had turned unusually cool. He greeted her cordially, taking in every detail of her appearance, "Good evening, Audra, you are the epitome of beauty."

With a charming smile, she greeted the dashing soldier, "You flatter me, sir. Did you have a good trip?"

"Yes, I had to take a later train because of business at Camp Cavalry. There was trouble within the ranks; two enlisted men were fighting over a debt owed. I had some counseling sessions. Finally, the issue was resolved."

"Since I had not heard from you, I wondered if you ever wanted to see me again."

Then Derek touched her face with a caress and spoke tenderly to her, "My feelings for you will not change. Audra, don't ever doubt my love for you. You are the one I revere."

With a cocky grin, Derek took her hand and led her to be seated on the Victorian sofa. She tried to hide that she was under a heavy burden, that she might be dismissed from the school.

He studied her. "What new knowledge did you gain today?"

Tears welled up and fell from her lashes. The sergeant immediately moved towards her and wrapped his arms around her. She wept on his shoulder as he gently held her. Like the fire that warmed the room, she was warmed by his nearness. Being in his strong arms, she forgot all of her cares. Audra became aware that she was being held tightly in Derek's grasp and slowly pulled away. She apologized for her tears and explained what had occurred at the operating theater and how Dr. Carlton had threatened her.

"I am sure that God will vindicate you." His confidence placated her.

"Thank you. I needed to hear that. It gives me peace."

The two young people visited late into the evening. Then Derek informed her, "I have to leave on an early train tomorrow morning. There is some business on our ranch that I have to attend to."

He brought her fingers to his lips. "May I see you again?"

"Yes, you may continue to call on me." She blushed at her boldness.

"I will look forward to it. Goodnight my sweet." And his lips brushed her face.

Later in her room, Audra prayed for sleep to whisk her far from the disconcerting feeling of being held in Derek's embrace.

She marveled, "He is so persistent in his pursuit of me! It is very impressive. Still, my attitude toward him is lukewarm. My vow has not lost its power. Yet the day has turned from ashes to gold."

22

While Audra was working for her friend in the hospital, Lisette, Kenton, and his parents were enjoying their trip to the rodeo in Santa Fe. The corporal's parents, Zane and Kimberly Lott, readily befriended Lisette. They quickly established a rapport with the young nurse.

Before the event, Kenton and Lisette walked through a market area to gaze at the wares of the vendors. A certain vendor had a large assortment of cowboy hats.

Kenton mentioned, "You need a hat for your fair skin. We will be in the sun most of the day."

Lisette fancied the idea and chose a hat. "I would like one, but I can buy it."

He insisted, "I will pay for it."

She donned her western hat and asked, "How do I look?"

Viewing her with admiration, he declared, "Miss Dodd, you could rival a fashion model."

At the rodeo, there was much drama and trauma in the arena as the cowboys competed in the bronc riding contest. The horses were large and rambunctious with their twisting and bucking.

Then Lisette turned to Kenton, "I was engrossed in viewing the well-trained horses in the calf roping event. However, it is difficult for me to watch this bull riding competition. I consider bull riding an extremely dangerous sport."

One of the contestants was bucked off, and limped out of the arena. Another man narrowly escaped the bull's horns. Lisette began to fidget and look away. As the event continued, she found herself gripping Kenton's hand. The contest was almost over when suddenly a huge, ferocious bull burst out from the shoot with a cowboy on its back. He only rode for a few seconds and was thrown to the ground. The bull swiftly turned and began to gore him in the abdomen. Before the clowns could distract the animal, the bull's horn ripped into the fellow's leg. The bull rider lay still on the sand of the arena. Two men picked him up, put him on a stretcher, and carried him to the exit.

Slinging her purse strap over her shoulder, Lisette grabbed Kenton's wrist. She pulled him from his seat as she stumbled over his boots. "Ken, help me to find that wounded bull rider!"

They hurried from the bleachers and found the young man lying on the stretcher outside of the arena. Lisette knelt down and took his pulse. She yelled to Kenton, "The victim's heart has stopped, and he is not breathing! Begin compressions to his heart!" Then she lifted up the man's head and blew into his mouth. Yet he still was not responding.

The parents hastened to the scene in order to help. Zane, the father, put pressure on the bleeding leg.

Lisette murmured, "Kenton, pray that any internal bleeding will stop." And he nodded his assent.

The crowd around them reported, "The ambulance has

taken another cowboy to the hospital, and the doctor here is treating another injury."

They continued their therapy for several minutes. The bull rider's lips had started to turn blue, and a rodeo attendant put his hand on the girl's shoulder to make her stop her remedy. "Miss, it's no use for you to try any longer. I am sorry, but the young man is dead."

She screamed at him, "No, leave me alone!"

In desperation, Kenton prayed, "Lord, revive him in Jesus name! Send an angel!"

At that moment, a tall, fair-haired man came up and laid his hand on the bull rider's brow. He was there only briefly and then gone.

Lisette checked the pulse again, and there was a heartbeat. The cowboy began to breathe, and the bleeding in his leg stopped.

An old hearse came to the scene that was to be used as a backup ambulance. The attendants inquired "Where is the dead man we're supposed to pick up?"

An onlooker pointed to the injured bull rider who was now sitting up. He had survived the ordeal. It was truly a miracle.

After the near-death accident, Lisette was tearful and shaking. Kenton held her close until she became calm. The corporal comforted her, "Lisette, you saved the young man's life."

"No! It was the angel!"

The Wild West Show in the evening was to romanticize the epic days of the old west.

Lisette commented, "The trick riders, on the backs of horses, were the most spectacular."

Kenton nodded. "Yes, and also the cowboy riding into the arena on a buffalo."

Upon leaving Santa Fe, Lisette overheard Kenton's dad teasing him, "Oh, my word, Ken, how did you win this girl's affection? You need money for a ring? Don't let her get away. All you need is a pretty wife, a truck, and you are set for life."

He snickered. "That is quite an exaggeration, but I get your point."

The train ride from Santa Fe to El Paso was five hours in duration. Lisette rested with Kenton's arm around her and her head on his shoulder. It was comfortable for her and pleasing for him to have her close by.

~~~~~~~

Anxious to visit with Audra, Lisette was waiting for her at the hospital. She was like a joyful little girl who had received a pony for Christmas. There was much excitement in her words, "Audra, thank you so much for your service to me. My weekend was marvelous! I am so enamored with Kenton! The more I get to know him, the more I desire to be with him. I think that he would be a wonderful husband. I once heard an old wives' tale, 'Your future husband will behave towards you in the same manner that his father treats his mother'. Ken's father is superbly nice to his mother. They appear compatible and totally in love. His parents were kind to me, and they were genuinely interested in my life and career. It was impressive."

"That is wonderful, Lisette, but be careful not to become
~~~~~~~

too infatuated too quickly. You will be devastated if Kenton betrays you like he did me."

Her expression changed from gleeful to fearful. "Yes, I will keep myself guarded. By the way, how did your con sultations go with Dr. Scott?"

"Very well, indeed. I met his son, daughter- in- law, and their year-old baby. Since Dr. Scott was on call and could not leave, they brought lunch to us at the hospital."

Eager to share some news, Lisette announced, "Today, I became aware that the board asked for Dr. Carlton's resignation. He only had a few clients."

"Really?" Audra was astounded.

"Yes, the doctor resigned and has effectively retired from his practice."

"Did Derek come to call on you last weekend?"

"Yes, he did!" Her reply was enthusiastic.

Then Lisette assumed a serious tone, "Incidentally, there is another subject that I wish to talk about. I am glad that you and Ian have reconciled your friendship, but you must beware of his attention to you."

"Ian and I are now in harmony. Being in his presence is stimulating. When we go on rounds together, it is like 'iron sharpens iron.'"

23

The first Saturday of each month, the hospital had a benefit clinic to treat Mexican children and the elderly who were ill. Many parents crossed the border with their little ones for this free clinic. They would walk for miles and line up at the hospital door as early as three in the morning. Audra relished this day to help the poor and the sick. In the clinic inquiries, the parents would describe the children's symptoms, and the medical students would give their diagnosis. The hospital pharmacy would furnish the medicines.

Derek and Kenton had traveled to El Paso to help Audra and Lisette in the clinic as Spanish interpreters. With only a couple of interpreters, the consultations were slow, and the people had to wait for hours for their youngsters to be diagnosed. Dr. Kirk, who was bilingual, would also help with the clinic. The medical students would be divided into groups.

Entering the hospital, Derek spied Joshua and went to greet him. The sergeant heartily shook hands with the student in friendship. "How are you, man?"

"I am well, sir. How is army life?"

"Never a dull moment."

The two men exchanged small talk in congenial conversation.

Thereafter, Joshua went to find Audra. "Did you mention any of my problems to the soldier boy?"

"Not a word."

Dr. Scott had appointed Derek to interpret for Ian, and another student. Joshua quickly approached that student and asked, "Would you please trade places with me in your clinical group?"

He frowned and shook his head. "Ian is in my group, and he will surely antagonize you."

"I can tolerate Ian. Sergeant Rands is the interpreter for that group, and he is a friend of mine."

"All right, but don't say I didn't warn you."

Lisette, Kenton, and some students composed another group. Audra, and three other students were in a third group. Dr. Kirk took the remaining students under his 'wing'.

Ian and Joshua were outstanding in examining the children. In one case, Joshua quickly noticed something strange. "This elderly lady keeps scratching the top of her head." Inspecting the cause, he exclaimed, "A worm is embedded in the woman's scalp." He skillfully implemented a surgical removal, and a grin broke out of her toothless mouth.

After the medical students examined the children in their group, Derek also checked them over. He found more ailments that the parents had not disclosed and that the students had overlooked. He observed that one little girl had sores on her stomach. He called the students over to see her, "Impetigo is a disease that spreads on the skin." Then Derek furrowed his brow in anger as he spoke, "The mother forgot to mention these sores. Take care to be thorough in each examination." In another case, he explained, "This is thrush in the baby's mouth." On still other consultations, he detected fungus the size of a saucer on a boy's back and scabies on a child's wrist.

In regard to treatment of the patients, Derek had prayed for discernment. He was so proficient in diagnosis that Joshua was puzzled. "Sergeant Rands, I know that you are a chaplain, but are you also an army doctor?"

"I will explain. My father is the Indian agent on the Apache reservation where I lived as a youth. There are some medicines at the agency to treat the Indians when they are sick. We were trained in first aid and how to set broken bones. I read a lengthy book on diseases and their cures."

Audra experienced the hardest case of the day. It was three o'clock in the afternoon, and the medical students and interpreters were closing their clinics. She was detained for one more patient who had come late. The recorder insisted, "This child is in urgent need of care!"

In evaluating the little girl seated on her mother's lap, a sense of dread came upon Audra. She immediately began to pray against death. The child, Reina, eight years old, had an extremely elevated fever.

There was a ragged gash on her arm that oozed with yellow infection. She wiped her infected eyes with an old handkerchief. As Audra examined Reina, the little girl whimpered and trembled. It was apparent that her body was septic. To Miss Kirk, death seemed imminent. So, she told the medical students, "Go and find Dr. Kirk and Dr. Scott! Tell them that I need immediate help!"

Both doctors came quickly to her exam room. They saw the dire situation and took over the examination. Audra went to find Derek, and the group began to pray. In a loud voice, Dr. Kirk rebuked the spirit of death in regard to the child. The room seemed charged with the presence of God. The medical students grabbed Reina's mother as she began to fall to the floor.

Dr. Scott ordered, "Admit the little girl to the hospital with IV antibiotics, eye salve, and dressing for the wound. This child will live." The doctor was optimistic for the outcome.

Wiping back her tears, Audra exited to the hall. Derek followed her and held her close. He whispered to her, "The prayer of faith will heal the sick."

The two companions walked to the doctors' lounge so that she could regain her composure. Lisette saw her friend crying and brought her a cup of tea. Audra squeezed Derek's hand. "I am thankful that you are by my side and for your encouragement."

Upon leaving the hospital, Joshua approached Derek and asked if he might speak to him, "Sir, not long ago I was in a depraved, depressed state of mind. Shamefully I did not study, dozed in class, and was almost flunking the medical course. Audra was made aware of my drinking and gambling. She told me to go to the church altar to pray. In desperation, I went, and a church deacon shared Christ with me. It has changed my life."

"My friend, you made a wise decision that you will never regret."

"I planned to be an engineer, but upon examining the

cadavers, I had a sensing of how God engineered the human body. I have a photographic memory, and now, the intricate parts of the body fascinate me. My talent for surgery has become apparent. I have started to diligently read my medical books. I am questioning whether I want to spend my life building roads and bridges. I know that you are a chaplain. Would you pray that God's vocation becomes known to me?"

Derek nodded. "Yes. Amen. I will pray, but you must seek; you will surely find the will of the Lord for your life."

The young man was uplifted in the conversation. "I am glad to know you, soldier."

"Keep in touch; you will make a fine doctor." Joshua's face beamed with that comment.

Audra and Lisette expressed gratitude to Derek and Kenton who had come to help with the clinic for the Mexican families "You both were a tremendous asset to the hospital benevolence program."

The soldiers and the young ladies returned to the mansion and visited over supper.

The elder Kirks had gone out. So, Kenton and Lisette chose to visit in the upstairs parlor.

Retiring to the main parlor, Derek and Audra talked about the events of the day. Then the sergeant broached a question, "Audra, would you accept a courtship with me?"

"I will think about it and give you, my answer." She appeared so serious that Derek wondered if she still felt resentment.

"I appreciate your consideration." His dark eyes and male countenance were filled with satisfaction.

She rose from her chair. "Please excuse me sir, good night."

He reached for her arm. "Audra, if I need to give you a thousand kisses to kiss away your hurt, then I will do it."

Smiling sweetly, she replied, "The hurt is gone."

With that answer, Audra felt Derek's hands on her waist bringing her near to him. He wrapped his arms around her and molded her soft body close to his hard chest. It awakened a desire that they both felt, and she did not want to leave his embrace. His fingers threaded through the silkiness of her hair. He began to kiss her face starting at her temple and going to her chin. Finally, his lips reached hers, and she was in awe of his affection.

"You are so precious to me," he whispered huskily. "In the mountains of Mexico, I prayed that you might still be free. To the ends of the earth, I would have pursued you."

Audra sensed his love for her, and it pierced the veil that hid the vow. She glimpsed the vow of fear that had engulfed her. Thinking about it, she questioned, "Am I ready to let it go? Though free of resentment, I cannot yet tell Derek that I trust him."

Later she brought tea to the parlor, and their conversation was easy and affable. The flames of the fire seemed to crackle with applause and approval of their relationship. The sparkling lights of the huge chandelier also illuminated the infatuation.

~~~~~~~

The next day was Sunday, Matthew and the musical trio planned to minister at the garrison in Columbus. Therefore,
~~~~~~~

Derek was free to accept an invitation to preach at Christ Church in El Paso. His companions came with him to that assembly.

The pastor gave the invocation, and then Audra and Lisette sang a hymn that they had composed. They accompanied themselves with the mandolin and piano.

Derek's sermon was entitled 'It is God's will to prosper you'. He quoted Psalm 105:37, "Then He brought out Israel with silver and gold, and there were none among his tribes who stumbled." He also cited Deuteronomy 28:12, "The Lord will open the heavens, the storehouse of his bounty, to send rain on your land in season and to bless all the work of your hands. You will lend to many nations, but will borrow from none."

When the meeting ended, a middle-aged man approached the young people and introduced himself, "My name is Carl Patton; I am the director of an insane asylum here in El Paso. I have prayed for some time for a cleric to come and minister deliverance to the male residents oppressed of the devil in the asylum. I believe that there is a whole nest of 'vipers' in that place. I mean demonic activity. I know that there are many causes of mental illness and some of the residents are truly physically impaired. Yet others are institutionalized criminals. When some of the men are evaluated to enter the penitentiary, they pretend to hear voices so that they can stay in the asylum. There is continual strife, fighting, and cursing in the institution. I abhor the bullying and the perversion that goes on among the men. Most of the residents' families rarely come to visit them or write to them. In the Bible, I have read about deliverance ministry from the oppression of demons. Jesus cast out demons and commanded his disciples to do the same. I invite the four of you to come and minister to the men. They would appreciate your music, but only the soldiers will have direct contact with the men. You will have no contact with the institutionalized women as they reside in another building. My brothers, you will have complete liberty to preach and to pray."

The group discussed the opportunity. "We agree that we will come to minister at the asylum. We will devote a whole day on the following Saturday for this ministry."

Derek had a request of the director, "Sir, would you contact some church members who would fast and pray for this meeting?"

"Absolutely, I know of several who will stand with us in this deliverance ministry."

Kenton also interjected a petition, "Mr. Patton, could you bring some Bibles for those men who are able to read?"

"Yes, I will have them available when you come."

Before leaving the church, Kenton encountered Lisette's father and asked him, "Sir, may I have permission to court and subsequently marry your daughter? I love her most ardently, and I will protect her and take good care of her."

Mr. Galt seemed content with the prospect. "I graciously give you, my approval."

~~~~~~~

There was a stir among the residents as Derek, Audra, Kenton, and Lisette walked into the men's dining hall of the insane asylum. Most of the fellows were seated at small ta-
~~~~~~~

bles while others were standing. The director addressed the group, "These men seldom see any women. Once in a while, a mother might come and visit her son. For young women to enter their domain is a rare phenomenon."

Two men were seated together, and they immediately began to comment on the visitors. The first man spoke with excitement to his companion, "There are two new girls here, and they're real pretty."

"Why those soldiers here? They take us to jail?" asked the second man, suspicious and fearful.

"No, they guard those girls," replied the first man.

To greet the men, Derek and Kenton went around and shook hands with the fellows. They asked, "What is your name, and where are you from?"

One man tried to assault Derek, reaching for his throat, and growled, "I'm going to kill you!" The sergeant quickly caught the attacker's hands and brought him to sit in his chair. The residents who were close by saw what happened and clapped.

Some of the men begged the soldiers, "You sit down with me. You stay here. I like you, soldier."

In the background, the visitors could hear one man moaning and another man sporadically speaking gibberish. A few of the men just stared into space.

A hush fell over the audience as Audra began to play the mandolin, and she and Lisette sang hymns. A few of the residents sang with the young ladies. The men applauded and then chanted, "Sing more, sing more."

Kenton shared a message on the love of God and the gift

of eternal life in heaven from Romans 10:9, "If you declare with your mouth, 'Jesus is Lord,' and believe in your heart that God raised Him from the dead, you will be saved."

He asked the men to raise their hands if they wanted to pray. "Men, repeat this prayer. Father God, come into my heart and be my Savior. Forgive me of my sins. I believe that Jesus is the son of God. I believe that Jesus died on the cross for my sins and rose again. I trust Him as Lord. Thank you, God for eternal life. Amen"

Then Derek preached on the Biblical account of how Jesus delivered a man possessed with demons, referencing Luke 8:26-39. The sergeant boldly proclaimed, "We have come today in the power of the Holy Spirit to set the captives free. Those of you men who want prayer for healing and deliverance, please come forward."

A number of the men made their way to the front for prayer.

Derek and Kenton prayed for each man individually in this manner, "Demons, infirmities, I command you to come out of him in Jesus name."

As the prayers went forth, there were demonic manifestations: men falling to their knees, shrieking, crying, cursing, and vomiting. In the end, several of the men began to praise and thank God. Some of the men exhibited a change in their demeanor. Others said that they felt peace.

The director then asked Derek and Kenton to minister and pray for other men who were confined to their rooms. The women were not allowed to enter that area of the asylum. The group spent the greater part of the day ministering in the insane asylum. The fruit of their endeavor would be made known later.

24

In the hospital, the child Reina was slowly recovering. The doctors, nurses, and medical students maintained a constant vigil of the little girl. They also showered her with flowers, gifts, and toys. Lisette brought her treats. Audra and her grandfather read the Bible in Spanish to her each day. To the child's delight, the elderly doctor taught Reina how to play checkers.

In the medical school, Dr. Kirk had exhibited his ability as an outstanding teacher, communicating his knowledge from years of medical practice. The doctor quickly became very popular among the students. He was also trusted and approved by the hospital staff. His astute medical practice and wisdom even became known in the community. The hospital board contacted Dr. Kirk. "We unanimously offer you a position as teacher in the medical school and as a practicing physician in the clinic and hospital."

After much prayer, Dr. Richard Kirk replied, "I will take the offer. Training prospective doctors is a worthwhile pursuit. Therefore, I will move to El Paso just as soon as I am able to notify my practice in Columbus."

Audra reported the news to Lisette, "I have mixed emotions over grandfather's career change. I realize what a great contribution he will make to the medical school. Yet, I had hoped to go back into practice with him in Columbus."

As she prayed about her destiny, she remembered the scripture, Revelation 3:7, "These are the words of him who is holy and true, who holds the key of David. What he opens no one can shut, and what he shuts no one can open."

~~~~~~~

In the cool of the spring day, Kenton and Lisette were seated on the porch swing of the mansion. He assumed a serious composure. "Lisette, when you think you can trust me enough, I desire to ask you for a courtship. My prayer has been made, and I could love you so easily. Take your time in answering me."

In a sober pose, Lisette stuck her finger into his chest. "Be it known to you, soldier, I do not need to wait to answer you in this matter." Then she paused and fear struck his heart, but a grin tugged at the corners of her mouth. "I trust you completely. I am honored to accept your courtship."

Breathing a sigh of relief, Kenton inhaled the sweetness of the girl as he grasped her close to him. He caressed her face with his fingers. His lips initiated his kiss, and Lisette yielded to the intensity of its pressure. The courtship was a promise and sealed with a kiss. The young man and woman had an anticipation of a happy life together.

Holding his beloved's hands, Kenton kept his focus on her. "Lisette, I will not be able to call on you in El Paso for a time. I have a commitment and guard duty at the garrison for the next couple of weeks."
~~~~~~~

"All right, until we meet again."

~~~~~~~

Two weeks had gone by, and Elizabeth requested that Audra and Lisette come to Shiloh ranch. The young ladies would spend the weekend with their paramours. Derek would also lodge at the ranch. However, Kenton had guard duty but hoped to meet Lisette on Sunday afternoon at the train station.

Graduation at the medical school was fast approaching, and Elizabeth had a surprise for Audra and Lisette. "Girls, I have sewn dresses of high fashion for your upcoming event."

Dress fittings were in order, and the young ladies were well pleased with the designs. In viewing the gorgeous dresses, Lisette queried Elizabeth, "Mrs. Kirk, I am in a courtship with Kenton Lott. Would you be interested to sew a simple wedding dress for me? If possible, I would need to give you payments."

"Of course, Lisette. You expressed much gratitude for the flamenco dress."

Also in attendance, Raquel interjected an idea, "Lisette, my wedding dress from my first marriage is here. It is ornate, covered with seed pears, and a genuine piece of art. Would you like to see it?"

"Oh, yes, it sounds fabulous."

She brought out the wedding dress, and Lisette tried it on. It fit her perfectly. The young lady exclaimed, "This is like a Cinderella dress, so fantastic! How much do I owe you?"

Raquel smiled coyly. "It is gratis. I have wished to give it away and get rid of it. I want no memory of it."
~~~~~~~

Overcome with thankfulness, she hugged Raquel. "I will think of a gift for you, dear friend."

The family traveled to the church in Columbus on Sunday morning. After the church meeting, three young adolescent girls, Rebecca, Monta, and Scarlet came to visit with Miss Kirk and her guest. Introductions were made, and Audra casually mentioned, "Lisette is now in a courtship with Kenton Lott."

Thereafter, Elizabeth motioned to her daughter to come to the other side of the church to visit with friends. Lisette stayed to continue the conversation with the girls. Rebecca studied her. "Miss Galt, would you please tell us your beauty secrets?"

"Yes, walk with your head up, stay out of the sun, and obey the Ten Commandments."

Monta seemed perplexed. "Miss Lisette, I was surprised to hear that you are in a courtship with Kenton Lott. Last Sunday he sat in church with Penelope Adams, and she snuggled up next to him. Then she put her arm around him. I sing in the choir, and I saw them together."

Lisette's eyes widened in astonishment. "I thank you for telling me this. I shall inquire into it."

Two of the girls had to leave with their parents, but Scarlet lingered to talk. "Miss, there is more that you should know. After church, Penelope was fawning over Kenton. She took his hand to introduce him to her relatives that had come for the Adams' anniversary reception. She acted as if he was her beau. Please keep this in confidence."

The blonde beauty sighed deeply. "Scarlet, your kindness is much appreciated."

"Penelope hates us girls because we are competition for her in flirting with the young men. Miss Lisette, I hope you are the winner of this romance. I do not want to see you get hurt." Lisette hugged Scarlet and bid her goodbye.

Not walking far, Lisette was stopped by Penelope who asked to speak to her. The young woman had a scathing look on her face. "May we talk? Ken spent two days with me last weekend. He stayed overnight at our home on Saturday. The corporal asked me to share his room for the night, but I refused. However, there were a lot of kisses. Ken and I have a special bond. I know how to please him and build up his ego. I am his first love. He ended his courtship with Audra and returned to me. We have rekindled our love, and he will end his courtship with you soon. Bow out now and save your dignity."

Lisette was flabbergasted, but she kept her poise. "Miss Adams, your story is false. Kenton has already asked my father for my hand. I call your bluff; you may go on your merry way with your lies."

By the time that Lisette got into the surrey with Audra and her parents, she was sobbing. She confided to her hosts the conversations of the girls and Penelope's at the church, "Penelope was like a witch, tempting me to bite into her poisonous apple to destroy my life."

Having compassion for her friend, Audra tried to comfort her. "Lisette, Penelope has lied and manipulated. She is jealous because Kenton rejected her in favor of you. Some time ago, the girl came to me, and told me not to steal Derek from her. She claimed that the two of them were infatuated with each other. When I told Derek this news, he had a laughing fit. He later rebuked her, and now she avoids him."

"What about the observations the girls at the church made concerning them being together?"

"Kenton will refute Penelope's lies, but he will have to explain the other."

Daniel also tried to console Lisette, "My dear, I pray that the Lord will give you peace. Think on this scripture found in Psalm 37:1, "Do not fret because of evil doers."

She nodded. "Yes, I will write it down."

After preaching at the garrison, Derek arrived at the Kirk ranch for the noon meal. Audra summarized her friend's dilemma for him. Lisette was resting with a headache and had no desire for food.

After their dinner, Derek asked to counsel her in the parlor. He had prayed about the situation and had some insight to share with her. "Lisette, we don't fight against flesh and blood but against the powers of wickedness in the heavenly places. I believe that the devil has sent an assignment against you and Kenton to destroy your love, your trust, and your future marriage."

"Yes, I agree."

"My question to you is, will you allow it?"

She put her hand on her forehead in frustration. "No, I will not, but I feel so hurt."

The sergeant spoke in a serious tone, "You must say this: No weapon formed against me shall prosper." He referenced Isaiah 54:17.

"I will."

A knock was heard on the parlor door. "Ladies, the surrey is ready to take you to the train station for your trip to El Paso."

When the group arrived at the station, Kenton was waiting for them. With a big smile, he ran to help Lisette down from the buggy. She tried to be brave, but broke down and started to weep.

He was distressed to find her so distraught. "Sweetheart, are you ill?" He tried to embrace her, but she stiffened against him.

"Do not touch me!" And she peered at him angrily.

"What is it? What is wrong? Come, let us sit down on this bench to talk."

Approaching her friends, Audra informed them, "Derek and I will be nearby." She whispered to Kenton, "Pray, you are in bad trouble." He looked up at her mystified.

Directing her gaze to Kenton, Lisette asked, "Where were you last weekend?"

"I helped some friends get ready for their wedding anniversary reception."

Then she divulged in detail what Penelope had told her. As she talked, deep anger rose up in the young man, and he almost shouted, "Lies, all lies! That woman is despicable!"

"Did you stay overnight at the Adams home?"His aspect was sheepish. "Yes, Mr. Adams and I had just finished a long list of jobs and repairs. I was about to leave at dusk when a storm blew in with lightning. It was too dangerous for me to ride my horse to the garrison. Then it grew dark with much rain. I was compelled to stay the night."

"All right, I did not believe Penelope's lies, but that's not all." And she began to cry again, using a handkerchief to wipe her eyes. He tried to put his arm around her, but she would not let him. She told him about the eye witnesses' report of Penelope and him together at the church.

He ran his hands through his hair in frustration. "At the church, Penelope and her family came and crowded in next to me in the pew. When she put her arm on the back of the pew, I got up and left."

"When was that, at the benediction?"

"No! Two minutes after she sat down. After church, Penelope took me by the wrist to introduce me to her relatives. Then I left."

"You let her manipulate you, and allowed her to touch you, to compromise you."

"My love, you are overreacting. It did not mean anything."

Pressing her lips together, she argued, "Apparently, she thought it did. You did not resist her advances, but chose to stay by her side. Why did you not leave, because you liked her flirtation and fawning?"

"This is not worth discussing, my darling."

"Do you not care that I feel betrayed?" Lisette was wringing her hands.

The corporal's eyes flared. "You insult me. Betrayal is far from a soldier's code of honor."

But his fiancée was not pacified. "If you did not have the will power to withstand this temptation, then what will you do when the next vixen comes along?"

Gritting his teeth, he retorted, "There will not be a next

time. I assure you!"

Lisette could not keep back her tears. "I can't conceal that this pain in me is real. Do not come to call on me again. I no longer trust you."

Kenton became nervous and made his plea, "Sweetheart, I am sorry that I hurt you. It was not intentional. I see the error of my poor judgment. Please forgive me."

She looked at her watch. "I must go. It has been an experience knowing you. Goodbye."

"No! You will not leave like this. Lisette, you are precious to me, and I love you!" And he took her hands into his, but she pushed them away.

"I forgive you, Ken. Now let me go. My head is pounding, and I do not feel well."

As Lisette boarded the train, she looked back; the tears in her eyes matched those of Kenton's.

In the distance, Derek was about to help Audra get on the train, Kenton came near and made a plea, "Audra, will you convince Lisette not to end our courtship?"

"I will certainly try. Ken, I hope you have learned your lesson."

"I guess so."

Perplexed, Kenton fixed his gaze on Derek. "Do you agree with what Audra just said to me?"

"Completely, a man does not dally with one female when he has a courtship with another. Read in Proverbs about the wanton woman."

Kenton shared his account of the disastrous weekend with the sergeant. "I did not reveal this to Lisette, but Penelope came to my bedroom in the night. The door was locked, and I told her to go away. I left the house at dawn."

Shaking his head in dismay after hearing his friend's story, Derek remarked, "What were you thinking? At the church, you should have left the pew the minute Penelope sat next to you. Flee temptation and the seductress!"

Bewildered, he asked, "Oh God, I repent of my careless and unwise actions. What do I do now to win Lisette back?"

"Continue to tell her you love her, and let the Holy Spirit lead you."

"My pursuit of Audra has taken relentless prayer. I keep telling her that I love her. Lisette is an exceptionally fine young woman. Do not give up on winning back her love. I imagine that it will not happen in a day."

~~~~~~~

The following week, Derek and Kenton traveled to El Paso; Dr. Kirk and his granddaughter met them. The sergeant greeted Audra with a kiss. It was a poignant moment.

Except for a few moments at the train station in Columbus, it had been two weeks since Kenton had seen Lisette. With flowers in hand, he knocked on the door of the Galt family. The mother informed him, "My daughter has walked to the mansion."

So, he hurried to that home. He encountered Jenny and asked, "Is Lisette here? I wish to speak to her."She returned with a glint in her eye. "She will meet you in the parlor."

When Lisette saw Kenton enter, her mind was in turmoil. "My longing for him is so real".

He nervously spoke, "I brought red roses for you which
~~~~~~~

symbolize love."

"Thank you. They are radiant." She brought them to her nose to smell the fragrance.

"Lisette, I am extremely penitent for the hurt that I caused you. I apologize for my callous attitude about the incident. I have repented before God for my stupidity. My friendship with the Adams family has come to a close. I pray that you will not end our courtship. My love for you is deep, and I want you in my life."

"Presently, there will be no courtship between us, but maybe in time I will consider it again."

"May I at least call on you?

"No." And she walked from the room.

Kenton was headed to the door when Audra called to him, "Ken, please stay and have supper with us. You are a guest, and I beg you to visit awhile. Be patient with Lisette. God will soften her heart."

"All right, ask Lisette if she minds if I remain for the supper."

When Audra asked her friend if the corporal might join them, she nodded her assent.

The conversation around the table was enjoyable and congenial. The four friends enjoyed being together again.

Yet Lisette was unusually quiet, and after the supper she excused herself, "The meal was delicious. I shall take my leave."

However, Derek interrupted her plan. "Lisette, we need you to play rummy with us. It will be partners, the girls against the guys." His eyes pleaded with her to stay

"I guess I could play a couple of games."

There was competition and laughter around the table. They played several games. As it was getting late, the group decided to adjourn.

Derek turned to Kenton, "Would you walk with Lisette and escort her home?"

"Yes sir, I would be pleased to accompany her."

Glaring at Derek, she had to be polite. "Thank you, Ken."

As the two walked toward the door, Lisette stopped. "I must get something." She returned carrying the bouquet of red roses. As they left, Derek gave her a meaningful grin. The young couple walked slowly in the direction of her home. The street lights guided their steps. The stars glistened above, and the full moon gave extra light for their short journey.

Kenton broached the silence, "Did you receive my letter?"

"Yes. Thank you for your thoughtfulness."

"How was your week at the hospital?"

"It was busy, but we only admitted a few geriatric patients. How was your week?"

"It was tiring. I kept wondering how you were. I have missed you, Lisette."

She wanted to say, "Good." But instead, she paused. "I just need some time to let the memory fade."

"You take all the time you need. I love you, sweetheart. Good night."

Her voice was pleasant, "Goodnight, Ken."

As Kenton descended the porch steps, he turned, and she looked back at him.

The next morning Lisette came early to the mansion with

an apple pie that her mother had baked for the guests. As a hired girl, she came often to help with tasks for Dr. and Mrs. Kirk. Audra spied her in the kitchen preparing breakfast. No one was around since Derek and Dr. Kirk were reading the morning newspaper, and Jenny was watering her flowers. So, Audra asked her, "Would you please sit down at the table for a serious talk? Lisette, my grandmother used to tell me a proverb when I would magnify a problem larger than it really was. She would say, 'My child, don't make a mountain out of a mole hill'. Part of Kenton's offense was that he was of a victim of circumstance. The other part was his lack of wisdom. If you make his mistake too big of a mountain, he may never climb it."

"Is that what I am doing?

"Yes, you are, dear friend, I have known Kenton longer than you have. He is an honorable man. I rate his character the same caliber as Derek's."

"I am sincerely afraid to trust him."

"You already know how noble he is, and he has chosen you for his beloved. If you cast him off over a petty offense, you will regret it. But all is not lost. You took some baby steps last night toward unity: the supper together, the card game, and the walk to your home. Was it not enjoyable being in his presence?"

"Actually, it was."

"My advice to you is not to let Kenton dangle too long so that he grows weary. You have to put away the hurt and the memory of it. I struggled with hate and anguish for several months over an offense. I am thankful that Derek persevered with me."

"Do you think that Kenton will return to see me?" Doubt clouded her face.

Audra gave her a cunning look. "I will make sure of it. Derek has mentioned that he would like for you and I and also Raquel to perform a concert for the soldiers at Camp Cavalry. The garrison has acquired a piano. Next Saturday night is the date. While we are in Columbus, we can pick up our graduation dresses. You and Kenton can spend some time together. We can study for our final exam on the train. What do you say?"

Lisette appeared enthusiastic. "It sounds terrific!"

"By the way, pack your flamenco dress."

"Oh my, what will the soldiers think about our fancy dresses?"

Smiling coyly, Audra retorted, "We shall see."

In his parents' presence, Kenton imparted the history of the incident with Penelope. When Kenton's dad, Zane, heard the reason why his son and Lisette had parted, he was extremely disgusted with Penelope's behavior. In anger he burst out, "That brazen hussy tried to make a nincompoop out of you! She strived to lure you into the claws of her lust!"

Kenton sighed in remorse, "The whole thing turned into a disaster. I know that a man is not supposed to cry, but I had to resist it."

His mother, Kimberly, was encouraging. "Ken, the Lord can restore your romance with Lisette. I will pray for her to love you again."

"I appreciate that, Mother."

A solution popped up in the father, "Son, go and purchase something expensive for Lisette, a keepsake."

His mother was demurely secretive. "I have the perfect piece of jewelry for this lovely girl."

25

From sunup to sundown, the week passed quickly, and Audra and Lisette once more boarded the train to travel to the Kirk ranch. Derek came to pick up the young ladies at the station in Columbus, but Kenton did not come to meet Lisette. She remembered that she did not come to see him off when he left El Paso.

The next day Kenton arrived at Shiloh ranch on an army motorcycle with a side car. He asked to speak to Lisette, and she greeted him cordially, "Good morning, sir."

"You look gorgeous today." And she gave him an endearing smile. In the cool of the day, they strolled to the patio where fuchsia Bougainvillea flowers trailed down from the tile roof. It was a serene setting. A three-tiered fountain bubbled nearby, and a cardinal flashed his plumage in a low-lying bush.

Kenton silently debated, "I desire to renew my bond with Lisette. Yet I am leery of showing any affection to her".

However, when she ran her finger across the back of his hand, it ignited a spark. He brought her hand to his lips and kissed it.

The pretty young woman gazed at him. "Ken, I will agree

to your courtship, if you still want it."

He was insistent, "Yes, I want it, but we must establish one thing. Either you will trust me or you will not!"

"I will trust you."

With those words, he leaned over and kissed her rosy cheek. "I would wish to start every day kissing you good morning."

"Yes, I would like that, too."

Abruptly Kenton got down on one knee and handed a small wrapped gift to her. When she opened it, a ring with a large diamond sparkled up at her.

Searching her face, he promised, "Lisette, I do pledge my life to you forever. There is no one alive that I love as much as you. Will you marry me?"

Visibly surprised, she quickly agreed, "Yes, I give you, my love." And he placed the ring on her finger.

Then Lisette felt his hands on the back of her shoulders as he eased her close to him. Encompassed in his arms, she submitted to his touch. Holding her gently, she clutched to Kenton like a woodpecker grasps a tree. He responded to her embrace with tender kisses. She caressed his face with her fingers, and he stroked her hair to the bottom of her long curls. Their hearts were joined together again.

Lisette held up her hand to gaze at her engagement ring. Kenton could tell that his fiancée was impressed with it. In awe, she turned to him. "How do I merit this? This ring is the most stunning thing I have ever seen!"

A grin slid across his lips. "It befits you as you are the most dazzling thing I have ever seen!"

"Let me explain. There is a history to this ring. It is not old and worn, but quite new. Not long ago, my elderly aunt was in the hospital gravely ill. My uncle purchased this diamond ring and brought it to her where she lay in the bed. When my aunt put it on, she seemed to perk up. Since her husband was of the miserly sort, she was extremely happy for such an expensive gift. He was vastly satisfied as his wife talked of little else but her ring. She showed it to the nurses and the doctor. The ring magnified the love of this wedded pair."

"How romantic! The story is enchanting."

"My aunt passed away a short time later and also my uncle. He left the ring in his estate to my mother, but she never wore it. She thought that it was too fancy for her."

In this joy filled moment, Lisette confessed, "Ken, to be in love with you is what I dreamed of and hoped for."

~~~~~~~

When the soldiers at Camp Cavalry found out that young ladies would give a concert on Saturday night at the garrison, they lined up three hours before the event. The mess hall was packed with an unprecedented attendance. The men were awed when Audra, Lisette, and Raquel entered the hall wearing flamenco dresses. Their gospel music was met with much applause from the soldiers.

Derek delivered a message on spiritual warfare, citing James 4:7, "Submit yourselves, then, to God. Resist the devil and he will flee from you." He implored his audience to act on God's word.

Glancing around, Audra saw that the soldiers gave him their rapt attention. None of them fidgeted or looked bored.
~~~~~~~

"He preaches as one with authority," she surmised.

Ending the meeting with the salvation message, Derek quoted John 3:16, "For God so loved the world that he gave his one and only Son, that whoever believes in him shall not perish but have eternal life." He then gave an invitation, "If anyone wants to receive Christ into his life, come to the altar".

A soldier came forward to pray. The man confessed, "I have been under a heavy burden of sin from my past. I have repented of my wrong doing. Forgiveness has given me peace in my new life in Christ."

The young ladies sang a closing hymn, and Matthew prayed the benediction. After the concert ended, the soldiers formed a long line to thank the musicians.

A certain officer, Lieutenant Asten, introduced himself to Audra. What he boldly said to her made her gasp, "Miss Kirk, you are the essence of beauty. I seriously want to propose a courtship and marriage to you. You will know the depths of my passion and my love."

Audra quickly replied, "Sir, I have a beau. His name is Sergeant Derek Rands."

The lieutenant sneered. "You need a real man, not that pipsqueak chaplain."

Her hands flew to her hips, "He could make you bite the dust! Now, I must greet the other soldiers. Good night, sir."

However, the officer pressed the subject. "I will speak to you later, pretty lady."

Riveting her eyes onto the man, she declared, "Sir, I see that you have a problem with lust; you need Jesus!"

The lieutenant walked away with a smirking grin.

The soldiers next in line heard her comment. First, they began to chuckle; then they broke out into roaring laughter. One of them spoke up, "Miss Audra, we gave you an ovation for your singing, but after hearing your remark to the lieutenant, we applaud your spirit. That soldier has boasted many times of his conquests of women."

The dialogue between Audra and Lieutenant Asten spread throughout the garrison like wildfire. Derek later questioned her about the incident, and he snickered at her pluck. He then made an astute observation. "Audra, no one will ever be able to bamboozle you."

~~~~~~~

A note came to Matthew and Raquel from Reverend Barr. "I want to meet with you both at the church at your earliest convenience."

They looked at each other nervously and perplexed, "Have we done something wrong?" They made an appointment to meet with the reverend in his office.

When the wedded couple entered the church, Pastor Barr kindly welcomed them. "My friends, I am resigning my pastorate at the church soon. My wife and I will move to Colorado to be closer to our family. Matthew, you are an excellent preacher, and you have a servant's heart. I beseech you to consider becoming the next pastor of the church here in Columbus. You may still live at your ranch as the congregation is widely scattered. If you are interested, I will give my recommendation to the board. However, the church body will vote. I understand that you will be released from the army in the coming days. You can obtain your minister's
~~~~~~~

license by correspondence. The two of you can pray and let me know of your decision."

Raquel looked at Matthew in dismay, but his attitude was confident. "We shall pray and hear from the Lord."

To become a pastor's wife gave doubts to Raquel. "My dear, will the parishioners give credence to a divorced woman in the ministry?"

"Yes, I believe that they will. Most of them know that you were abandoned. I am favorable to take the position. If the church body votes to receive us, then it will be a confirmation of God's will."

On the following Sunday, Pastor Barr again met with the wedded pair. Matthew reported, "We have prayed, and I will apply for the pastorate. I will be discharged from the army in two months."

The pastor immediately contacted the board who presented the soldier's petition to the congregation. The decision was unanimous; Matthew would become their next pastor.

26

Returning to her home in El Paso, Lisette was in high spirits. She flashed her engagement ring in front of her parents. Their mouths fell open; they were so astounded. They congratulated their daughter, but her father was skeptical as he viewed the large diamond. "Lisette, army pay is lower class income. Your soldier must have spent his whole life savings on this expensive ring. It looks like a vanity item, a rich man's status symbol."

"No, daddy, it was left to his mother in an estate."

"That woman should have sold the ring for a large sum and given the money to the poor. It says so in the Bible."

"Who said it, Seth?" Kate, the wife, was frowning.

"Jesus?"

"No, it was not Jesus, but Judas!" Kate was a Bible scholar.

"Oh, I guess I was mistaken." Her husband appeared sheepish in his error. "By the way, daughter, when do you and Kenton plan to marry?"

With anticipation, Lisette's face glowed. "Kenton will the leave the army in one month and will not re-enlist. We want to marry as soon as we can find a suitable place to live here in El Paso."

Fear eked into her father's demeanor. As head of the household, he felt like a cat on a hot tin roof about to slide off. "Lisette, darling, we cannot afford to pay for a wedding. You and Kenton will have to elope. You know how tight our finances are around here. Also, if you no longer help us with your nursing job, we will have our electricity turned off. Until your mother finishes night school and obtains a better job, we will be in dire straits. Could you postpone your wedding for a few months? Besides, your courtship has been of a short duration."

Tears started to immerse her lashes, and she hurried from the room. She could hear her parents arguing. Kate was angry and withstood her husband. "Lisette will not postpone her wedding. She has helped support this family's livelihood for years while you spent money on your hobbies. There is a scripture in the Bible, 2 Corinthians 12:14, 'After all, children should not have to save up for their parents, but parents for their children'. Go ahead and turn off the electricity You will not mooch off of our daughter any longer!"

He started to pace the floor. "That would be a difficulty for the family."

The wife put her hands on her hips and stepped up close to her husband's face. "My dear, you have a motorbike in the garage that you rarely use because we cannot afford the gasoline. There is transportation to your job, and that motorbike should be sold so that Lisette may have a traditional wedding."

He argued, "I cannot sell my motorbike. That's my 'baby'. I have put a lot of time and expense into building it."

"You are undeniably selfish! While on this subject, you can also sell your gun and coin collections."

The next day, Kate inquired of her husband, "Have you made plans to sell any of your possessions?"

He scowled at her. "No, Lisette can pay for her own wedding."

With those words, she decided to take action. She brought out a kerosene lantern and contacted the electric company to cancel the service. After her work, she went to the pawn shop and hocked her wedding ring. When the children returned from school, she explained, "Do your homework while it is still light. Then do your chores later. I cooked a meal on the gas stove. Your supper of beef roast and baked apples is ready. Potatoes and scrambled eggs are left for your papa."

Kate left a note for her husband. "You must wash your clothes in a bucket and pack your own lunch of bread and cheese."

The older brother was accustomed to caring for his younger sister, so their mother rode her bicycle to her night class. When Seth Galt returned in the evening from his work, he was in for a rude awakening. His wife had rebelled, and he was now confronted with deprivation and discomfort. He was pacing the floor when Kate walked in from her night class. There was only a lantern for light.

"What in the world is going on here?"

An argument was about to ensue. "I will no longer put up with your selfish ways. You are not a bachelor, but a father with three children. Do you want your daughter to remember you as a self-centered ogre?"

In defeat, her husband threw his hands into the air. "All right, my darling, I will sell the motorbike. I seldom ride it anyway. I will also sell some of my guns."

"Thank you, I appreciate this noble gesture."

He frowned, "Where is your wedding ring, Kate?"

She stared at him in a self-righteous manner. "In the pawn shop."

He breathed a sigh of exasperation. "Please call Lisette to come into the living room. I want to talk to her about her upcoming nuptials."

The daughter entered and wondered what conversation would ensue. With compassion, her father spoke, "Lisette, go ahead and make plans for your wedding. I will pay for it."

He then turned to his wife and snickered. "I thought I married a 'kitten', but in reality, you are a 'tiger'."

~~~~~~~

It was the day of the graduation for the First Phase medical students. Many family members and guests had come to El Paso to see Audra graduate. The Kirks, Raquel and Matthew, Dr. Kirk and Jenny, Pablo and Maria, and Derek with his parents were in attendance. For Lisette, her family, Kenton, his parents, and the grandparents made an appearance. Some of the guests had reservations at the hotel.

A group of students crowded around Lisette to view her large diamond engagement ring. A classmate exclaimed, "Very nice, Lisette! How does that diamond measure?"

"It is one carat."

Ian commented, "That ring does not look paid for."

Lisette glanced up at him. "It is paid for. I hope that I
~~~~~~~

deserve something so costly."

He chuckled and nodded his head. "You are worthy of it, Lisette."

"Thank you for your kind words, Ian."

After Ian walked away from gazing at Lisette's engagement ring, he felt a deep pang of regret in his gut. He speculated, "If it had not been for my indiscretion, the lovely nurse could have been my fiancée. I have no doubt that Lisette would have made me a superb mate. I wonder if I will ever find a wife as fine as Miss Galt."

In the graduation ceremony, Dr. Scott announced the top students: Audra Kirk, Ian Dodd, and Lisette Galt. All of the students had completed the First Phase of the medical school. Ian, Joshua, and Lisette were among those who would go on to complete the second year of the school. Audra had plans to take the state exam to receive her physician's license.

Dr. Kirk and Jenny hosted a graduation tent reception at their mansion for Audra's and Lisette's families and friends. It was a celebration with much food and merriment. Ian and Joshua came to the party to visit for a short while. Derek made an effort to converse with them to continue their friendship.

Finding Elizabeth, Lisette embraced her fondly. "Mrs. Kirk, I am very grateful to you for this gorgeous dress that I am wearing today. I only had one, old, Sunday dress for this occasion."

With tears, Lisette encountered Kimberly, Kenton's mother, and kissed the woman's hand. "Mrs. Lott, I am so thankful for this precious diamond ring. It is truly amazing."

The soldiers with their paramours circulated and chatted

with the guests. Then the two couples joined each other for refreshments. Dr. Scott and his wife came to visit at their table.

Audra inquired of the doctor, "How are your son, daughter-in-law, and their baby?

"Very well, indeed. As a matter of fact, they are expecting again." With a sly grin, he continued to speak, "I bought a Chinese checkers game and Dominoes for them, but that didn't help."

The young people burst into laughter, and Mrs. Scott rolled her eyes.

After the doctor and his wife left, Lisette remarked, "I have never seen the lighter side of Dr. Scott. He is always so serious, austere, and stoic at the hospital. In a nurses' meeting, he stated specifically for us not to confide any personal problems to him. I applaud his wisdom of not getting personally involved with any woman."

Coming to her daughter's table, Kate Galt sat down next to Kenton, "Ken, Seth has worked in the coal mine for many years, and he has a chronic cough that medicine cannot cure. I am concerned that he may have 'black lung'. If there is ever a job opening at your lumber yard, would you please consider him? He is honest, friendly, and hard working."

"Mrs. Galt, we do have future plans to open a gas station. I believe that there will be many more cars on the road in the future. Have Mr. Galt come and apply."

As the group conversed, Derek pulled out a letter from the insane asylum director and read it to them.

To the Soldiers and the Ladies:

Greetings to you ministers in the name of the Lord. Here

is a report of the results of your ministry to the residents of this institution. The greatest improvement is that there is more peace in the asylum among the men. Three of the men have gained so much sobriety and self -control that they have returned to their families on a trial basis. One fellow who claimed that he heard voices, no longer hears them. Most of the criminals have stopped fighting, and will be re-evaluated to enter the penitentiary to serve the remainder of their sentence there. The cooperation of the men can only be credited to God's grace. Several of the men are constantly asking for the soldiers to return, and they beg for more music. Would you please consider returning as soon as your schedules permit? I have applied for a stipend for the four of you.

With much gratitude and appreciation,
Carl Patton, Director, Institution for the Insane

27

In El Paso, Audra packed her trunk and returned home to Columbus on the train accompanied by her parents.

Even though it was almost evening, she wanted to visit Doreen at the Clarks' home. Welcoming Audra, the woman was bubbling over with excitement, "Wade and I are in a courtship, and we will be married soon in California. Mrs. Clark has given me her elegant wedding dress. Even though it is old, it is in pristine condition."

Audra frowned. "Doreen, I am skeptical; I do not want Wade to mistreat you like he did my sister."

She assured her friend, "Much prayer was involved in my decision. I am happy, and I have peace."

"I am very glad for you."

"There is other news that I want to tell you. Mr. Clark passed away seven days after the couple's fiftieth wedding anniversary. Mrs. Clark is collecting her things and will soon go to live with her son. The dear lady has long wished to be near her grandchildren. And listen to this! An amazing thing has just become known to me! Mr. and Mrs. Clark left their grand house to me in their will! Their son, a busy merchant did not have the time or the desire to fix it up for sale. He also expressed his appreciation to me for restoring health to his parents."

"That is marvelous."

"This is my question for you. Would you be interested in buying the house from me for $500, which includes the furniture? It is worth much more even with the repairs, but it is my favor to you."

"This is extremely generous of you. Yes, I do not even have to think about it. I will definitely purchase the home."

"Confidentially, I did not tell Wade about this inheritance. I want him to love me for who I am and not for my money. I already have some savings to bring to the marriage."

"I totally understand."

The young woman handed a large envelope to Audra. "Enclosed are the keys to the iron gate and to the front door of the property. You may deposit the money in my account at the bank. I will leave the bill of sale and the deed there for you to pick up. I have cleaned the house from top to bottom. It was quite enjoyable since I had never lived in such lavish surroundings before." Then Doreen began to giggle. "As you can see, the house is filled with antique European furniture. Mr. Clark's son called the large, ornate pieces 'dinosaurs'. Also left in the home is a Civil War collection upstairs. However, the room is locked. The key for that room is missing, but neither his son, nor I, had any desire for the memorabilia anyway. I am sure that, Derek, your beau, will find it interesting. I wish you much happiness as you live in this home. Please keep in touch with me. We must continue to write to each other."

Audra nodded. "Yes, we will always be friends."

In her good-bye, Doreen's eyes clouded up. "My past, sordid, life is so changed because of you. I will always remember how you picked me up when I had fallen so low and had no hope."

~~~~~~~

At Shiloh, the Kirk household was a stir with a weekend reception for the marriage of Dr. Kirk and Jenny. The celebration was a lively party with friends and family present. The guests expressed best wishes to the newlyweds and also to Matthew as their new pastor. In the large dining room, Raquel sat next to her husband. Sofie and Andrew were both seated on their daddy's lap and rested against his chest with his arms around them. They looked content and secure in this setting. The children only jumped down when it was time to serve the supper.

Daniel had invited Derek to attend the festivities, but as the evening grew dark, Audra knew that he would not come. She would travel to El Paso in the morning to help Lisette with her wedding plans. There would be no chance for her to visit with the sergeant. It was probable that he was detained for some business at the garrison. However, Audra lamented to her sister, "I am very disappointed that I have not seen or heard from Derek this entire weekend".

The next day, the Kirks were ready to take their daughter to the train station when a message came for her.

Dear Audra,

I quickly write this note. I just received news that may be of interest to you. This next Saturday, Mr. and Mrs. Allen will come
~~~~~~~

with the children and a social worker to the church. Some couples in the congregation have expressed an interest in adoption. My parents will request custody of Gabriela. When I am married, I will adopt the child and raise her as my daughter.

Derek

Wrinkling up her nose, Audra appeared flabbergasted, and she brooded, "Derek did not say that he and i would raise Gabriela together. My negative past experience with the sergeant has kept me from loving him. I have hardened my heart against him, and it feels like a heavy chain around my neck. I delayed in giving Derek an answer to his courtship. Though I allowed him to call on me, my decision was to let the chaplain dangle. Now I am keenly aware that my vow may have caused me to miss out on an exceptional husband. If my relationship with him is indeed over, it's my own fault."

As the carriage rambled along, she kept thinking about Derek's message. With tears trickling down, grief was clinging to her like a grave cloth.

At the station, Audra bid her family goodbye and boarded the train; she scanned the area for an empty seat. As she walked down the aisle, she was aware that everyone was gawking at her. Everywhere she went, her red hair, ivory skin and beautiful profile brought her stares. Actually, she was quite used to the attention and often greeted the people. Audra spied an empty seat behind two Mexican men. They were dressed in expensive suits and were probably wealthy ranchers or businessmen. The pretty *señorita* did not escape their view, and they smiled up at her.

Suddenly, the train lurched forward and she fell into the

lap of the Mexican man in the aisle seat. He helped her up, and she meant to say *perdóneme* (pardon me), but instead she said, "*Con su permiso*." (with your permission).

The man grinned. "*Como no, señorita, en cualquier momento.*" (Sure lady, anytime).

Blushing bright pink, she murmured, "I meant to say *perdóneme*." The men went from grinning to chuckling aloud. The people on the train turned around to see what was happening, and all eyes were on her. The funny incident broke her melancholy mood. She would tell Lisette about it, and her friend would laugh and think it hilarious.

Yet alone in her room at the mansion that night, Audra's mind was racing, "If Derek has forsaken me, I fear the notion of becoming an old maid." Finally dismissing her distress, Audra turned her thoughts to the coming week, "Aside from studying for the state physician exam, I look forward to helping with the wedding preparations for Lisette. We will also visit the orphanage, and I will offer to accompany the orphans on the train ride to the adoption meeting in Columbus."

~~~~~~~

An incident had occurred on the previous Saturday at the garrison. In the barracks, Private David lay in his bed with his face down trying to stifle his weeping. On Friday night, he had gone to visit his fiancée. With little regret in her words, the young woman informed him, "I am sorry, but there will be no future for us together. I am now in love with a prominent man in the community, and we will marry in the coming days. I am giving your ring back to you."

Private David was devastated in the rejection of his be-
~~~~~~~

trothed, and he began to mourn his loss. He kept repeating, "I was not good enough for her. I wish I could die."

The private's army buddies were worried since their friend had skipped breakfast and the noon meal. They tried to talk to him, "David, this sorrow will pass. You have your whole life ahead of you."

Later in the day, the men sought out Chaplain Sergeant Rands, "Sir, come and talk to our friend, Private David. He has taken to his bed and is sobbing over the loss of his sweetheart."

Derek came and counseled the young man, "Pray for victory in this matter, son, and God will undertake; you will get through this." However, the sergeant's advice was to no avail; the private could not get control of his emotions.

A commanding officer came to the barracks and discerned that the private was despondent. So, the officer confiscated David's rifle and pistol. He left an order for the chaplain, "Keep a vigil over this young man. Get another soldier to assist you."

During this time, Derek prayed, "Lord, in Jesus name, intervene on Private David's behalf."

The sergeant thought about the party at Shiloh, "Missing the reception at the Kirk ranch is a regret, but duty has called."

Private David kept his bed all day Sunday and would not eat any meals. By Monday morning, he was in a weakened condition. He reported for duty, but his eyes were bloodshot and his head was aching.

In the inspection, the commanding officer observed that the soldier was trembling. "Son, I command you to bed rest and to take food. I warn you to stop grieving, or you will be shipped out to a special army hospital."

On Tuesday morning, David barely made it through the inspection; in the physical exercises, he fell to the ground. Because he had been an exemplary soldier, he was allowed to stay on duty. However, by noon, he slumped over, and his buddies carried him to the barracks. An order came for him to be transported from the garrison to enter a hospital the next day.

Yet later in the afternoon, something happened that changed everything for Private David's state of mind. A letter came from a girl named Sarah. She was the younger sister of his former fiancée. The private was incredulous as he read the note.

Dear David,

I hope that you are not sorrowful in the breakup with my sister. Life goes on, and this memory will soon fade. I am hesitant to write this, but I have admired you for sometime. You may write to me if you so desire. In two weeks on Saturday evening, there will be a box social for the young people in the town square. The ladies will invite the gentlemen to share a box supper of tasty food. Would you care to join me and try my fried chicken and chocolate cake?

I pray the Lord bless you as you serve our country.

Yours truly,

Sarah

The private's mood went from despair of life to delight in his destiny. He was ecstatic as he showed the letter to his buddies. He excitedly told them, "The younger sister is prettier and sweeter than the older sister to whom I was engaged! I apologize for indulging in self-pity and negative behavior."

He also expressed appreciation to Derek, "Thank you, sir, for persevering with me in my anguish."

The young man went to the mess hall for supper, and his letter was passed from table to table with whoops and hollers from the men.

Derek snickered at the scene and reflected, "The letter was the answer to my prayer."

Instead of being shipped out to a special army hospital, Private David was allowed to go back on duty.

28

On Saturday morning, an orphan meeting was scheduled at the Columbus church. The Allens, the children, Audra, and the social worker, Miss Selina, traveled by train. The youngsters enjoyed the train ride, peering out the windows to see the desert cacti.

Audra was waiting by the church steps for Derek to arrive. When he saw her, he quickened his step; he drew her into his arms and kissed her tenderly and ardently.

When he released her, she whispered, "People are staring at us."

"Do you really care?"

She began to giggle. "No, but the meeting will start soon." Breathing a sigh of relief, she considered, "The sergeant's kiss has melted away all of my anxiety, and my mood is exuberant. My doubts about the future are erased."

Eyeing her beauty, he commented, "You are like the rose of Sharon."

Her lovely face was wreathed in smiles.

"Derek, I have something to tell you that is of immense importance. You will be very pleased, but I guess it can wait until later."

When the couple entered the church for the meeting, she glimpsed her childhood friends, Wyatt and Ruby Grant. Derek was introduced to the couple, and they chatted briefly.

Only a few people were in attendance at the meeting. They were mostly young married couples. Garth and Elena Rands came to petition for custody of Gabriela, with the pretext that Derek and Audra would eventually adopt her.

Mr. and Mrs. Allen brought the children to meet the prospective parents. These included Timothy, four, Caleb, five, and Ethan, six. The little boys were rowdy, running up and down the aisles and between the pews of the church. It was like herding a bunch of cats. After introductions were made with children and adults, the couples filled out an application for their preferred child. The participants were then interviewed by Miss Selina, the social worker.

Calling to the rambunctious boys, Mr. Allen offered, "Let's go play in the church yard."

The cemetery adjoined the church, and the children immediately discovered it. The little boys climbed onto the tombstones, straddled them, and pretended to ride on them like they were horses.

When the Grants finished their interview, they returned to their seats to await the results. Wyatt put his arm around Ruby, and she started to weep. She buried her face into her husband's shoulder to hide her sobbing.

Noticing this, Audra went to investigate. "Ruby, what is the matter? Why are you crying?"

Wyatt replied, "We have a six -year-old son. For the past four years, our attempts to have another child have been in vain. Ruby had her heart set on adopting the baby girl. We have been informed that the child is not available."

With boldness, Audra retorted, "I will arrange for you to adopt baby Gabriela." Ruby perked up, and both husband and wife gazed at her in utter incredulity.

Explaining to Derek that her friends had petitioned for the baby girl, Audra pleaded, "Would you mind if we allowed the Grants to adopt Gabriela? We will have our own baby."

His eyebrows rose, and he gave her an astonished look. "What did you say?"

"Did you not hear me?"

"Yes, I heard you. Say it again."

With a coquettish grin, Audra reached up and caressed his face. "I love you. We will have our own baby."

"Well, if that's the case, then by all means, we shall see that the Grants are able to adopt Gabriela."

The orphan meeting was very successful. All of the little boys were adopted and grinning as they went home with their new mommy and daddy.

The Grants were effusive in their thanks to Derek and Audra, "Dear friends, we sincerely appreciate your sacrifice. We are overjoyed in this adoption." The wedded pair had gleeful expressions on their faces as they left the meeting carrying baby Gabriela.

As they exited the church, Audra pondered, "When I told Derek that I love him, I finally unveiled the vow and cast it down. I will no longer cling to it. The sorrow and heartache of the vow held me captive for many months. Now the chains are broken, and I am free from the bondage of the vow. It is a liberating feeling. All of my fears are gone."

~~~~~~~

The surrey was ready take Audra and the Rands to the Kirk Ranch, but she drew near to Derek instead. She gazed up into his handsome face. "Sergeant, will you take me for a ride on your horse far into the desert today?"

"You want to sit next to me in the saddle with my arms around you, is that it?"

She started giggling. "Yes, of course. Will you at least take me to Shiloh on Rio? My dress has a full skirt."

Taking the ends of her skirt, she stretched them out, and twirled around. "See, they will fit over the horse. I want to talk to you about an opportunity for us."The sergeant glanced at the frilly dress and shook his head. "No sweetheart. I have a counseling session with two recruits; they have been arguing and cursing each other. I will come to the ranch later today. I will get my Bible, sermon notes, clothes satchel and spend the night. You need to rest. We will spend the evening together."

Derek's thoughts were encompassing him as he rode his horse to the garrison, "My pursuit of Audra has been long and tumultuous. However, the story of my nursery rhyme is now a reality; the soldier has captured the fair lady's heart. It gives me colossal satisfaction that Miss Kirk confessed her love to me today."

The sergeant traveled to Shiloh ranch in the late afternoon. Audra had dressed in much finery. She sensed that this would be an important evening.

When Derek's arrival was announced, she ran to him, and it was very satisfying for the him to hold her close.
~~~~~~~

In speaking to her father, he asked, "Sir, may I have permission to wed your daughter? I will love Audra and care for her as she deserves."

"Son, you have my blessing. You are worthy of my daughter. Welcome to the family."

Entering the parlor, Derek sat down next to Audra on the love seat, and they chatted for a couple of minutes. Then he got down on one knee and searched the face of the beautiful young lady before him. He pulled a small case from his pocket with a marquee garnet ring inside.

With expectancy he presented it to her. "Audra, you fulfill all the hopes and dreams I could have prayed for. No man has ever been so in love as I am with you. Will you do me the honor of becoming my bride?"

Her eyes glittered in amazement as she looked at the ornate garnet ring. "Yes, nothing can hold me back from your love. I truly want to be with you forever."

"You are a treasure to me, and I will cherish you."

Drawing her into the circle of his arms, he bundled her close. She submitted to the intensity of his caress. There was such passion in his touch that it left her with a heady sensation. He kissed every part of her face. With his hands enmeshed in her hair, he found her lips, and it moved her to submit to his possession.

Derek's kiss came again and again as he breathed words of adoration. She never imagined that his love could be so exciting. Audra slid her arms around his neck, and he picked her up and swung her around. His joy was rapturous. This would be a marriage made in heaven. With his arm around her, she snuggled into the clutch of his side.

"Audra, I will have two weeks of furlough for a wedding and honeymoon. We can take it all in one fortnight or break it into two. My father has offered for us to have a wedding on the reservation, and that he would pay for it. Therefore, we would have another week for a wedding reception here in Columbus including a honeymoon. I will leave the choice up to you, and you can think about it."

"I would choose to have a wedding on the reservation. The Apache would enjoy our marriage celebration."

Derek gave her a broad smile. "I hoped that would be your decision. A wedding on the reservation would show the Apache people that we care about them, and that they are not forgotten. When would you wish to be married? Do you have a date in mind?"

"Yes. I will travel to Santa Fe and take the state physician exam next week. The following Saturday is Kenton and Lisette's wedding. I desire that we shall be married the weekend thereafter."

The sergeant expressed surprise. "You only need a short time to prepare for the wedding?"

"Yes. My mother and sister will help me. I just want to be with you."

Then, he seemed to be genuinely concerned. "I will need to quickly find a place for us to live."

"I already have a grand house for us!" Audra appeared excited.

He glanced at her puzzled. "Do not keep me in suspense, my lady."

"Doreen inherited the Clark's house, and she sold it to me for $500. I used my savings to pay for it; I have the deed with both of our names on it. The house is thirty years old and needs repairs, but it is a Godsend. This is what I wished to tell you today."

Followed by Derek, Audra pranced into the ranch's dining room, displaying her garnet engagement ring to her family. Her parents' reactions showed that they were thrilled. Daniel Kirk silently thanked God, "My prayer has been answered. I will finally have my long-awaited 'son.' Actually, I am doubly fortunate since Matthew is also in the same high caliber as Derek."

Smiling, Garth and Elena Rands were equally delighted for the match.

Telephoning the mansion, Derek and Audra shared the news of their engagement with grandfather Kirk and Jenny who were overjoyed with the announcement.

~~~~~~~

In the afternoon on Sunday, Audra suggested going to the Clark home to survey it. "I am anxious to explore the stately brick home." As they journeyed to the great house, she exclaimed, "In the distance, the home appears grandiose." The atmosphere exuded drama for the young couple as they traveled toward it.

The sergeant whistled. "Well, Miss Kirk, you are moving from one mansion to another. Every time I passed this way, I wanted to tour the inside of that dwelling. It is a place of intrigue and reminds me of a manor house of the Lords in England."
~~~~~~~

A red brick wall surrounded the five-acre estate. When Derek opened the large iron gate, Audra peered in and gasped; she was beset by fear. The yard was overgrown with weeds and cacti, tall trees covered the windows, and some of the shutters were partly hanging off the hinges. The board walkway that led to the entry was broken up and crumbling.

Gazing up at Derek mystified, she murmured, "Did I make a mistake in this purchase? I bought the property on impulse. Will this house become a money pit for us to refurbish? It was almost dusk when I last visited here, and I did not realize how bad the place looked."

Ignoring her pessimism, his attitude was dynamic as he inspected the outside of the house. "This estate is an excellent investment! The roof, bricks, and porch are in good condition. I will contact my army buddies to come and help revamp the yard and paint the iron gate."

Opening the front door, Derek took Audra's hand to explore the interior. They were awed by the exquisiteness and magnitude of the house. Her eyes wandered. "Come and see this woodwork; it is intricately carved. The parlor is furnished with Victorian furniture, and the fireplace supports an ornate mantel. The Renaissance paintings hung on the walls are classic, and the velvet draperies that bedeck the windows look expensive."

He escorted her into a dining room. "Here is a long table with upholstered leather chairs that seat twelve. This massive, European antique furniture reminds me of royalty. The oriental rugs on the hard wood floors do not look worn. I see that this main floor has three bedrooms, and an antiquated bathroom."

Entering a large kitchen with a pantry, Audra declared, "This room is decadent!"

"Yes, the floor is mostly rotted. I will build a new one and cover it with ceramic tile from Mexico. The back porch door will have to be replaced where a dog scratched and chewed it. I'm writing down notes of the repairs and upkeep to have this home ready before our wedding."

The couple climbed the staircase to the upstairs living quarters and encountered four bedrooms. Audra exclaimed, "The four poster beds, armoires, and marble inlaid dressers are magnificent! The brocade draperies are elegant."

Derek peered into the bathroom "There is no water hook up, and it appears rather decrepit."

As they continued to stroll, they encountered a door that was locked. "This must be the room with the Civil War collection. Let me kick the door in."

Audra swiftly put up her hand. "No, wait; let us search the desk in the parlor. But before we go back downstairs, I see one more closed door." They opened it and walked into a huge attic almost stepping on a mouse that scurried past.

Surveying the attic, Derek picked up a dusty sign that read, Antique Emporium. "The Clarks must have had an antique shop at one time. This room is full of old, European furniture. Look at all of these trunks against the wall. It will be interesting to open them and see what is inside. We could sell some of this furniture to offset the expense of refurbishing the place."

"That is a superb idea, but let's first see if Raquel needs

any of it. She has only a few pieces of furniture. Matthew plans to purchase furnishings when he is released from the army. This could be a wonderful savings for them!"

"Certainly. Also, Kenton and Lisette might like some of these antique pieces. They could have them shipped by rail to El Paso."

"I agree. They would appreciate the generosity."

After returning downstairs, Audra headed towards the parlor. She had an eerie feeling seeing Mr. Clark's eye glasses on his desk as if he would return for them at any minute. They hunted through the desk and Derek discovered an item in a cubby hole. "I found a key, and scratched on it are the initials, WAR, but our time is running out. We will put off our search for the Civil War collection until another time."

Outside on the grounds behind the house, they approached a brick carriage house and a small stable. Inside the carriage house, Derek examined a surrey and harness. "These are in fine condition."

Then they stepped into the stable, and Audra held her nose. "This place stinks! It is full of manure that has not been cleaned out for some time."

Walking outside, Derek stated, "This large pasture will be perfect for Rio, but the fence is in shambles and must be repaired first."

Doubts assailed Audra about the cost of living in such a huge home. She knew that a soldier's salary would be modest. Derek and his father owned a ranch, but she had never visited there. "My love, I do not want to put all of my life savings into fixing up this house. I only want to work part time in the Columbus clinic until children come along. Should we put this property up for sale and buy a smaller home? The taxes will be high on this estate. What about the expense of maintaining it?"

"Do not worry, my darling. I have savings, and our ranch is profitable. As we give our tithe to the church, we will always prosper. There will be many benefits of living here. It is close to the garrison. We have the perfect place to entertain and minister to the soldiers. If a man is converted to Christianity, then usually his whole household will follow the Lord. Besides, our grand home can be a gathering place for family and friends during weekends and holidays."

"Yes, celebrating Christmas here would be magical, indeed. But I want time with you, not always cleaning, dusting, and taking care of the things in this house."

"You flatter me with that statement, Miss Kirk." Derek stepped towards Audra and gingerly placed his hands on her face. At first his kiss was subtle, and then it deepened as she put her arms around his neck. "Sweetheart, I will help with the work here or hire someone to assist you. We can close off some of the rooms. The place is somewhat cluttered with furniture. Eliminate some of it as you choose. This home will be very useful for us. We must have faith to enjoy and manage it."As the engaged couple departed, Audra looked back at the great house wistfully. She mused, "I will be Mrs. Derek Rands soon, and we shall dwell in that home. What a joy it is for me to be this soldier's wife."

29

"There are three things that are too amazing for me, four that I do not understand: the way of an eagle in the sky, the way of a snake on a rock; the way of a ship on the high seas, and the way of a man with a young woman." Proverbs 30:18-20.

On the Apache reservation, Indian agent-pastor Garth Rands set out to prepare wedding festivities for his son. The attendance at the church had grown so much that it was overcrowded. So, the agent built a balcony and also constructed a covered entry where the children could be taught Bible lessons.

In writing the invitations, Garth instructed Elena, "Mark them with a seal for each family who are members of the church. The invitation must be in hand in order to enter the wedding ceremony and to enjoy the feast. When the news of the wedding is known, the whole reservation will show up for the celebration."

"Yes, I see the wisdom of this."

"I have commissioned men from the church to work on the surrounding roads, filling in the pot holes with gravel. Some of the young fellows have offered to use their machetes to cut the grass and weeds in the church yard."

Elena added, "My plans are also going forth. Several church women have offered to help prepare and serve the food. Miriam will provide piano music for the ceremony. I have hired young girls to assist here in the agency."

There was vast excitement on the reservation in anticipation of Derek and Audra's wedding. The Indians considered it to be an extravaganza occasion.

The date came that the wedding party would travel to the reservation. Derek drove one truck with Audra, Kenton, and Lisette. Matthew drove another truck with Daniel, Elizabeth, Raquel, and the children. Dr. Kirk and Jenny brought Pablo and Maria with them. Each truck was filled with luggage and food supplies.

Arriving at the agency, they encountered ample rooms to house the guests. The families spent the following day in wedding activities: decorating the church with crepe paper flowers and streamers, cooking, and baking.

In the evening, Derek and Audra went to the veranda to relax. As they chatted, Audra began to giggle. "My love, listen to this story; I overhead some of the young girls talking today. Can you imagine what their favorite part of the wedding ceremony will be?"

"No. I cannot guess."

"They are most excited to see the groom kiss the bride."

Derek chuckled. "I certainly will not disappoint them."

The next morning, Elena gave instruction to the hired girls. "Take baskets to pick flowers to be used for the bridal bouquets. Also, Audra wants a vase of roses to be brought to the bride's bedroom."

At a very early hour, the Apache guests could be seen in the distance traveling toward the church. The wedding was scheduled for noon, but the Indians started to arrive by ten o'clock. It took four grown men to control a line at the church door. Those who had no invitation had to wait until the legitimate guests were seated.

Miriam played the Wedding March on the piano with much gusto. Matthew and Kenton served as best man and groomsman. Agent-pastor Rands, the groom's father, officiated the wedding. Raquel and Lisette entered the church wearing long, violet satin gowns. Sofie, as flower girl was donned in a white, ballerina style dress. Andrew, as ring bearer, marched boldly behind his sister.

A hush fell over the congregation when Audra and her father came into view. The bride appeared regal in her exquisite white Spanish lace gown. Her beauty glimmered like the tiara on her head with her red curls shining underneath a long veil. There was never a more resplendent bride. As Audra made her promenade, it was as if she were a queen going to her coronation. The people looked back at her in admiration.

When Audra met Derek at the altar, he took her hands. His face mirrored his intrigue of this lovely woman who would walk through life by his side. He beheld her elegance and was well pleased. The groom directed his gaze to his bride to begin their nuptials. "I take you, Audra, to be my beloved wife, forsaking all others." The intensity of Derek's words was so real that it moved her to tears as he spoke the vows.

The moment totally engulfed her, and she imagined, "I

must be in a dream."

Finally, the pastor announced, "You may now kiss your bride."

Drawing her close, Derek whispered, "I love you."

Placing her arms on his, Audra murmured, "And I love you."

His kiss was long and slow, full of passion.

The Apache guests seated in the church stared in amazement. The young girls looked at each other and squirmed in their seats. There was no wiping the grin off of their faces. This is what they had come to see.

The guests exited the sanctuary and waited in the yard to shake hands with the bride and groom. As the wedded pair came down the church steps, the well-wishers threw flower petals into the air. Suddenly Derek lifted Audra into his arms and carried her to the end of the board walk. Then he kissed her on the lips and let the kiss linger before letting her down. The Indian people craned their necks to see them. They started laughing, and Matthew and Kenton whistled. Indeed, Derek showed the Apache nation that he was in love with Audra.

Agent-pastor Rands announced, "The wedding dinner will be served in the church so that the people may sit on the benches, out of the sun. At the wedding feast, everyone will receive a bowl of goat stew accompanied by tortillas and mangoes. Your mugs will be filled with sweet tea, and each adult will receive a cloth napkin as a souvenir."

A long table arrayed with flowers showcased a large wedding cake with six smaller cakes surrounding it. The cakes featured a sweet plum jelly icing with crushed nuts on top. Candy mints garnished the sides. Miriam and Sheyla cut the cake and tore pages from a Sears Roebuck catalog on which to serve the pieces.

Guitarists provided music for the festive event. For the Indian guests, it seemed like a fancy party at the opera house. Derek and Audra circulated to greet and visit with the guests. The Apache seemed glad to renew their acquaintance with the newlyweds. The bride hugged the women, and they acted like she was a dear friend. Several of the Indians asked when the couple would return to the reservation.

It was quite spectacle when two little girls took Sofie's hands and walked around with her inside the church.

A table near the altar of the church held some wedding gifts. The church ladies had pieced together a large quilt from fabric scraps. There was a carved wooden jewelry box, some painted pottery pieces, and a blanket made of sheep's wool. The women, seated on the wooden benches in the church, were keenly focused on the opening of the gifts. On the previous day, Joseph and his father, William, had delivered four goats as gifts for the wedding dinner. The chief and his son, Thomas, arrived at the agency carrying seven guineas and a large basket of eggs for the festivity.

After the dinner, some activities were planned. Elizabeth called to the children, "I brought pinatas filled with candy for you little ones."

They immediately started jumping up and down and clapping. Kenton helped the children to break the pinatas in the church yard.

Then Lisette and Raquel gathered the boys and girls. "Come, let's play Pin the Tail on The Donkey."

They also played a game with a large button on a string. Sofie and Andrew had fun participating. Louis, who was injured by the sheep, was among the children.

Previously at the ranch, Matthew had crafted three sets of horse shoe games, a macho sport. He beckoned them, "Men test your skill; each winner will move up to the next team."

The inhabitants of the reservation who attended the wedding stayed for hours; they did not want to leave the merry making. It was late afternoon when all of the games were over.

Finally on the agenda, Agent Rands recruited some young men. "Boys, bring out a large table from the church. Then go and fetch watermelons from the pump house. Cut slices to be eaten in the shade of the trees."

As the sun was going down, the guests began to leave for their homes. Derek and Audra felt humbled as the Indians expressed their gratitude for the wedding invitation. The indigenous people said over and over how much they enjoyed the celebration. Some asked, "Will there be another festival next year?"

Garth and Elena addressed the wedding party. "This has been a most joyous occasion. The wedding and the feast have been a great honor for the people of the Apache reservation."

The wedding entourage spoke of their agreement, "It was our great pleasure to be a part of this memorable day."

The bride and groom readied to retire for the evening. As Derek pulled back the sheet on their bed, he was surprised to see it covered with rose petals. He peered at Audra with a cocky expression and swiftly snatched her up. Still holding her, he brushed her face with a kiss and murmured, "It's going to be a romantic night, my darling."

The next morning after the wedding, the bride awoke in the comfort of her husband's arms. Her mind was searching for the words of love that Derek had whispered to her in the darkness of the night. For Audra, it would be a lifetime of wedded bliss to be loved by this soldier.

THE END

www.ingramcontent.com/pod-product-compliance
Ingram Content Group UK Ltd.
Pitfield, Milton Keynes, MK11 3LW, UK
UKHW020145250726
13967UKWH00002B/874

9 781957 497778